Entangled
Lives

Entangled Lives

Imran Omer

Winchester, UK
Washington, USA

First published by Roundfire Books, 2018
Roundfire Books is an imprint of John Hunt Publishing Ltd., No. 3 East St., Alresford,
Hampshire SO24 9EE, UK
office1@jhpbooks.net
www.johnhuntpublishing.com
www.roundfire-books.com

For distributor details and how to order please visit the 'Ordering' section on our website.

Text copyright: Imran Omer 2017

ISBN: 978 1 78535-784 8
978 1 78535 785 5 (ebook)
Library of Congress Control Number: 2017944839

A CIP catalogue record for this book is available from the British Library.

Design: Stuart Davies

Printed and bound by CPI Group (UK) Ltd, Croydon, CR0 4YY, UK

We operate a distinctive and ethical publishing philosophy in
all areas of our business, from our global network of authors to
production and worldwide distribution.

Contents

In memoriam: Asifa.
Mother, protector, friend.

I

I, Suleiman, and Him

I took my coffee and went into the living room, leaving Sebastian and my mother in the kitchen. Another morning and another cup of coffee. Another day with just a little work—too little work. My career felt frozen, my self irrelevant. Motherhood agreed with me, but it wasn't enough. I had led a life of adventure—not danger so much, but excitement, curiosity, the thrill of discovery, and the satisfaction of unraveling the truth from the threads of lies. I used to step from airport to war zone, from lie to truth, the way I now went back and forth from kitchen to living room to bedroom.

I had a moment's opportunity to listen to some news before Sebastian finished his breakfast and demands for Cartoon Network began. Between his cartoons and my mother's fervent love of *Law and Order*, I felt like my own TV was some kind of front line in a battle of wits and stamina.

The four-and-a-half-year-old was winning.

I flipped through the news channels. On a Saturday morning, in an election year, every studio was full of pundits forecasting the ever-changing political weather. Some were stuck like a needle on a broken record, crying for change while the others competed in a contest over who was the most patriotic, insisting that only the most conservative could save America from the shameful enemy that had attacked us—the enemy that dragged the country into two wars and a few hundred billion dollars in debt.

Chris Matthews tried to squeeze from his guests what he wanted them to say on one channel. David Gregory reported from the campaign trail of one of the Democratic candidates, searching zealously but sometimes unsuccessfully for differences among the three major candidates. Meanwhile Bill O'Reilly harangued his guests with his own answers to questions no one could

1

remember him asking. Then on another channel I caught a glimpse of a familiar face—I couldn't recall where I had seen him—that vanished the next moment when the moderators moved on to the next story.

I left the TV on but stepped out of the living room. As I passed the kitchen, I heard my mother trying to convince Sebastian to finish his cereal. I went upstairs and picked up my laptop the moment I got into my room. The last news channel's website yielded a photograph of the man I had recognized. Soldiers hustled him into the notorious prison that one of the Democratic candidates promised to close.

A breath I didn't realize I was holding hissed through my lips.

The caption on the photo gave no relevant information and I was left asking myself, Was he the man?

Was he the man who let me live, probably out of pity? The man who saw me as a fragile creature, just "a woman"? I went through a couple more websites to see a few more shots of him. Despite his haggard appearance—torn clothes, long beard, scattered hair, dark pockets under his eyes—I did recognize him. I clearly recalled the young man's face, framed by a turban. It was the face of the man who had broken into Laila's house with his comrades in arms to wipe us out, but who had ended up killing his partners in crime instead.

* * *

Through the glass in the door, I watched as they took the black bag off his head. He blinked then squinted against the light as they hustled him through the door and pushed him onto the chair in front of us. He wore a dull orange jumpsuit, dirty and worn at the knees. Shifting on the cold metal chair, he still kept his chin close to his chest.

"Take those handcuffs off, please?" I asked the guards.

The two men, dressed head-to-toe in black, looked at each other.

One of them shrugged and the other fished in his pocket for a key. While he unlocked the handcuffs, the prisoner leaned away, turning his face down even more, clearly trying to protect it. "The leg iron, too," I said.

The guard who'd now removed the handcuffs and stood up glanced down at the chain that was strung between the prisoner's ankles, then turned a grim, cold-eyed look to me and shook his head. My throat went dry and I swallowed. I tried not to look at him but the hint of a self-satisfied smile on the guard's face was plain to see. Then the two of them stationed themselves behind the prisoner. Two more stood outside the door.

Once the prisoner's eyes adjusted to the light, they rested a few moments on me, and then slid to the side to look at my interpreter, Suleiman.

This young man looked very different from the man who saved Laila and me on the other side of the world. The man who had the courage to help me seemed bitter and angry, but the man in front of me now had lost all hope, exhausted beyond measure.

"*Kiya hall chall ha, Raza?*" I asked him using one of the few full sentences of Urdu I had learned.

"*Behtreen,*" he said with a smirk.

"Fabulous," Suleiman interpreted.

I realized the ridiculousness of the greeting.

He looked around, seeming to take in the décor of the room. A blue plastic tarp covered the floor, its implications making my skin crawl. Four chairs, upholstered with a pyramid design in red and orange fabric, were crowded on one side of the table, facing the chair in which the prisoner sat. I'd set my bag on the chair on the right end. The walls were cinderblocks painted in a thick coat of cheap paint, the color of stomach medicine. From the look on his face I knew this man had lived long enough in an environment of concrete walls, iron bars, razor wire, orange uniforms, and black bags that nothing there—even, strangely enough, me—seemed to surprise him in the slightest.

"This is Suleiman," I said, blushing at the struggle to begin our conversation again. "He will interpret for us."

I pushed the cup of tea I had brought for him to the other side of the table. He only watched me, not looking at the tea. I forced a smile and worried it looked more like a grimace.

He asked something of Suleiman, but I could only understand the word "Muslim."

Suleiman did not respond to him.

Then the prisoner added something to his question.

My interpreter scowled at him, forcing me to ask, "What did he say?"

When Suleiman only shook his head, I asked the same question again.

His eyes locked on the prisoner's, Suleiman cleared his throat then said, "He has asked me about my faith in a very demeaning manner, and that he does not want to talk to me or you."

I took a few books from my bag and said, "I went online to find books in Urdu, Pashto, and Arabic, but didn't know which ones you would like. Here are some . . . fiction and non-fiction . . . I thought might interest you."

This seemed to pique the curiosity of the two guards in the room, and the prisoner turned his head almost imperceptibly.

Through Suleiman, he said, "I don't speak Arabic and can read little Pashto."

"Oh! Okay . . . but you can read Urdu, right?"

The prisoner folded his hands in his lap and sat up straighter in the chair, glancing back behind him when he spoke.

"They won't let me have them," Suleiman translated.

"I'll see what I can do about that," I said, making brief eye contact with the guard who'd unlocked his handcuffs. The man in black shook his head, wearing a tight-lipped frown. "You helped me and I want to help you," I said, turning my full attention back to the prisoner. "I want to know about your life. . . . Who you are, why you fought in the war, and . . . Why did you save us?"

He listened to the Urdu translation with an increasingly furrowed brow then shook his head and asked a question Suleiman translated as, "And how will your knowing my story help me?" "I want your story to be heard," I said. It felt like a lie even though it wasn't. "You must have something to say to the world." He barely waited for the translation to finish before rattling out an answer.

"No, I don't." But his words sounded even shorter than the ones Suleiman chose in English.

I shook my head and spoke directly to the prisoner. "Your story may help you in court."

I swear I saw the two guards smile—one of them might even have laughed a little. I closed my eyes waiting for the translation: "Which won't happen. Not before my death."

I sighed and told him, "You never know . . . elections are coming up, and a new president, a Democratic president . . . a more liberal president, may allow proper trials to begin, and even grant access to civil courts."

"Change of governments won't change the attitudes of Americans towards us," he translated back from the prisoner. I heard the doubt in Suleiman's translation and I sighed again when he looked at me sideways.

"Don't you want people to know your side of the story?" I asked. "Don't you want to tell people your experience of this war?"

Another long pause while he looked down at the floor. He sagged for just a second then sat up straight again. When he spoke this time he spoke directly to me, while before he mostly looked at Suleiman.

The translation, which came in parts, had Suleiman's inflection matching the prisoner's for the first time in the interview. "I had no views about this war when I became part of it and I still don't understand it . . . but even if I tell you whatever I think, and what they think, your prejudice will corrupt it."

"No," I said, maybe a little too harshly. The guards looked

up. I shook my head, leaned in over the table, and said, "I will tell your story in *your words*—a book, not just an article. And the book won't be published, not a word of it, until you approve it. Suleiman here will translate it for you to the last syllable." I patted Suleiman on the shoulder, who looked at me with the narrowed eyes of undisguised surprise.

While he translated the two guards looked at each other and some kind of silent conversation passed between the two of them. They both shrugged and turned their attention back to their prisoner.

"And I am supposed to trust you"—Suleiman translated the prisoner's smirking reply, then smirked himself when he finished—"and this man who shies away from his faith?"

Suleiman added, "I never agreed to—"

"Yes, you can trust me," I interrupted. "I can't let you down after what you've done for me . . . and Laila."

While Suleiman translated that I added, "Don't you remember?"

"It's hard to remember anything in this hell," was the translated reply. Then Suleiman hesitated, thinking about what seemed to be a difficult-to-translate word. "It's . . . *comical*, though. That's exactly what *they* want us to do, to remember and tell."

I could clearly see that he was struggling with the decision even as Suleiman struggled with the translation, the emphasis—while ignoring the feeling.

We sat in silence long enough for the guards to seem impatient.

"Do you think it was easy for me to get permission to come here?" I asked. I let Suleiman translate the question but didn't wait for a reply. "Do you think I would have left my child and come to Cuba if I didn't think what you had to say was important?"

The prisoner winced a little at one of Suleiman's words and I imagined it was the word *child*.

"I didn't ask you to come here," Suleiman translated, nodding along with the prisoner. "And anyway don't you journalists sniff around everywhere to smell stories like dogs, to make money and fame . . . to sell private lives of people with extra dressings as a malicious butcher sells rotten meat under a good wrapper?"

The young man didn't look as angry as his words sounded in translation. His eyes, dark and cold but shimmering with intelligence, never left mine.

"I have no interest in fame," I said, and I meant it but at the same time didn't think he would believe me. "And I'm not doing this for money. In fact, I'm happy to have all proceeds of the book go to paying a lawyer to defend you."

One of the guards let loose an exhausted sigh and the prisoner chuckled grimly as he listened to the translation. He remained silent for a while, pondering his options. Then Suleiman slowly translated his answer.

"I don't know your reasons and up to a certain limit I don't care . . . telling you my story can be a good amusement for a dying man; it's not a bad idea to spend some hours of the leftover life in this comfortable chair of this comfortable room. . . . But you have to promise me one thing: If you really get any money by writing about me then you will not spend it on me in any way. I want you to use it to get my son out of that *madrassah* . . . bribe that bastard Bayfazal, he is very greedy, he will give up my son if he finds it profitable enough. . . . If you do that for me, I'll not only tell you whatever you ask me but I'll also be thankful to you for the rest of my life . . . well, the rest is short but you know what I mean."

"Where is that *madrassah*?" I asked Suleiman, then whipped my head back to the prisoner.

I didn't need Suleiman to translate: "Karachi."

"Who is Bayfazal?"

The prisoner frowned and closed his eyes. His lips moved a little as though he was silently speaking, then he spoke and Suleiman translated, "I will tell you all about him."

A smile crossed quickly over my face, but I couldn't allow myself to celebrate what I knew just from the fact that it was being told to me in an interrogation room in Guantanamo Bay wouldn't be a happy story.

I looked him in the eye, leaning forward again, and said, "I promise I'll do my best."

I took a tape recorder from my bag and turned it on.

II

Massi Museabate—Maid Miserable

And then one day I found myself living in a hovel with my mother in the Gizri neighborhood in the center of Karachi, a slum surrounded by the posh areas of Defence and Clifton.

My mother was ill, and lay in bed most of the time. I never knew precisely what illness she had. I was only a child, and this was just one more thing that was beyond my comprehension. Long days would become longer weeks and she barely stood, didn't leave the house. Then she would seem to recover, just enough to get a few full breaths, and she would go away to find work, leaving me with Massi Rehmatea who taught the Quran to children and lived in the hovel next to ours.

Rehmatea was a stern prison guard, and she had a way of looking at me that made me feel like some kind of sinner despite the fact that I had no understanding of sin in my little body. It took only a few slaps and half a dozen of those disapproving glares before I decided not to offend that woman—or at least try not to. I knew she would use the same cane on me sooner or later that she lavishly applied to her students.

I kept myself busy in what was really only a three-meter radius around that little shack. My only toys a rubber duck and a lion that my mother brought with me to Massi Rehmatea's hovel.

Though her name, Rehmatea, means *blessing*, as I grew up ⟩ discovered that all her students called her Massi Museabat "Maid Miserable"—behind her back.

It was an apt name. She certainly made me miserable not to think about that time, even though I was so ⟩ memories are hazy and unreliable.

At the age of seven I learned that however terri' might seem, it can always get worse.

When I was seven, my mother died.

When I look back to find an image of my mother in my mind, I see her in bed, sick, staring blankly at something only she could see, and whatever it was, she wished she couldn't. I think she wanted to die, wanted to be done with it all. I don't know why—and that's not the only thing I don't know.

I don't know who my father was, and I don't know who those people were that Museabate took me to after my mother's death.

Who was the man that yelled at her when we visited that big house? His growling voice made me hide behind Museabate—to seek refuge with what seemed to be a lesser ogre.

Who was the crying woman that pushed him to get hold of me, to take me away from both Museabate and the man? Why was she doing that?

I knew the man would not let her get to me. Finally Museabate dragged me out of there, the sound of the crying woman fading behind us.

After that, Museabate reluctantly took me in. She beat me when I wouldn't read the Quran. She made me work all day, inside and outside the house. And to describe where we lived as a "house" is to be irresponsibly generous. The wood frame was patched with whatever materials could be harvested from the filthy streets. The "door" was rough and dirty sackcloth. But it was a roof over our heads in a city where not everyone enjoyed such a privilege.

Museabate set me to the task of carrying water back in a big bucket from the water tap—a mile away from our little shack, and I used some of that time finding the necessary detritus to keep our little hovel standing. Thin and desperate, I was fast and soon found my circle expanding as I went a little farther out every day and came back with a little more of use. I once came back with a full two-liter bottle of orange Fanta and this was the only time I remember seeing Museabate smile.

With only my mother to compare with, I think in her own way seabate was good to me. I had enough to eat, good enough clothes to wear, a clean bed to sleep in, and on *Eid* and *Barri Eid* she gave me a little bit of money.

Never going to school, existing only in the makeshift hovel and in the streets of Gizri, it's difficult to keep track of time. I think I was ten years old when a knock on the wooden panel that was the frame for the hanging sackcloth, changed my life.

Museabate had her students in that day, and they sat in a circle on the floor, dutifully if half-heartedly reciting from the Quran. They all stopped and looked up at the sound, but Maid Miserable clapped her hands, looming over them. They began again, but more quietly, their eyes darting, like mine, between the door and Museabate.

Museabate asked the visitor's name and a husky voice replied, "Respectable lady, I am the new *maulana* of Medina Mosque."

Museabate gasped and quickly covered her face with her *duppatta*, the strip of cloth that was wrapped around her neck. From behind this camouflage she shoved me gently toward the door and whispered, "Bring him in, boy!"

I took a few quick steps and was out the sackcloth door—straight into the arms of a man who, from my ten-year-old's memory seemed like a giant, or like some kind of circus bear wearing a man's clothing. His rough black beard hung to the middle of his chest and his black eyes locked on me.

I swallowed and bowed and swept the makeshift door open. Without a word, the man bent forward at the waist and went through, seeming to be careful not to touch any part of our little house for fear of getting his traditional white clothes dirty.

"Please have a seat, *Maulana Sahib*," Museabate said. Her voice sounded strange—thinner and weaker than I had ever heard it.

"*Bismillah!*" he rumbled, and carefully sat down on the *charpie*, the light wooden bed, lying near the door. It was the only thing available to sit on. I hadn't had much luck finding furniture on the streets.

The children reading the Quran stopped their recitation.

"Why don't I hear you?" she yapped at the children. "Memorize your verses!"

The stranger smiled when they began to read again, much louder this time—even louder, in fact, than Museabate actually liked.

"How are you, *Maulana Sahib*?" Museabate asked the man, practically groveling.

"I am fine, sister," came his deep-voiced reply. I thought then that his voice sounded like thunder. I think it might have been the first time I heard a grown man speak in such close quarters. "You are doing blessed work, teaching these children the holy book."

"God is merciful, *Maulana Sahib*." There was no other reply.

"I have decided to open a *madrassah* by the mosque," the man said while I kneeled next to him, listening intently but trying not to look him, or Museabate, in the eye. "By God's blessings we will soon get the empty land connected to the mosque for the living quarters of the students who don't have homes to go to. Perhaps we could hire your services to teach the girls' section."

Museabate blinked at this, clearly startled by the invitation, coming without a change in the man's booming monotone.

"Girls will live in the *madrassah* too?" Museabate asked in a shaking voice.

"No, no," the man was quick to reassure her, "but the girl students will be visiting us daily."

"Many, many thanks, *Maulana Sahib*. I'll be glad to teach at the *madrassah*. I have no other way to earn my living." I had never heard Museabate speak so quickly.

"There is no need for thanks, sister . . . I'll need a *hafiz* woman like you to teach our students, I am lucky that you are here right across from the mosque."

Museabate looked down and her fingers seemed to claw lightly at the dirt floor.

"You are doing a very good job for the poor," she said, and my eyes went wide as I saw her *duppatta* starting to unravel. "There are only a few *madrassahs* in the city," Museabate finished, quickly rewrapping her falling *duppatta*. Without asking, she moved to make the *maulana sahib* a cup of tea.

"I used to teach the Quran in the refugee camp to the Afghani children, then the party sent me to Peshawar, and now to Karachi," the man explained. "Our leader *Maulana* Fazlur Rahman is keen to establish *madrassahs* all over the country. President Zia-ul-Haq is very kind to provide us as much help as he can. I have also seen your son in the mosque," he added, gesturing to me. "Very obedient, a very good boy."

I wanted to scream at him that this woman was not my mother, but swallowed instead as Museabate spoke for me. "Thank you, *Maulana Sahib*, but he is not my son. I have never been married. He is the son of my neighbor who died a few months back."

I saw exhilaration cross his face and for some reason that look created an unknown fear inside me.

"*Wah, wah, mashallah . . .*" he said, smiling. "You have done lots of good deeds in your life. Heaven will be your abode, sister, I am sure of that."

"Thank you, *maulana sahib*, Allah is merciful."

I swallowed again and remember being terribly thirsty. When the man opened his mouth to speak, my heart threatened to stop in my chest.

"Maybe you can give this child to the *madrassah* so you won't have to support him."

And it felt as if my heart did stop.

"We will have other orphans there," the man continued—and the word "orphan" made me want to cry, but I held my tears back. "They will be preparing themselves to be the workers in the path of Allah. This boy will be fine with them."

A silence fell between them that seemed heavier than the big water bucket I carried back and forth for Museabate.

"I love this boy, *Maulana Sahib*," Museabate said, and I couldn't help it—my face shot in her direction so fast I felt a little twinge of pain in my neck. "I can't even think of separating him from myself . . . but if I get the job of teaching the holy book then I guess it won't be a separation, I will be at the *madrassah* daily and I could see him daily . . . after all I also have to think about his future, he has no one else in the world."

I closed my eyes and bent my neck back down, wondering if I had just been rescued from slavery, or was simply being sold to a new master. Museabate certainly never said she loved me, but after all, a mile is a long way to carry a bucket of water . . .

The man seemed to be looking at me when he said, "Sister, don't worry about your job at all, it's done. Once the construction is completed I will come and tell you the date you can start."

"Many, many thanks, *Maulana Sahib*."

"I should go now, it's time for *zuhur* prayers."

Without another word from anyone, he stood and left the shack.

I followed him out, ignoring Museabate's calls for the very first time in my short life.

I watched the man walk away and stayed out till dark. When the bullies of the slum came out of their sheds and started calling me *harami suer*, "illegitimate swine," I ran back to Museabate who took out her cane and beat me to her satisfaction.

A week later I was sent to the mullah . . . and the very next day he dragged me into his bed.

III

Bayfazal—Anti-Blessing

The *madrassah* was called *Roshni Kay Minar*: "Towers of Light."
The mullah who had taken me from Museabate was named
Fazal, which meant "blessing." But all the boys at the *madrassah*
called him Bayfazal: "Anti-blessing."

Bayfazal had probably never trimmed his beard in his life,
but he dyed it regularly. A few folds were ingrained on his lean
forehead, which never went away no matter if he was happy or
angry. His thin lips often turned inward in a sort of permanent
sulk.

I saw Museabate at the *madrassah* every day, and every day I
would tell her I didn't want to live there.

And every day she would scold me for asking to go home with
her.

"Stop pouting, you are good here," she kept saying. "*Maulana
Sahib* will remake your life." Then she would throw a slap at the
back of my head.

Soon more boys came to the *madrassah*. Some were orphans
simply abandoned there. Some were brought by their crying
parents, who could not afford to feed them, and hoped that at
the *madrassah* their boys might get three meals a day. What kind
of education they might be getting along with those meals never
crossed their minds. Starved minds drowned in the abominable
life of the slums put little thought into education. Their focus was
food.

For them, the government was the sole possession of the feudal
lords, and lately industrialists. Politicians ran after their own
schemes, loans, and commissions. The intellectuals of the nation
sought only awards and ceremonies. . . . Only the clergy were
ready to feed their children and provide a roof. They were surely

15

grateful to people like Bayfazal.

I am ashamed to admit that I was happy when more boys—younger boys—came to the *madrassah*. The younger boys took over the business of Bayfazal's bed, and my older classmates and I were given the responsibility to clean, cook, and care for the younger ones.

Bayfazal was just as inclined to use the cane on his students as Museabate was. A slight deflection from routine, a small mistake, an incomplete memorization of the words of the holy book would anger him, and he would use the stick. He would use it mercilessly.

One day a student was stupid enough to complain to his parents about the beatings. He was sternly told to follow his teacher and stay out of trouble. If they had listened to their son, tried for a second to understand what we were all going through, they would have had to go back to providing his meals and a roof over his head—an insurmountable task for them.

When the parents left, Bayfazal pointed fingers as thin as a hawk's claw at the room where every student of Bayfazal's dreaded to go. The boy fell to his knees, begging forgiveness. Bayfazal bent down and pulled the boy up by one of his ears, and dragged him to the room. Screams and shrieking pleas for forgiveness ripped through the *madrassah* for a while then everything went silent.

And for me, at least, the silence was worse.

* * *

I went through the hall where we learned our lessons, ate, and slept, and went through the narrow door that opened onto the back courtyard to get to Museabate; I had a message from Bayfazal. While I waited for her, I noticed a new girl in the group of students. Her hair, moist with oil, was tightly woven in a long snake behind her head. A soft dimple appeared on her round face every time she smiled. Her face held a tiny birthmark—not an imperfection but somehow a way to identify her as one in a million, in a billion, in all of God's Creation. In the middle of the group, she moved her body back and forth, clearly pretending to be busy reading the holy book. Her big eyes peeked through long lashes—and something happened to me then. Bayfazal would probably say that I had discovered sin, but what I discovered was, to me, the most precious treasure of all. What I discovered was beauty.

"What are you staring at, Raza?" Museabate demanded.

I blinked and looked up at her as if waking from a trance. "*Maulana . . . Maulana Sahib* wants the attendance of the girls for this week."

"Come later," she answered curtly. "I haven't taken attendance today."

"Yes, *Massi*."

After this visit I would look for excuses to go to Museabate so that I could have a look at that new girl. There were times when Museabate was late a few minutes, and I tried to talk to her. She never answered my questions. I realized that she wouldn't talk to me in front of the other girls.

One day I told Bayfazal that I had to get groceries for the evening meal and followed her from the *madrassah*. She crossed the street and took the path to the slum. Before she could enter it I ran and went in front of her. "You are a student of Museabate," was all I could think of to say.

"Museabate?"

"Don't you know? Her students call her Massi Museabate."

She laughed. "Good name . . . aren't you afraid I will tell her?"

"I know you won't."

When she gave no sign of a reply, I said, "Let me buy you a Popsicle."

"With what money?"

"I buy groceries for the *madrassah*."

"No . . . you should go now . . . *Massi's* house is not far. If she saw us here, she would make the sky fall."

"I know. I lived with Massi."

She didn't pay any attention to my response and started moving faster in what I figured was the direction of her hovel. I stopped and let her go, making sure I wasn't too obvious watching her walk away.

While I was shopping for the meat that was cooked daily for Bayfazal, I bought some TwoTwo candies and hid them in my loose *shalwar* trousers.

The next day I went back to the section of the *madrassah* where Museabate taught and slipped the candies to the new girl. She hid them under her shirt. The two girls on either side of her, reading and waving back and forth, looked back at me then at the new girl. I could tell they had seen the candies, but they remained silent.

I hoped the new girl wouldn't have to give all the candy to these other two to keep them quiet.

IV

Perveen

I know now that there are some people who would think that at the time I was too young to have fallen in love. Can a boy of thirteen experience real love, or a sort of budding, sinful lust, some kind of chemical passion best prayed away? But I also know now that I was in love. It was as real as any love experienced by someone twice the age I was when I first saw this new girl at the *madrassah*.

I remember that time in a sort of haze, a cloud that carried me along on what felt like the wings of an angel—wings under which I could retreat from the hostile environment that was my life. I would drink in her face, her eyes, her hair as if I were sipping some secret elixir of the ancient alchemists. Drunk with the look of her, intoxicated with the idea of her, I clung to the thought of her with both hands.

I would follow her to her shack at the other end of the slum whenever I could, stopping to talk to her only when I could do so without attracting anyone's attention. Every passerby—and there were thousands crowding the dusty streets and narrow, crumbling pavement of this wrong side of Karachi—might be a spy. They might be a spy for Bayfazal, or for Museabate, or for God Himself. And if either of the first two knew how I felt about her, they would take her away from me, or take me away from her. I knew this the way I knew the sun would rise in the east and set in the west. They would do that just to hurt us.

What God might do, I was afraid to ask.

The terror of Bayfazal and Massi Museabate and the fires of Hell hovered over me and kept pushing me away from my center. It was as if they were Hajjis doing *tawaf*, encircling Kaba, pushing back those of us in the outermost circle, never letting us change our orbits, never forgiving us anything.

Meat prices went up every week those days, and it was easy for me to claim I'd paid more for lamb each time I went out for groceries for Bayfazal. It was naïve to think he would never be able to catch me, and that I would never become a lamb myself under the boot of Bayfazal.

One day I brought the groceries, told Bayfazal the cost of all the items, and gave him the change.

"So lamb is two rupees higher than the last time, right?" Bayfazal said.

"Yes, *Maulana Sahib*." Something was wrong. I could smell it.

"Faqira, come in."

The butcher appeared from the next room. He had a big scar on his left cheek. His thick dry hair stuck out from his scalp like the spikes of a porcupine.

"Tell him how much you are charging for the lamb."

"Sixty rupees, *Maulana Ji*," the butcher said.

"But he was not there. His intern charged me sixty-two."

Bayfazal looked at him.

"They can't do that, *Maulana Sahib*. I am sure the boy is lying," he said.

Bayfazal turned his head to me. I could see in his face that he was enjoying the sight of the growing tension in my young body that made me breathe heavily.

"I am sorry, *Maulana Sahib* . . . I am sorry . . . forgive me." I threw myself on the floor and grabbed Bayfazal's feet. "I'll never do it again."

"I know you won't . . . Allah is forgiving." He pulled his feet away. "You will be forgiven too, but after a price."

Bayfazal waved Faqira away and the butcher backed out of the room quickly. Then Bayfazal called in a tall man with a black pointy beard and thick eyebrows. This man stayed in the room next to Bayfazal. Nobody knew his name. We all called him *Jallad*, the executioner.

"Raza needs to learn a lesson," Bayfazal said to Jallad, sliding his hand over his long beard, coiling the longer hair around his forefinger like snakes around a pillar.

"Of course, *Maulana Sahib*." Jallad put his right hand on his chest and bent down a little to show his respect to Bayfazal.

I stood up and stepped back to get away from him.

"Boy! Don't make it worse," Jallad said.

I froze where I was. Nobody could come to my rescue, no one was on my side. I was the end of an unfortunate progeny.

Jallad brought my wrists closer together to tie them with a rope. The fragile wrists of a thirteen-year-old trembled like a house of straws at the first sign of flood. I knew what was about to happen, I had a glimpse of this kind of torture before. Bayfazal left his comfortable chair and picked me up, grabbing me from my hips. Jallad tied the other end of the rope to the hook in the ceiling. I hung eight inches above the floor; the pressure on my wrists made me cry. One moment I felt my bottoms slipping down to my legs and the next my buttocks bore a hit from Jallad's boot, and then another. After a few more, the pain made me loose count.

Water splashed on my face brought the pain back. Bayfazal's piercing eyes stared straight into mine. Even in my feeble state I thought if I could grow eight more inches, the distance from my feet to the floor, I would be as tall as Jallad. If I were, I would beat him to death.

"What did you do with the money?" Bayfazal kept repeating. "Don't test my patience, Raza."

He waved his hand to stop Jallad, who was surely about to hit me again.

"I . . . I bought . . . bangles."

"Bangles? For whom?"

"For a girl."

"I know bangles are for a girl. Who is that girl?"

I remained silent.

"Rascal! You're barely over three feet tall and yet the desire for a woman is in your head . . ." He laughed at me. "Who is this girl? Tell me!"

I remained silent.

He waived his head in disappointment, signaling through his eyes to Jallad to get back to his cruel work.

The pain rippled through brittle branches from my buttocks to all my extremities. I was soon hanging unconscious and bleeding.

* * *

Late at night, when I finally drifted back to the cruel reality of my life, I found one of the students, Ahmed, placing bandages on the cuts all over my body. I closed my eyes again and let him do his work. The cuts would heal, but my heart . . .

"If you had told them the name of the girl, this would not have happened to you. Do you have a wish to die?" Ahmed asked. I heard a note of Bayfazal in his voice that made my knees quiver.

I had no energy to respond to him, but his scolding made me realize Jallad and Bayfazal could have beaten me to death.

I didn't actually know her name.

All the boys took our lessons, and at night slept on the floor of a single big hall. The walls were still unpainted, unfinished, rough concrete that showed old water stains, older cracks, and patches of white lye seeping out. Rough spun rugs that might once, long ago, have been black and white were now grey and slightly darker grey, faded and threadbare. The identical pattern repeated over and over meant they must have been made on a machine. The smell of mildew and old piss was always present, even when Bayfazal delivered his raging, angry sermons.

He demanded we fear God, and seemed sure in his own confidence that he had convinced us all that he, Bayfazal, was the only mediator in the path between us and God. His own bitter lamentations were all encompassing. That day he warned us for what felt like the millionth time to submit to his demands or he would use the power bestowed upon him to punish us. The sermon finished with accusations against . . . I wasn't sure who . . . names I didn't recognize.

And finally, "Tell me the name of the girl for whom our impenitent Raza savors his desire, the sin of thought that will lead him to the unforgivable sin of fornication unless we—all of us, all of you—help me help him."

He motioned for me to stand and I saw no choice but to struggle up to my feet.

"Do you all want to learn your lessons the hard way . . . as he did?" Bayfazal gestured at my aching body while delivering this threat.

Ahmed looked at me and I looked away from what I saw in his eyes. He raised his hand.

"Yes, Ahmed."

"Her . . . her name is Perveen, she comes to learn the Quran from Massi Mu—from Massi Rehmatea."

Bayfazal sighed, and so did I. Now I knew her name. Whatever happened next, I knew her name. I clenched my teeth so my lips wouldn't move as I rolled her name back and forth across my mind: Perveen . . . Perveen . . . Perveen . . .

"Ahmed, you are Raza's watch-buddy now. He should never be able to go to the girls' section, and he should never be able to get out of the *madrassah* unless I personally allow it. If I ever find that he went out, he will be the one who will be placing bandages on you. Have I made myself clear?"

"Yes, *Maulana Sahib*," Ahmed said.

"Now all of you go and do the revision of the previous *paara*, the chapter of the Quran you have finished. I will call each one of you to teach you the new verses."

The boys all sat in line along the walls of the room, except for me. They allowed me to stay in my comforter for the day. This was all the mercy I had ever found there.

Students took their *rehels*—small cross-legged supports—

from the wooden box resting in the corner, then they took out their copies of the Quran from the cupboard, kissed them twice, placed them on their *rehels,* and started swinging their heads and shoulders back and forth while reading the verses.

Ahmed, my watchdog, looked at me from the corner of his eyes and bent down to whisper, "I had to do it . . . for the sake of all."

The next few months I remained imprisoned in this poorly named Tower of Lights. I saw the sky only from the windows; visits to the courtyard were also banned. The *madrassah* became a holy prison.

One day, before commencing lessons in the morning, Bayfazal announced that we would all be going to a gathering where we would listen to crucial words of wisdom from the leaders of the Islamic *Jamat* group. Here we would be enlightened to tackle the troubling times ahead. They would tell us about the agony of war in Afghanistan and the chaos it was bringing to our own country. There would also be representatives from Saudi Arabia, the country of the holy city Makah and the holy center Kaba, that were sent by the king to help us fight the godless people.

On a Friday, after the afternoon prayer—the most important prayer of the week—we lined up and were herded onto a bus. As the shops and street carts awoke from their own Friday prayers, beggars rushed from outside the mosques to the shops and vendors, waiting for the paying customers to arrive.

It took us an hour to get to the old part of the city. As the bus trundled along, we boys spoke to each other only in whispers, so Bayfazal and Jallad wouldn't hear us. Then Bayfazal and Jallad, seemingly lulled by the sway of the old bus, fell asleep. This started a nearly silent festival among the boys and in a few minutes, someone slid a magazine onto the floor between my feet. It was Shoaib, a boy a few years younger than me who everyone blamed for bringing lice into the *madrassah.* He turned and winked at me and I picked up the magazine. It was called *Afsana Digest* and I only got a half-second glimpse of it—pictures of smiling men and women on the cover—before I was hit so hard on the side of the head my ears started to ring.

"I found it on the floor!" I yelled, pressing my hand against my burning ear.

Jallad ripped the offending magazine out of my hand and swatted me on the head with it—hard—but then the bus hit a hole in the road, or ran over something, and it jerked him to the side. I heard Jallad sit down and mutter something to Bayfazal, but then we seemed caught in the current of a river made of heads, caps, and turbans all moving toward and then pouring into the stadium. Men waited in the galleries and on the rooftops of the surrounding apartments for the show to start.

Before we stepped off the bus we were told to grab each other's hands and not to let Bayfazal and Jallad out of our sight while we followed them in. We were dragged through the crowd like tiny fish swimming through the teeming weeds in a sea. We were seated in a section reserved only for *madrassah* students. After all, we were the future lambs and needed to listen to the sermons much more closely than anybody else.

On the east side of the stadium was a big stage on which a dozen men in white clothes sat on big red velvet chairs. Under their feet was a green carpet, and behind them, a large banner that read: Afghanistan's Liberation = Muslim World's Liberation.

Four men with Kalashnikovs, wearing white clothes, stood at the back of the stage, keeping an eagle eye on the crowd, clearly ready to shoot.

The large ground was covered with rugs, and full of all sorts of people—men with green turbans, men with white turbans, men with white scarves on their shoulders, men with black wristbands, men with white hats that had golden embroidery, men with thick black turbans wrapped around their heads like a boa wrapped around a tree, and men with simple white caps—all the sects decided to come under one umbrella to fight against Soviet expansion.

At last, one of the men on stage stood and spread his arms in front of him, palms facing downward. The pulsating crowd settled down and silence took over its buzz. In this silence, the matrix of the aromas of different of kinds *itirs*, the indigenous perfume, felt stronger than before.

The man spoke a few introductory words, inviting the representative of the Saudi government to address the people. The representative sitting closest to the speaker stood up and came to the podium. He wore *thawb*, the long loose shirt coming to his ankles, and *shemagh*, the headscarf with a black band over it. The representative spoke in Arabic, which was translated by the man who had introduced him. He thanked Zia, the president of the country and the chief martial law administrator, for his contribution to Islam by mobilizing people to fight the godless Soviets. He placed the dictator just a few notches below the prophet in his role of serving *Ummah*, the Islamic Nation.

Later, leaders of different Islamic *Jamats* addressed us, exhorting us that we should have only one cause in our lives on which we should spend all our energies, the expulsion of the Soviets from Afghanistan. They offered their appreciation for the money coming from America and Saudi Arabia for the blissful cause of fighting the communists. The invasion of the godless people brought men of Allah under the banner of the people of Jehovah to fight a holy war—or a holy war for one banner, the hope of being the one and only superpower for the other. The enemies of the Crusades became allies in the twentieth century.

The speakers offered quotations from the Quran to stir the emotions of the people, enticing them to fight their *jihad*, convincing them about the holy legitimacy not only of the war but also of the military dictator of the country. The crowd chanted slogans at every pause and to me they seemed to transform into a molten mass under the power of the speakers. The men in the stadium shouted their zeal, emphasizing its determination to roll over the communist forces like a boulder crushing cockroaches, scattering the bodies of the hated Soviets into thousands of pieces, not letting them ever rise from their perfect demise.

The religious parties, for the first time in the life of the nation under Zia, were determined to expand their religious agenda and become a part of the mainstream politics of the country.

At the end of the presentation, a few young men came onto the stage, young men who were about to become the fodder of war, who would live their lives in the mountains, come down from them to strike the enemy, then retreat back to the mountains to live a life that would leave them little more than wild animals. And in this process of coming down and going up the mountains, they might sacrifice life and limb to years in which hearts should blossom with love, eyes search for hope, and minds expand horizons. They were about to vanish into the smog of war, and a war that was not really theirs.

It was my first day out in a few months, so I enjoyed the show, despite the dark shadow it threw across my future—and on the futures of all the students of different *madrassahs* who sat there with me. We were the soldiers in the making, soldiers like the young men that appeared on stage. I could sense that danger like a lamb seeing his mother under the butcher's knife, but somehow more frightening to me was the realization that I was unable to accept that notion of sacrifice in the path of Allah. If He was omnipotent, He did not need any help to be the Almighty. Couldn't He bring about the desired result in the spur of a moment, without butchering young men in war?

V

Shahbaz Khan

Bayfazal's strategy was to put the rebellious ones or those he suspected could be rebellious to the task of *hifzing*, memorizing the Quran verbatim. It was a challenging task that consumed its victims day and night.

I became one of his chosen ones that year.

It took me four years to *hifz* the Quran. I often got into trouble in those four years. Despite my efforts I remained unable to fully adapt to the rules of the hellhole, Roshni Key Minar. Ahmed continued to serve as a watchdog over me, and quite often healer.

By 1988, when I was seventeen years old, the first group of Bayfazal's lambs was ready. It was his time to pay back the support he had received from the *Jamats*, and send fuel to the fire of war.

All the students older than fifteen were collected in the courtyard. Two visitors with beards longer than Bayfazal's gave us a sermon on the blessings we were about to receive by participating in a holy war against *kafirs*, the godless people. They told us that we would leave Karachi a week later.

The very next day the *madrassah* took on an uncharacteristically festive feeling. Parents and relatives of the students—who had no say in Bayfazal's decision to send them away—came to meet them one last time before their departure. Museabate, whom I didn't want to see, came and gave me her blessings—blessings that had no value to me.

"You should be proud of yourself." She patted my back.

"I am being led to the slaughter, what's there to be proud of?" I said, taking care nobody else could hear me.

She slapped the back of my head. "You are rebellious, like your mother."

"My mother?" I asked, and clenched my fists, working hard not to hit her back. "Who was she? Who was my father? Some of these boys at least get to say goodbye to real family, real parents, but me? All I have is some miserable . . ."

She reached up to slap my head again, but something in my eyes must have made her think better of it.

"You never even told me about them," I said quietly, forcing myself to relax.

"There is nothing to tell," she said—and, I think, all too quickly. "I don't know anything about your father at all, and your mother was . . . a neighbor."

She always used these ambiguous words to describe them. She was the only link to my parents, but that link insisted on silence. In my memory there is a picture of Massi Museabate sitting next to my mother. It is the only distinct picture of my mother in my mind.

"You have the beard of a young man now," she said, "but the heart of a baby, still."

Before I could respond, other people wandered too close to us. I couldn't be seen to be rude to her, and she took that chance to turn her back on me and walk away.

* * *

At the end of the week two men came to the *madrassah*. It was evening and I was in the kitchen. My group—myself and three other students including Ahmed—were preparing dinner for the students, and for Bayfazal and his friends.

The door of the *baitahak*, the room where Bayfazal received his guests, was open. I was curious. I told Ahmed I was going to the bathroom but went out into the yard. I started taking down the dry clothes hanging on the rope and heard Bayfazal say, "What am I going to do? I have spent so much money on them already."

"This is not something against you, *Maulana*. The war is ending," one of the men answered. "The Russians are leaving Afghanistan.

29

America and Saudi Arabia have stopped sending money. The government is not prepared to send any more *mujahids* across the border."

"Who is going to pay me the money I've spent to prepare my boys for *jihad*?"

"Don't be greedy, *Maulana*. You have been given more than enough to look after your students," said another man with a sharp voice. "And you are not going to get any more as there is no use to keep these *madrassahs*, no need of any *mujahids*. You need to close the *madrassah* and learn to live on the salary of the Imam of Medina Mosque."

"Do you know how much the government pays an Imam? It couldn't feed a kitten for a month!"

"Well then, you'll have to go out to the public for funds to run your *madrassah*."

"I thought that when I received the money from the heads going across the border, I would expand the *madrassah*. There are so many children out there that need help . . ."

"We should be going now," said a man with a husky voice.

"Fellows . . . have some tea, please," Bayfazal said.

"Sorry *Maulana*, we have to go to a lot of other places, this is not something that can be broadcast on the daily news."

I rushed to the kitchen.

A couple minutes later I heard Bayfazal shout, "Who piled up these clothes on the *charpie*?" He was coming back from the gate after saying farewell to the men.

"I am sorry, *Maulana Sahib*, I wanted to get the meal ready first," I replied while coming out of the kitchen.

"I have told you so many times—don't take them off if you don't have time to fold them."

"Sorry, *Maulana*."

"Fold them *now*!"

I followed his command without wasting a moment.

* * *

At night when we went to our comforters I whispered the news to Ahmed, who was lying next to me. Then I asked him, "Is he going to throw us out?"

"If he doesn't earn twice what he spends, he will," Ahmed said.

"I wonder if it's a good thing. . . . No free labor for Bayfazal, that's not bad."

"The world outside is not so pleasant either." He turned around and pulled the sheet over his head. The discussion was over.

The next morning Bayfazal told us that our chances of martyrdom were taken away by the authorities, and we were no longer entitled to get new clothes and old boots, coats, and blankets. He also announced a list of students that were now "adults" and should leave the *madrassah* and "find their own place in the world."

I wished my name was on the list.

* * *

Bayfazal turned out to be quite the entrepreneur. He started a few projects to earn money. He sent students to rich houses across town to teach the Quran to their children. Some new students came to the *madrassah* in morning and evening shifts. He made me their instructor. We cleaned the beds along the wall of the courtyard and planted vegetables in them.

He made a team consisting of Jallad and two other men to beg funds from rich families. He closed the girls' side all together, and Museabate was jobless after working ten years at the *madrassah*.

Despite the income from his projects, our rations were reduced and we seldom ate any fresh vegetables, let alone meat. All the vegetables that were harvested in the *madrassah* were sold in the market. We had lentils day and night, and occasionally rice—the stench of our flatulence overpowered all else.

All the money received from these enterprises, of course, went in Bayfazal's own pocket. At the end of the year two young men who had gone to teach the Quran never came back. Bayfazal cursed their names but spent no time or energy trying to find them. One day I suggested to Ahmed the notion of running away.

"What are we going to do out there? There is no work . . . and we have no skills," he said.

"We will at least be out there."

"Out there begging! If you want to run away, go ahead. But you have never talked to me about it, and never say any such thing ever in the future. I don't want to get in trouble."

* * *

I very well remember it was an unusually cold day for Karachi, a city where winter passed by with a whisper. Bayfazal told us we had to prepare some *Hamds*, poems in the praise of the Lord, and *Naats*, poems in the praise of the prophet, to present them in a *jalsa*, a gathering, to a "big man" who might provide money for the *madrassah*.

Bayfazal supervised the preparation of our side, whereas Museabate supervised the girls' presentation. Bayfazal promised he would hire her back if he received a handsome endowment as a result of this show. Whenever we failed to express enough emotion we were smacked on the backs of our heads for our lack of gratitude. We shook our bodies back and forth to bring vibrations to our voices that conveyed our warmth for God.

On the day of the *jalsa,* a heavyset man with two bodyguards came in a black Pajero, the SUV that had become the symbol of the feudal class in Pakistan in those days. Shahbaz Khan was a tall man, whose bushy eyebrows overshadowed eyes cloaked by thick, fleshy lids, giving him the look of a lizard. He was warmly received by all the adult men in the *madrassah,* led by Bayfazal. It was the *maulana* himself who seated the man in the front row on a red velvet sofa rather than the ordinary chairs left for the common people who had no money to offer the *madrassah*. We put on the show diligently. But the man for whom the show was held appeared carved from stone. I saw no movement in his face, no expression of the slightest emotion. He was either incapable of feeling or trained to keep his emotions deep inside. Only later did we come to know that Shahbaz Khan was the son of the man Bayfazal had been expecting.

* * *

One month after the *jalsa,* and two days before the commencement of Ramadan, the one who was an informant became a messenger.

Ahmed placed a piece of paper on my palm and pushed my fingers to make me clasp it. "I have *not* given this to you," he whispered in my ears.

The note was from Perveen, and when I realized that, my eyesight blurred and my heart raced. It took me several minutes to calm down enough to read it—just a sentence saying she wanted to meet me as soon as I could get away.

After considerable begging I convinced Ahmed to take my message to her that I would meet her behind her shack on the evening of *tarawi*, special prayers that began on the eve of Ramadan, which lasted throughout the month.

There was a lot of preparation for *tarawi* at *madrassah* as every year three to five new *hafizs* led the prayers and recited the holy book accompanied by experienced *hafizs* supervised by Bayfazal. The *tarawi* started the very first day after seeing the new moon, or after the announcement of the appearance of the moon from a committee established by the government.

I was expected to lead the *tarawi* and recite that year, but Bayfazal had taken me aside a few days before and said, "You are out. You need another year."

"But *Mau*—" I tried to argue.

He interrupted me with a wave of his hand and said, "You gulp down words—sometimes even phrases—without pronouncing them." Then he mocked me with some sort of tense face, as if he were going to vomit on me. "You'll embarrass me in front of the congregation."

And I knew he couldn't afford that. Ramadan was the month he collected most of the funds for the *madrassah*, and in that time of dwindling resources, he needed to make sure the visitors were happy and decorum was maintained. This was a blessing. I could sneak out during those long prayers to meet Perveen and no one would notice my absence.

The *madrassah* was cleaned to its core a couple of days before Ramadan, and new prayer mats were used for the worshippers. Bayfazal decided that one *hafiz* would lead the prayers in the rooms of the *madrassah*, another outside in the rear courtyard, and the third in the Medina Mosque, located next to the *madrassah*.

That year the moon clothed itself in gray clouds and refused to show a glimpse to the eager population. We waited for the decision of the committee. When the announcement of the eve of Ramadan was heard, the mosques turned on their sirens, and everybody in the *madrassah* fell into preparations for *tarawi*—there was less than an hour to complete the preparations.

I placed myself in the last row of the rear courtyard, close to the back door. When the *Isha*, the last of the five prayers of the day, was over, and the first *tarawi* was about to start, I sneaked out of the *madrassah* and walked fast through the alleys to get to Perveen's shack.

A few feet away from her family's little hovel I saw her two brothers, chatting with a few of the slum's resident delinquents. Making myself as inconspicuous as I could, I listened in on their conversation.

"This white powder is all over the place since the surge of refugees from Afghanistan eight years back," one of the boys said, his eyes shifting quickly back and forth as though he expected police or soldiers, or Satan, to come out of the darkness and take him.

One of the others was much calmer, leaning with his back against the rough brick wall of Perveen's shack. "How to take advantage of the market, and control demand and supply in the slum," he said. "That's the real question."

A third boy shrugged, looking his nervous companion up and down. "There's no need to fear the police, as long as they get their regular share . . ."

I swallowed, afraid to move. These were not boys anymore, but dangerous criminals. They were in no position to let me slip away peacefully. I was protected in the four walls of the *madrassah*, but I knew if they saw me out there . . .

I turned to an alley going right to make a big circle to get to the back of Perveen's shack.

In the reflected light coming from the big houses across the street, I saw an eye peeping through a small hole in the wall.

"How are you?" I whispered.

"I am all right," Perveen whispered back. The sound of her voice made me smile in the darkness. "We don't have much time, my brothers will be here soon."

"Where is your mother?"

"She's sick . . . sleeping."

I remained silent.

"They are marrying me to that man."

"What man?" I asked—almost too loudly. The blood seemed to freeze in my veins.

"The one who came to the *madrassah*."

"Shahbaz Khan?" I almost gagged saying his name.

"Yes . . . I'll be his third wife. He is giving a lot of money to my brothers."

We remained silent for a while, trying to find the depth of the feelings we experienced for each other more than four years ago when it was difficult for us to even give them a name.

"I'd rather die than get married to that reptile."

"What can we do?" I asked.

"Let's . . . let's run away."

"Think about it . . . you may be his third wife but—"

"And half his age."

"But you will live in a mansion, better than living with me on the streets like dogs."

"I'd rather beg on the streets with dogs than live in a palace with that vulture."

"Who are you are talking to, girl?" The voice of a woman struggled with a cough to complete the question.

"It's Zarina, *Amma*."

"What is she doing out late in the evening?" her mother asked.

"Her husband is out of town."

There was silence in the shack.

"When is the wedding?" I was now more careful.

"Just after *Eid*."

"Even if we decide to run away, where will we go? What will we do?"

"Anywhere . . . anywhere away from here, and anything . . . anything that can feed us," she whispered.

"We need some money to get away from here. I have none."

"I have saved some," she said.

"That *behenchod* Sultan thinks that it's his territory. I'll beat the hell out of him if he ever steps into this area with his stuff," one of her brothers threatened. He must have been entering the shack from the other side.

"Our product is better than his anyway, we can beat him anywhere," another voice said.

"I'll meet you here during *tarawi* next Friday," I whispered.

Then I ran away from there as fast as I could. I never felt more terrified, and more excited, in my life.

* * *

Perveen was waiting for me the next Friday.

"What have you decided?" she asked.

"I can do anything for you."

"No, I want you to make up your own mind."

"Yes . . . yes, of course I want to get away from here."

"When should we leave?"

"Everybody is distracted on the night of the new moon, that's the best day. They would only find us missing long after our escape."

"Right. My brothers stay out late too. What time do you think you'll be able to get here?"

"Just after breaking the fast, when they're all on the roof to see the new moon."

"You should go now," she said. "My brothers will be here any minute. I'll see you on the *Eid* eve."

* * *

Bayfazal usually loosened his reigns on us the night of the new moon. He had to prepare for the prayers and festivities of the next morning. I hoped he wouldn't come to realize my absence till they all went to bed, which was usually late on the eve of *Eid*.

I didn't tell Ahmed anything, so he wouldn't be tortured after our elopement. He would have nothing to tell them except that I might have met with Perveen.

On the eve of *Eid*, when everyone else was on the roof focusing their eyes on the western horizon to see the new moon after breaking the fast, I slipped away and came down. After a few minutes I heard the uproar of the younger boys, and later the not so young ones. The moon was apparently eager to see the circus my life had become, and showed itself quite early that year. I rushed out of the east-open front door as everyone's eyes were still on the crescent moon to the west. I ran when nobody was around, and walked when I found people hanging out in the alley.

Women congregated outside the front of Perveen's shack—just a few, probably trading idle gossip. Avoiding their attention, I reached the back side of the shack and barked like a dog, which was our signal. The inside of the shack was silent. I barked again.

I heard a male voice say, "These fucking vagabonds."

I rushed, and stood along the wall of the shack so he couldn't see me through the holes in the wall.

"*Bra*, you are not going out with your friends today?" It was Perveen's voice, somewhere quite close to me.

"Since when are you worried about my going out?"

"I was just asking."

After a couple minutes I heard the siren, which was the confirmation that the evening belonged to the festival.

A few minutes later I heard her brother again. "I am going out. When Rahim comes, tell him I'm at Suleiman's place."

"All right, *bra*."

A few seconds later, she whispered, "Stay there, I'll be out soon."

Every second of the few minutes she took was increasing the tremble of my legs. I kept strolling in the small space behind her shack, peering into the alley every few seconds.

She wore a shirt with a pattern of large sunflowers, covering her head and shoulders with a black *chadur*, and carried a small, worn-out bag. I looked around and came out of my hiding place. I took the bag from her and we moved into the alley fast. A couple minutes later, when I found her falling behind, I stopped.

"Keep moving," she whispered. "Keep the distance."

I started walking.

"*Areea*, where are you going *bacha* at this hour?" It was one of the women I had seen standing outside her shack talking to her neighbors.

"I am going to Zarina, *chachi*. I need to get my brothers' clothes from her."

"How is your mother?"

"The same, *chachi*."

"Allah will send His blessings . . . it's all in His hands."

"*Chachi,* I should go, otherwise it will be too late for me to come back alone."

"*Haan bacha,* go ahead."

We almost ran through the alleys of the slum, one after the other, and crossed the big road, moving fast for the bus stop.

We stood for fifteen minutes at the bus stop, a block from the slum, and around a mile from the *madrassah,* but then we decided to go to the next stop, another half a mile away. We walked as fast as we could. We did not want to miss the bus while we were on our way to the next stop.

We waited another fifteen minutes at the new stop. At last the bus arrived. Perveen stepped onto the women's section in the front and I went into the men's. There weren't many people on the bus, and I sat in the first seat, next to the iron grill that divided the two compartments. The conductor came to me and I pointed at Perveen. He bent down over the grill and asked for the fare. She took a small purse from her bag and gave him the money.

At the station, Perveen gave me money and I bought two tickets for Lahore. We went through the flyover to the platform. The train was scheduled to leave at 9:30 p.m.

We sat on the bench and waited for the train to arrive. There were very few people on the platform. Nobody wanted to travel on the eve of *Eid,* even the window of the small tea shop next to our bench was half opened, and the man behind it was dozing.

Around 9:00 the train settled at the platform, and people started to hop on it; we got in on one of the third-class cars. A couple with their three children, two boys and a girl, were sitting two seats away from us, and a young man pushed his bag on the rack over the seats on the other side of the isle.

It was 9:40 but the train was still motionless, it was already ten minutes late. Through the window I saw four men on the flyover that took people from one platform to the other. Bayfazal grabbed

Ahmed's arm, and Perveen's two brothers were next to him.

Bayfazal caught my eye for a moment—the next I turned my head and slid backward. Perveen looked at me and must have seen the fear in my eyes. She pushed her head back.

A few seconds later I peeped out through the corner of the window. They were running for the train. My heart writhed in my chest like a fish out of water. Perveen's face seemed drained of all blood.

VI

Hajji Badruddin

Her back was straight and her eyes were glued to the vacant seat in front of her. I peeked out the window again. They were on the platform now, running for the third-class cars, which were all in the front, behind the engine. Just when I grabbed her hand and stood up to get away we heard the whistle and the train took a jerk forward. She pulled my hand and I sat down. The train accelerated out of the station.

Besides some excursions for *jalsas*—shows of religious intoxication—and the political rallies of religious parties, we *talibs*—students of *madrassahs*—had little exposure to the world outside the *madrassah*.

The eyes that I had fallen in love with were innocent, but the eyes of the girl sitting next to me now blazed with conviction. We had both changed since we'd met more than four years ago. We had grown up, because we'd had to. Maybe there really never were any children in the slums of Karachi or in the slums of anywhere.

The third-class cabin was a sort of monument to the lives of the third-class citizens, grasping to survive in a third-class neighborhood in a third-class power. The seats were as haggard as the women of scary stories—witches that had lost their youth a long time ago, and were now jealous of the young travelers sitting on them. They pierced their uneven edges into our flesh to take revenge on the new life dawning on us.

The ticket checker came, punched our tickets, and disappeared.

When the three noisy children of the couple sitting across us went to sleep, they started dozing too. A young man about my age, sitting in the row across the isle, was reading a copy of *Afsana Digest*.

I had once been beaten by Jallad for having a copy of that

magazine. The incident led to long lectures from Bayfazal over the next few days. According to him these magazines were filled with filth, no young boy of our age should read them. When the young man put the magazine down on the seat next to him, I asked his permission to see it.

He handed it over to me with a mischievous smile. "Enjoy yourself, *Maulana Sahib*."

Maulana sahib? My hand went to my beard. I must have looked much older than I was. I decided to get rid of that beard—and the age that went with it—at the first possible chance.

The magazine was full of stories of criminal valor and sexual conquest. I skimmed through it and placed it back on the seat next to him. He was already fast asleep, probably enveloped in a dream of one of the characters he had read about, a straw man offering him power over the forces of life—at least for a few minutes.

I rested my head on the side panel and closed my eyes. I shifted in the seat and my hip touched Perveen's. She glanced at me—not sharply, not angrily, perhaps not even surprised. The proximity of our bodies was intoxicating in a way I couldn't describe. With my eyes still closed, I determined to make a knot of this memory in my mind, to recall it whenever I wanted to for the rest of my life. And not just in some transient dream of fictional characters, fictional lives.

* * *

"You are getting too loud . . . is it a nightmare?" Perveen was shaking my shoulders to wake me up.

"No . . . No . . . I don't think so. I dreamt about two women, whispering in my ears," I said even before I was fully awake.

"Whispering what?"

"I couldn't figure out . . ."

"I wonder if it's a good omen."

I remained silent. The train lurched and clattered on.

"Do you know those women?" she asked.

"In the dream I felt I knew them."

She rested her head in the corner and closed her eyes. The black mole under her lower lip near her chin was the most prominent feature of her face. Her wide forehead was partly covered with the *duppatta* she was wrapping around her head and shoulders. I smiled when she wasn't looking at me.

A few minutes later when the train stopped at a small station she said, "Soon the train will be at Bahawalpur, and from there it will take around an hour to get to Multan. We should step down at Multan."

"Multan? But we planned to go to Lahore. It's a bigger city, and far from the reach of Shahbaz Khan."

"Nothing is far from him. They will look for us in Lahore first, some relatives of ours live there . . . but they may not consider Multan."

"Why didn't you tell me? I wouldn't have spent money on tickets for Lahore, Multan's fair is cheaper."

She shushed me gently. "Don't talk so loud . . . I wanted you to buy tickets for Lahore. They will try to get information from everywhere . . . from Ahmed, from the train station . . . everywhere. It's better if they keep thinking that we are in Lahore."

This time I didn't hide my smile from her. "You have planned everything already, I guess. But Ahmed had no idea about our plans. I never told him anything."

"Well, it didn't take them long to find out where we'd gone," she said. "They missed the train by seconds."

I remained silent. She seemed to be much more practical than me. Smarter.

"We should go to a shrine and stay there until I find some work," I said eventually.

She nodded and said, "For a couple of days . . . then we can find somewhere to stay."

"We have no money," I had to remind her. "It might take a long time to find a decent place."

She came close and whispered, "I have brought the jewelry Shahbaz sent for to me for the wedding. If we can sell—"

"That was not a smart move," I interrupted.

"A few thousand in jewelry is nothing for that reptile," she said, a little too loudly. Then she calmed herself and said much more quietly, "He will come after us no matter what."

I remained silent.

The couple and their children stepped down at Nawabshah, the area where Shahbaz Khan's father ruled. It was said that a long time back, when the British were expanding into India, the head of the family of Shahbaz's ancestors was told to ride his horse as far as he could into the sunset. In return for his loyalty to the British Empire, he could proclaim his sovereignty over the land he'd ridden through. Nobody really knew if this story was true, but the family did own vast tracts of land. The people who worked that land, farmers and their families, were barely more than slaves.

* * *

It was seven in the morning when we stepped out of the train on Multan Cantt. The sun moved slowly in the sky as if struggling to regain its dominance over the murky earth.

Multan was a city of Sufi shrines. The biggest, with thousands of followers in and out of the city, was Hazrat Bahauddin Zakariya. People flocked to this shrine by the hundreds every day, and by the thousands for festivals.

Shrines were havens for the downtrodden. They provided three things: food, shelter, and religious intoxication. Food and shelter, offerings by the privileged that were eager to receive more from God in return, kept the bodies of the poor going. Religion made them superhuman—with the help of drugs.

Shrines had always been centers of the cocaine trade, but those days, thanks to the war and refugees, heroin was popular everywhere, and gave additional charm to the shrines. When we came out of the station, we found the streets full of people. Worshippers and beggars were going to mosques and congregating in the city's open spaces. Men went in to offer prayers, and beggars camped outside to get the most out of the festival, when people are more wide-hearted, seeking blessings from God. The beggars on the streets guided us to the shrine.

The shops were closed, their goods still inside and not crowding the sidewalks, so the narrow streets of Multan seemed wider. A few vendors worked the sides of the streets, most of them selling fruit. The strong fragrance of *itir* wafted our way, putting our tired bodies, covered with old clothes soaked in perspiration, to shame. And that fought the aromatic food carts and fruit and vegetable stands to a stalemate. The latter only reminded me of a burning hunger—with neither money nor time to do anything about it.

We should have gotten to the shrine in ten minutes, but after twenty minutes there was still no sign of it. On the side of a street I saw for the first time those *tongas*—horse-driven carriages—that were the hallmark of the province of Punjab. They had two seats, like two jealous women refusing to face each other. One of them faced front, on which the driver sat, wide enough for two more passengers, and the other resting its back on the first and facing back, for three more people.

We stopped, and I asked one of the drivers about the shrine. Only after I managed to convince him we had no money for a ride there, he told us to go back the way we came and turn right on the main road to reach the Delhi Gate of Multan Fort. The shrine was located inside the fort. Delhi Gate was a reminder of the times when kings and viceroys ruled. Shops and houses crawled around it. Standing in the middle of the road, unable to block anybody coming in, it seemed miserable and guilty. We went through the crowded streets of the fort and came out into an open space.

The dome of Hazrat Bahauddin Zakariya blazed white against the brilliant azure sky. The pale sandstone walls were traced with green. The arched entrance and facade was whitewashed and welcoming. It sat on a wide plaza of stone the color of desert sand.

Dozens of shops outside the shrine sold spreads of fresh flowers and silver and golden thread, incense and candles of different aromas, and sweets and snacks. The shopkeepers buzzed about happily selling the most expensive item in their shops to the festival attendees to leave at the grave of the Sufi. Inside the shrine, the collection box was just as happy.

After 11:00 a.m., the shrine started serving *biryani*—spicy rice, rich with chunks of beef—and later, sweet rice. My whole body shook and I rocked back and forth as we waited in line. Perveen saw how hungry I was and held my arm, smiling, as if to make me stand still. Then we just started rocking together.

* * *

We stayed under the blue sky for three days, happily subsisting on the free food from the shrine. The fourth day, when the markets finally opened after the festival, we went to the shops to sell Perveen's jewelry.

The fifth store we tried sat off the city's center under a billboard advertising American soft drinks. The door was narrow and almost hidden behind a chaotic collage of advertisements for jewelry and watches, and even a camera and some kind of device a woman was using to curl her hair.

The jeweler was enormously fat—perhaps the fattest man I had ever seen. Sweat beaded on his forehead, but in fairness, it beaded on mine too. The days were invariably hot, made even more uncomfortable in this neighborhood by the thick smog of cars and trucks—vehicles of every shape and size—that roared around the traffic circle surrounding a small shrine.

Perveen eyed the man with a gloomy suspicion, and I flashed her a smile of encouragement, though I must admit I shared her skepticism. A cold certainty I didn't like appeared in the man's eyes as they played over Perveen's smuggled jewelry.

"I would like to sell—" I began, but was interrupted by the fat jeweler.

"No stolen jewelry here, my boy," he said, waving me away with his hand. "No, no, no."

Though to me they were stolen—after a fashion—I made an indignant face.

But before I could protest the fat man said, "Let me have a look at them." He held out his hand, but his face still wore a mask of stern disapproval. It was a face I knew all too well.

He gave our treasures only the most cursory glance then rumbled out a price that would barely keep us fed for a week.

"They must be worth ten times that!" I said, reaching out to take the jewels back from him.

He scowled at me, but didn't hand them back. "You think anyone else would even handle these stolen fakes?" he growled.

"Stolen?" I said, pouring as much outrage as I could into it, though indeed we'd been to four other jewelers already that day and none had even wanted to look at them.

"Fakes!" Perveen said. Her voice, sharp and high, startled me.

But that single word seemed to cause the fat jeweler actual pain. He stepped back and dropped the jewelry on his cracked glass countertop as though they were biting snakes.

"Get out!" he shouted, addressing me, of course, and not Perveen. "Get out of my store and take your trash with you!" With that last he glanced at Perveen and it was clear to us both what he meant by "trash."

Perveen stomped out, cutting off any chance I might have had to salvage the situation. I scooped the jewelry off the countertop with a scowl and as I followed her out of the store I said to the man, "You should be ashamed."

I closed my ears to the shrieked obscenities that followed me out, and they were quickly dragged under by the incessant roar of the traffic anyway. I took one step then half of the next, still with the jewelry in my hand, when a man touched my arm. I jerked away fast, bumping into another man passing quickly on my left. While I apologized to that man, the man who had grabbed me apologized to me, and the next thing I knew I was in another jewelry store, this one with many more cameras and a considerable selection of radios. Perveen followed me in.

"I hear everything through the wall," the man who'd grabbed me said with a smile that revealed many missing teeth. "He's as loud as he is fat, that one. And a crook, to boot."

I could only blink in response but when Perveen nudged my arm I handed the jewelry to this new prospect.

A few minutes later we left with barely more than the first man had offered, but something to start us off at least. And no more condemnations to remind me of Bayfazal, and nothing to remind Perveen of Shahbaz.

The very same day we rented a shack in one of the slums, not far from the downtown Multan. An alley from the main street led to the slum, which consisted of hovels on both sides of a narrow path. Our hovel was in the middle of the slum. Old plastic sheets were nailed onto the four wooden pillars to attempt the job of walls. An asbestos sheet rested on the pillars to hide the open sky.

The privacy this little hut—*our* little hut—provided made the proximity of our bodies haunting. At first we were both distracted by some basic housekeeping—enough to make it feel a little bit like a home and not what it was: a makeshift tent in another cruel city slum. Perveen set out our scant belongings and seemed to cordon off parts of the close interior. I could almost see them as she saw them, as rooms in a house: a kitchen, a sitting room, a bedroom for us, and another bedroom for a child . . .

My face grew hot when this thought came to me and I turned away from her, working to close off the bottom of the plastic walls in a surely vain attempt to keep the rats out. Then her hand was on my shoulder, soft and warm even through my shirt. I wished then that I could have washed for her, shaved even. I wanted to be wearing cleaner clothes, better clothes. I wanted to have something to give her, something to offer her, something more than someone to run away with, at least. I wanted to offer her someone to make a life with.

Very gently she turned me to her and I thought she wanted me to see her work, see the home she'd made for us, but when I turned her face was very close to mine. I kissed her without thinking I shouldn't, and without thinking I should. I kissed her because it had to happen, it was right, and we both knew it.

The feeling of her lips, then the very tip of her tongue, the taste of her, gave me a feeling as though my heart had stopped and my lungs had deflated and my eyes, though closed, were filled with light.

She drew away from me and she was smiling. Her hand pressed lightly against my cheek and I think I laughed a little, relieved that she wasn't offended or scared, and we kissed again.

This is when our little plastic and asbestos tent became all the home I could ever need, a place where Perveen and I could be together, not as lovelorn children, or impetuous runaways, or impertinent students, but as a man and a woman.

And that's how we started our lives together, in our imaginary bedroom in our imaginary house, as man and woman.

* * *

After a week of hunting for jobs I was successful in enticing a wholesaler of grains to employ both of us. Hajji Badruddin was a short man whose limbs and legs protruded from his bulky body like spikes from a football. He seemed to be pinching the people around him with these spikes to make them do what he expected from them. I started working at his shop, and Perveen at his home.

There was a big store behind the shop where different kinds of lentils, wheat, and millet were brought from the farms in big trucks and then cleaned, measured, and stored in bags to be supplied to retailers in Multan and other areas of lower Punjab. I had to clean the shop and the store, bring tea for the visitors, serve lunch to Hajji and his guests, and clean his car whenever he asked for it. I was also expected to help the workers in the store whenever I could.

Perveen went to his house early mornings, and came back in late afternoons. She did most of the chores of the house along with any whimsical commands of his wife.

Though there was something about Hajji Badruddin I didn't like, these days were good for us. We were both working and the little money we made—and it was very little—kept us in our plastic hovel, kept us fed, but most important it kept us together. I even managed to start saving. I replayed that day of trying to sell Perveen's jewelry over and over again in my mind, and though I'm not sure I remember making a conscious decision to replace it, I began to save just a little money at a time, not enough that Perveen would notice, to eventually buy her something, if only the sort of plastic bangles the other women of the Multan slums wore. This was the first time in my life I started to feel like a man and not a boy.

On days when I didn't see much of Hajji Badruddin, and there were a few, I felt better still. When I grumbled about my suspicions, that Hajji Badruddin wasn't all he seemed, Perveen gently dismissed me. She thought I had seen too many bad examples of men, and that made me suspicious. If I sometimes worked my full day without seeing the grain merchant, Perveen saw even less of him working in his home during the day. Hajji Badruddin's wife treated her well, and I didn't let on to Perveen that my suspicions about Hajji Badruddin weren't only because I was somehow spoiled against all men, but because of the way I had seen him looking at her, and the way I had heard him talking about other women when it was only men and boys in the shop.

Every evening when I reached home I would find Perveen outside our hovel talking to a few of the women who lived near us in the slum. We would eat dinner and talk for hours or we would go to the main street and walk a few blocks in air that was not overwhelmed by the stench of sewage. On Sundays, when the shop was closed, I would pick her up from Hajji's house and we would go to the shrine, just a few blocks from his house.

We were tired but happy. We did not want anything else from life. The passing months were making the life that we had left behind the landscape of a far country.

But life had its own will, its decisions were beyond our grasp.

* * *

One day as I was going home, I stopped at the bazaar to get some bangles for Perveen. It had seemed that every time I finally had enough money, some dire need would appear and I would have to wait, but finally I was successful in achieving my goal.

When I stepped down on the main street from the bus I saw two black Pajeros entering the alley heading into the slum. No car, let alone a Pajero, had ever entered the slum. I ran to the alley and watched the Pajeros disappear into the maze of hovels. I ran after them and hid myself under the protruding roof of a shack. I saw the vehicles stop in front of our hovel and the blood seemed to drop out of my face and into my feet.

Two men from each vehicle went in. Hajji Badruddin sat in the front passenger seat of one of the Pajeros. After a few seconds the men came out, dragging Perveen into one of the vehicles. I couldn't blame our neighbors for standing idly by, watching the struggle between four men with guns and a girl who had only fingernails to defend herself.

I jerked forward, attempting to take a step, but my legs seemed to reject the idea offhand. I opened my mouth but my tongue was dry and my throat closed around any attempt to call out to her.

I didn't have the courage to even try to rescue her. They would catch me, kill me offhand, and throw my body on a pile of trash,

51

then still take Perveen to Shahbaz Khan. And that was all the time I had being a man. As I stood there under that ramshackle roof, watching the Pajeros drive away, slowly, without concern much less fear of me, or anybody, I was a boy once more, frightened, and trapped in poverty and inconsequence.

I took the bangles from my pocket and it took me three attempts before I was able to let go of them, leaving them in the dust.

I went to the shrine to spend the night. The sight of them dragging Perveen to the car repeated itself over and over and over in my head. I wandered outside in the night like a sleepwalker, like some kind of undead thing shambling around without a will of his own. I felt my insides draining out, everything being replaced drop by drop with nothing but anger, a sort of impotent rage that made me feel as though I'd been set on fire. The crescent moon that hung in the sky seemed broken, and its two edges pierced my heart.

Finally a little cooler air, a little quiet, and some of my senses started to return.

I should have seen the connection between Shahbaz and Hajji Badruddin. Hajji must have sold grain from the fields of Shahbaz's wealthy family—surely they knew each other through their shared trade. But I had no clue how Hajji linked us to Shahbaz, how he could have recognized Perveen, who he'd never met before we wandered into his shop, two slum waifs in search of honest work.

Honest work . . .

All night I struggled with my desire to bring down those who had killed the only shred of happiness in my life, who took away the only person I had ever loved. But Shahbaz was far out of my reach. I had no refuge and no place to go, even if I found him, killed him, and took her back.

A few minutes before dawn came *azan*, the call for the Morning Prayer. I saw some of the dwellers of the shrine waking up, leaving their resting places, going toward the nearby mosque. I left the cool floor a few minutes later myself, and went to the east wall of the shrine. The sun seemed ashamed of the incessant drama of the earth and was hesitant to show his complete face, hiding behind the thick clouds that I imagined would soak the earth to clean some of the fever of human misery. I did *wazu*, the ablutions done for a prayer, faced west toward Kaba, and offered my respects to Allah in the hope of some advice, but no clear notion of the future appeared in my mind.

An hour later I went to the *chaiwalla* a block away from the shrine to have a cup of tea. Sitting on the *charpie* that lay on the sidewalk outside his small shop, I saw *tongas*, cars, and the carts selling vegetables, moving in two directions in front of me. Children and men were coming out of their homes to go to schools, shops, and offices. Here and there I saw working women moving among the men, getting onto the buses, rickshaws, and *tongas* to get to their destinations. I sat there long after finishing my tea. A man was arguing with the driver of a rickshaw, protesting the demanded fare. A boy was yelling at his younger sister who was slow and making him late for school. An old woman kept begging the man in a suit who was waiting for a rickshaw, offering lavish prayers for his family, repeatedly calling him "Babu" to appeal to his narcissistic stance. He waved his hands in desperation to get rid of her.

A shop, right across the *chaiwalla*, was opened by a tall man. His shiny products glared in my eyes in the virgin rays of the sun that had finally defeated the clouds just a few moments ago, giving vibrant life to the edges of knives and scissors of all kinds. I paid the *chaiwalla* and went across the street. Like a robot, I bought a sharp butcher's knife, hid it under my shirt, and went to Hajji's house.

I walked around it to see its weak points. Once I planned my means of entry I came back to the shrine.

At midnight I climbed up the electric pole and got over the boundary wall of the house. I grabbed the branch of the tree inside the house and slipped down on the trunk and landed in the front yard. The streetlight in front of the house helped me to find my way. The kitchen had an old-fashioned window with three one-square-foot panes fixed into each wooden panel. I carefully broke one of the panes, opened the window, and jumped in. I had brought some furniture from a shop with Hajji once, and had visited the residence. I knew the plan of the house; all the bedrooms were on the second floor and it was unlikely that anybody in the house had heard the small burst of noise of the glass breaking.

I faced no problem in finding my way to the bedroom, and the couple was fast asleep. I closed his wife's mouth, and pressed the butcher's knife to her throat with the other hand. Her cry remained stuck in her throat. She started pounding Hajji's chest with her hand. He awoke and sat up, struggling to understand what was happening.

"If you make a sound, I will kill your wife," I said, but it felt as though someone else was inside me, speaking for me—and speaking for Perveen.

"Don't, don't . . . I won't," he murmured.

"Go out and bring your children here."

"What do you want?" he said without getting off the bed.

"Do as I say if you want your wife breathing."

"Don't hurt my children," he said.

"I won't, but you need to bring the children here now . . . and listen, don't bother using the phone, it's not working anymore."

He went out, and after five minutes came with his three children: a teenage boy who I had worked with in the shop and who had always been decent to me, and two small girls Perveen sometimes called her "little nieces."

I locked his wife and children in the bedroom, and brought Hajji Badruddin into the living room. They started shouting and cursing through the door.

"Tell them to shut up," the voice form inside me said.

"Quiet!" he commanded.

The bedroom fell silent.

"How did you come to know about us?" I asked him at knifepoint.

"Your picture was in the papers from Lahore."

"And there was a prize for the one who finds us?"

He remained silent.

"You *pig*! Don't you already have enough money?"

"I didn't do it for money," the man blubbered. "Mehrab Khan sells most of his crops to me, I just couldn't remain quiet."

"Mehrab?" I asked. I knew the name. "Father of Shahbaz?"

"Yes."

The buzz of the sobs coming from the other room was making me weak, appealing to me to get out of the house before I went through with what I'd come here to do.

Staring at the knife, Hajji Badruddin said, "Take whatever you want from the house. I have some money, too."

"You think you can pay me for the life I had with her?" I said through a jaw clamped tightly shut. "Shahbaz could get any girl in the world, but I had only one woman to be happy with."

He clasped his hands and begged, "I am sorry. I made a mistake! Forgive me."

His hands seemed like claws, sticking out of a fat swine.

I hit his quivering belly with all my might—forgetting that I held the butcher's knife. But I felt a strange ecstasy piercing his flesh, padded with thick layers of fat. The blood soaked his clothes and dyed my hands black in the dark room.

He fell to the floor and tried to drag his bulky body away, but there was no way he could escape from my hands, which had the energy of ten men at that moment. He started hollering, but on my second stab his cries turned into the sounds made by a lamb whose throat had been cut and the air was gushing out of it.

I stabbed him again and then again. All my anger went through my arms and hands into the knife. The voices screaming from the bedroom seemed faraway and foreign to me, inconsequential, but they must have torn through the night like a siren.

I threw the knife over the dead grain merchant's still jerking body and ran out of the house.

VII

Ahmed

I ran into the alleys behind the main streets, using all my strength to get away from Hajji's house. I breathed in sharp, shallow pants that made my head spin, but I knew I couldn't stop so I just ran through it. My knees shook and I stumbled once, almost fell, and scraped across a rough brick wall. I almost fell to my knees when I pushed myself away from the wall. My body made the decision for me—I leaned against the wall and let myself breathe. Just a few real, deep breaths. I don't know how long I leaned there, in a dark alley that smelled of rotting food and dust. It was probably only a minute, then I went on, staggering at first, then walking.

When I finally reached the shrine I went to the communal water tap near the entrance. Using the cover of darkness I washed my hands, cleaned the drops of blood from my *qameez*, and with my eyes closed in the dark, by feel alone, I shaved my head, beard, and moustache. The homeless men and women were fast asleep in the shrine. That night, I added another body to the burden the shrine carried.

I went out of the shrine during day and begged, and went into the shrine at night and slept.

After a few days of this I saw a team of policemen approaching the shrine. I sneaked behind the shops pressed against the shrine and walked away fast, but not so fast as to be seen as running away. This was difficult to accomplish—all I wanted to do was run and run.

In the evening when I came back I saw two policemen sitting on the bench of a shop near the entrance of the shrine. Their black uniforms and golden badges seemed to glow in the bright lights of the shop. I turned around and went to Multan Cantt station. I decided to go back to Karachi, that ogre of a city. In its spreading limbs a fugitive might find better refuge than in Multan.

* * *

I stepped down at Karachi Cantt Station, and spent the last coins in my pocket on a light meal. Then I shamelessly begged money for a bus ticket. A few minutes later I was on the bus, heading back to Gizri.

I went to the bazaar near the *madrassah* and encamped in the alley next to the butcher's shop. The alley was full of all sorts of scraps and smelled like dung. All the windows of the houses that opened into it were closed. I kept looking out into the street until I finally saw Ahmed buying lamb from one of the modest shops. When he came out of the shop I grasped his arm and dragged him away into the alley. He throttled and shrieked at first but it didn't take him long to recognize me despite the change in my appearance.

"Do you have a death wish?" he said, still breathing hard as panic slowly faded away.

"I need to know what happened to her."

He sighed and looked down at the ground, but when I took half a step closer to him he said, "What do you expect? I wish I hadn't brought that note from her . . ." He paused and we stood there for a few long seconds before he finally sighed again and said, "She's in jail, under *Hudood* Ordinance."

"*Hudood* Ordinance? But I thought that snake wanted her to be his wife."

"Are you an idiot? Do you think this rich man would accept her as his son's wife after what you've done to her? She was no use to him once she ran away with you."

"But how did he manage to send her to jail?"

"I don't know. Nothing is impossible for a rich man in this country."

I started walking around in little circles, my whole body was trembling.

"Her brothers didn't try to protect her?"

"They were gone within a month of your elopement."

"Gone?"

"Police killed them in an ambush with some drug dealers. It was staged, actually. Shahbaz gave them a handsome reward to get Perveen. They couldn't keep their side of the bargain, so they had to go."

The thought of a staged drug deal, and Shahbaz paying the police to murder for him made it almost impossible for me to breathe.

"What do I do?" I grabbed my head and sat down on the ground, in the alley full of scum.

Ahmed remained silent.

A couple minutes later he patted my shoulder. "Bayfazal is sending a group of students to Afghanistan," he said, and I thought he was reluctant to tell me this, as though he didn't want me to know, but it was all he could think of. "He probably gets a big payday for each head. I'm sure he'll be happy to sell you off with the next group."

"But the war is over."

"War is never over," Ahmed replied with a little laugh that made him sound like an old man. "The Russians left and nobody cared about the civil war. But now the government has decided to send men there to support a new group trying to take over the country. They need warm bodies—anybody who can carry one gun and get shot by another."

"What do they call this group?"

"I don't know." By his voice I could tell it didn't matter to him, and in the end it didn't matter to me either.

"It's possible he may just let Shahbaz have me."

"If he gets a better offer for you he may," Ahmed said with a shrug. "There's no guarantee, but your only other choice is to run until Shahbaz's guys eventually catch you. And once they catch you, they *will* kill you, just like Perveen's brothers."

"Is he sending you away?" I asked, shaking my head, trying to erase an image of Perveen's good-for-nothing brothers dying in a hail of police gunfire, and me with them.

"Yes," Ahmed told me, "he is."

"How about the others, do they want to go?"

"Most of the younger ones are eager to go. Bayfazal's sermons have dug deep marks on their minds. Some of them are confused and afraid of war . . . but nobody can say no to him. You know that."

I nodded, and reached out to touch Ahmed on the shoulder. "What happened to you after we left?"

"The usual," he replied, forcing a crooked smile. "First Jallad beat the hell out of me, then Bayfazal doubled my workload . . ."

He paused again and we stood in silence for a little while until he finally said, "I need to go. Bayfazal will want to know why I'm late."

"Tell him you met me," I said. "I'm ready to go."

Ahmed nodded, frowning, and said, "Meet me here tomorrow."

"*Allah Hafiz.*"

"*Allah Hafiz.*"

* * *

The *Hudood* Ordinance was enacted in 1979 as part of the Islamization process of Zia-ul-Haq, the president, leader of the military regime, and the friend of America in the Afghan War. It intended to implement Islamic *Shariah* Law for *Zina*, extramarital sex, and *Qazf*, false accusation of rape. The ordinance provided a platform through which women who were raped were eventually accused of adultery. A woman alleging rape was required to provide four adult male eyewitnesses. Such proof was usually impossible. Moreover, to prove rape, a victim had to admit that sexual intercourse had taken place.

When the alleged offender was acquitted due to the lack of evidence, a woman who admitted that intercourse had taken place then faced charges for adultery. I heard about such cases in the discussion of Bayfazal's *Kuthbats*—sermons—before Friday prayers. In those days, the case of a blind woman, Safia Bibi, had made a lot of uproar from women's groups, who Bayfazal called "the evil daughters of the culpable Eve."

I knew it would be an easy thing for a man like Shahbaz to drag Perveen into some such case. The thought of it made my blood run cold.

I took a bus back to the train station where I begged for a little food money, and spent the night. The next day, early in the morning, I took the bus back to Gizri, and met Ahmed. He took me through the back door of the *madrassah* to a room upstairs that was used to store old prayer rugs and furniture.

When we entered the room, we found Bayfazal standing in front of us.

He waved Ahmed away and grumbled at me, "So, you are back. . . . How was the air outside?"

I remained silent.

"Nothing has changed here, except that you ruined that innocent girl. She was about to live in a palace and now she is carrying your bastard, sitting in jail awaiting sentence."

I blinked. Little sparkles of light intruded on my vision and I momentarily stopped breathing.

"She's . . . pregnant?"

"Yes."

"I will do anything you want . . . just help me to take her out of there," I begged, the words forcing their way out of my mouth.

Bayfazal responded with a cruel smile, "Nobody can help her now. She's in very powerful hands. But you can save yourself."

"It's my child . . . I need to do something."

"You do not know that."

"What do you mean?"

Bayfazal shrugged and replied, "She spent time with Shahbaz."

I swallowed and asked, "Willingly?" I felt stupid the second the word formed in the air.

Bayfazal just shrugged and my body shook and tears blurred my eyes. A sob burst out of me.

"Crying won't solve anything," Bayfazal said with a sneer. "You stink like a rotten pig. Go get a shower." He pointed to the door in the corner. "I am sending Ahmed with some clothes and food. And do not even think of leaving this room. I won't let you put me at risk again."

With that, he left. I heard the sound of the key turning in the lock, and didn't bother testing the door. I knew it wouldn't open. I dropped myself on a pile of old rugs and cried my heart out.

An hour later, Ahmed came with some clothes and a comforter while Jallad stood at the door. Apparently Bayfazal wasn't yet ready to trust Ahmed with my care. While Jallad waited, Ahmed left and came back with a tray of food—*dal* and two *nans*.

Throughout the day, I tried to sleep in the dark room, but couldn't. Any little sound startled me—I was sure it was the footsteps of Shahbaz's men coming for me. I never felt a moment's peace in that room. Even the haggard old furniture and the pile of threadbare prayer rugs seemed like monsters waiting for the command of Bayfazal to gulp me down.

The next morning, Ahmed brought some tea and bread along with a copy of the holy book. He handed it over to me and said, "Bayfazal says that you need this more than ever."

"Bastard," I whispered in response.

"You need to shut your mouth," Ahmed whispered, his brow furrowed. "Even the walls have ears in this *madrassah*."

"I don't care," I shot back, not keeping my voice down even a little. "What is he going to do, kill me? I'm marching off to my death anyway."

Ahmed swallowed and looked me in the eyes. "You're not the only one," he said. "You're lucky, you know? You fell in love, you lived with a woman, you saw the world. . . . The rest of us . . . we've never seen any of that. We're just going from one hell to another."

I felt the sadness of his heart. The numbness I was feeling after coming back to the *madrassah* and the memory of Perveen . . . I knew he was right. I saw a glimpse of life the other students of the *madrassah* would never see. They would never fall in love, never sleep with a woman. . . . Once they left, they might not even see a woman again, and they would never know how it must feel to become a father.

In the evening, after *Isha*, the last prayer of day, Bayfazal returned.

"I have made all the arrangements," he said. "You will leave with the group next Sunday. The train will leave for Quetta at six in the morning. I will ask Ahmed to get some things of use for you."

I knew what he meant by *arrangement.* He'd received the money for my head. He'd sold me like a goat.

"I want to see her," I said.

"You need to shut up and do what I tell you!" Bayfazal roared.

"Then let me go," I replied, taking my own turn to sneer. "Let them catch me."

Bayfazal used his huge hand to convey his anger; his fingers made a distinct mark on my cheek. "If you wanted that you shouldn't have come here. They will destroy me if they ever know I've given you refuge. Instead of letting you out, I'll kill you myself."

"What will happen to my child?"

"You keep saying 'my child'! 'My child!' Nobody knows whose child it is. You never know who else slept with her. And once she delivers, it will be sent to an orphanage. If it's a boy I will bring him here to *madrassah.* I will help your child as I helped you."

The hint of an abhorrent smile lifted the corner of his lips. I prayed from the depth of my heart for a girl.

"Can I please see Massi Rehmatea?" I asked, my voice barely

more than a whisper.

He remained silent, undecided.

"I may not come back from Afghanistan," I added to convince him.

Finally he said, "I'll send her to you before you leave."

Then he left me and I cried and cried. I was going insane locked in that room. If I could have opened the only window in the room, I would probably have jumped from the second floor to kill myself.

VIII

Tara, My Mother

On Saturday, Museabate came to my little room. Jallad stayed outside. She closed the door and took off her *purdah*.

"What a mess," she said, her voice burning me. "Just for a girl. Your mother would be ashamed of you."

"Have you seen her?" I asked, ignoring the rest.

"Yes, I went to jail to see her."

"Is it my child?"

"She says so," Massi Museabate said.

I took a deep breath and wiped a tear from the corner of my eye. "What will happen to the child?"

"You know what happens to such children."

"What do you mean?"

She remained silent, and I knew there was more being left unsaid besides the answer to my last question.

"Who was my father?" I asked her. "There's no use hiding anything. I will be gone soon enough."

"What's the use of digging up old graves?" she said, and something made her reach out and pat my shoulders.

"I need to know," I said.

Museabate threw up her hands in exasperation and said, "Your mother was from a very respectable family. She fell in love with a man who was not approved by her father. She lived in Dhaka. She got separated from her family in the ethnic violence of 1971, and later ended up here when they sent the refugees."

"Was the man she fell in love with my father?"

She looked at me closely and thought for a while before responding, "I don't know."

"Don't lie to me. Not now!"

Jallad pushed the door open and looked in, his eyebrows

meeting over his nose. He looked at me with such hate. . . . But Museabate waved him off and he closed the door, never looking away from me as though he were trying to kill me with his eyes.

"I have a few things of hers," Museabate continued when the door closed. "I'll send them to you."

"*Her* things?" I asked.

"Your mother's things."

"What *things*?"

"She forgot to take some things with her when she left," Museabate said, "but I guess it's time you have them."

"*Left?* You said she was ill and passed away in the hospital."

"Yes," she said, shrugging and nodding and not looking me in the eyes. "She did . . . eventually."

"What are you hiding from me?"

"There is a diary in her things," she said, "Maybe it will tell you everything you want to know."

I shook my head. How was I supposed to respond to this?

"What she would have thought of all this . . ." Museabate said, shaking her head.

"She wouldn't blame me for the love I have for Perveen," I countered. "She went through hell for the man she loved."

"And where did this love take her? To a slum! Where is it taking you? To the war!" She stressed all the right syllables to rub those facts in my face.

"Adopt my child once she is in this world."

"I will," she said, and just the barest trace of tenderness came to her face—or maybe I imagined that. "I shouldn't have given you away."

"Why not?"

Her silence told me she knew Bayfazal's secret—and mine. All of ours. There was no use pronouncing her guilty when I needed her to protect my child. I gulped down my anger like a sour medicine, and replaced it with thoughts of Perveen. We didn't say goodbye. Massi Museabate left, Jallad holding the door for her then locking it after her.

An hour later, Ahmed came with a plastic bag. In it was a diary, two books in English, a few envelopes with letters addressed to Museabate, a pen, and a photograph in which two young women sat on the floor in front of a middle-aged woman and an old man on a sofa. On the wall behind the sofa was a painting of a big rose vine in front of a green mountain and a river.

Was my mother one of the three women in the photo? Was this her family? Of course, who else could it be? I kept looking at the photograph, trying to find my mother in the three women. The middle-aged woman was probably too old to be my mother. Was I the son of one of the younger ones? The man and woman on the sofa were probably the parents of the young women sitting on the floor. The one on the right had long hair, and some strands fell over her forehead. The other young woman was leaning back, resting her palm on the floor. I wished that Museabate had brought my mother's things to me instead of sending them so I could ask her about the photograph. But it was too late for that. I had to leave the very next day and there was no chance to meet Museabate.

I opened the diary. On the inside cover was a little form to fill out. Under Name was written, in a careful and feminine hand: Tara. In the row for address: General History, University of Dhaka.

The few pages after that had some printed information—the things all diaries have. On the first page, January 1, the writer had scrubbed out the date and written "February-July, 1970." I flipped through the pages. After every few pages, she had scrubbed out the date and either wrote a new month or the duration of a year. The handwriting that was so careful on the inside cover quickly deteriorated. I could almost trace where she started to speed up and speed up, the words cascading out of her almost too fast for her hand to keep up. Then she would start again, a little neater, then worse and worse again.

Besides curiosity, I didn't know what I was feeling. I wanted to know about my mother but I was also afraid to know about a woman who had left her child.

But I was leaving my child, too, and I might never have a chance to get to know her. Was I different from her?

I started reading.

February-July 1970

My parents avoided each other, but kept the machine of the house running for us—me and my sister, Sumaira. Were they just the victims of an arranged marriage or was there more to this relationship that seemed to have a frozen ocean under its surface? I never knew. Sometimes the frozen ocean sent a chill our way, but the cold never overwhelmed us.

They were very practical regarding our needs but their approaches were starkly different. *Ammi*, our mother, was determined, sometimes even obsessive, to ensure our safety and comfort, and always concerned about our education. Our father was eager to provide for us the best possible facilities money could buy, but beyond that he expected us to find our way in life within the established parameters of his, which our mother forced him to broaden whenever she deemed it essential to provide us leverage in our lives.

Their disagreements regarding us were almost always about our social life, which he thought was too liberal, and about our education, which he thought was more than needed for future housewives and probably a hurdle in our finding suitable husbands in the community. He felt relieved when Sumaira got engaged to Shehzad, an army major stationed in Dhaka. He was eager to get a match for me as soon as possible.

My mother left behind all the cultural norms to keep him out of the way of my education. My father was against my going to Dhaka University and my study in a co-ed environment. Their struggle melted the frozen ocean, and its fierce waves ruled our lives for some time. It was the very first time I witnessed the strength that was hidden in her character. I was snatched away from her not long after that, and therefore I do not know, my friend, if there was a second time . . . I don't know what happened to her courage when I disappeared.

I very well remember that, in his rage, my father said to *Ammi*, "You were overeducated and couldn't get a husband, you were lucky I was there."

"I would be luckier if you hadn't been there—" My mother matched the force of his anger.

The first day I stepped out of the house to go to Dhaka University, I saw a world full of promises. The spring of Bengal was singing the songs of green pastures and cool air and the eucalyptus tree over the porch was rocking in the music. The earth was sending pleasant aromas in response to the shower of a few moments ago.

Our posh neighborhood, with speckle-free sidewalks, clean streets, and nice facades seemed an orchestration of a keen creator. I saw a Bengali girl coming out of the house two doors next to us wearing a college uniform. A boy waved at her and stopped his cycle to talk to her.

I got into the car, the Bengali driver closed the door of the passenger side and we drove away. The roads were full of cycle rickshaws taking students and men and women to their destinations. Two men were exchanging words on the roadside just before our first signal, pointing at each other angrily, using curse words. Bengali, which creates the most pleasant sounds, rarely adopts the harsh tones I was hearing. I waited eagerly for the signal to turn green.

I found my way to a small classroom in the history department of the university. There were never more than a few students pursuing the major in general history, so the classes were small. I noticed his presence in the very first class and then in every class—that presence sustained itself, and diverted my attention from lectures, books . . .

The girls had a hub of their own. I was the only West Pakistani in the group. In the beginning, all the girls thought I belonged to the Punjabi community, but when they came to know that my parents were from Delhi, their reservation toward me gradually phased out. In those chaotic times the space for West Pakistanis was squeezing down, but to be a Punjabi meant that she belonged to the ruling army, and therefore was destined to be shunned from the Bengali social circle. The hostilities toward the ruling regime in particular, and toward West Pakistanis in general, was increasing.

The very first time he approached me I found myself retreating. The conflict shook me to the core of my middle-class conservative roots. The voice in that core warned me repeatedly. I lived in a world that was divided in secluded spaces of communities, religions, and races, and though these factions of the society might be civil to each other, they insisted on keeping their blood pure. I could lose myself in the proclivity of its divisive nature, but I couldn't surmount it.

He refused to step back emotionally despite realizing my retreat. Every now and then he would invent something to talk to me about.

Shukuntala was our class fellow. We lived in the same neighborhood, and we took the bus together after finishing our last class. One Friday, when we were going to the bus stop, she said, "He is interested, Tara, are you?" She winked at me while asking the question.

"Who is interested? What are you talking about?"

"Come on! The world knows what's going on, you think you can fool me? I have a tusk larger than Ganiash—I smell things from very far," Shukuntala said.

"Nothing is going on . . . you have a weird imagination."

"Don't challenge me, honey . . . you will lose." She had a wide smile on her face.

"I don't know, Shukuntala, I don't know." I decided to be honest with her—I knew she was attempting to address the knot in my mind.

"What do you not know?"

"The differences in our lineages, our prejudices . . . they are very difficult to conquer. My mother had to fight like a lioness to make my father let me come to university to study in a co-ed environment, he won't accept a . . . he won't accept a—"

"A Bengali!"

I did not respond to her correct conclusion.

"Do you have problems with your father?"

I felt that she was crossing the border, that the affinity between us had been established, but then I reproached myself, I knew she meant well. "I can't call it a problem, but I am not close to him . . . he has a very different set of values than my mother's."

"I cannot decide in place of you . . . but you do not know the future, nobody knows it . . . you can live these years at the university by letting yourself experience something that you may cherish all your life or you can keep calling your feelings ghosts."

"I am afraid I will lose both ways. At least ghosts are safer to deal with, they are usually not real."

She remained silent.

We chatted about everything under the sky on the bus all the way to our homes—homes that were refuge for us women, but that also demand great sacrifices.

I remained curious about his inclinations. Didn't he hate this hide and seek of mine? This closeness and then hesitation to be close, did he have any idea of the struggle inside me? Men are usually immune to these struggles. They have the freedom to be what they want to be. They may fail in their attempt, but they don't have to hide their intentions. I felt jealous of their liberties.

The summer vacations of that very first year at the university brought relief. I had thought that the distance created by the break would make me phase out from this question of *to be or not to be* but the spare time during the vacations did not bring serenity. I decided to get away from Dhaka, and go to Karachi.

Almost every year during summer vacations I went to Karachi

with my sister, Sumaira, and quite often, *Ammi*, our sweet mother accompanied us, and every now and then father came along too for a couple of days. Since her engagement, Sumaira lost interest in our visits to Karachi, where my uncle (my mother's brother, Arif), and a large part of my father's family lived. I'd rather have my sister go with me instead of my parents. We had more liberties in Karachi without them, and our cousins entertained us like hell—or if you believe in heaven, my friend Rehmatea, then that's fine too.

That year, I bribed my sister with lots of gimmicks to make her go with me. We preferred to stay at our uncle's, and not at my father's family. My parents' families were very different from each other. Uncle Arif and his family were quite progressive in their outlook whereas my father's siblings always made it clear to us that it was not appropriate to roam the city of Karachi without any *chadur*, any covering.

Uncle Arif's three children were two to six years younger than me. I felt very comfortable with them. My uncle was as eager as my mother to send them to the best possible schools in Karachi. Most of my cousins on my father's side were educated till matriculation, the tenth and last grade in public schools, but I'd never seen them show any interest in college, despite my father's promise to support the male members of those families to further their education.

My mother's elder brother, Wasif, died in the disturbances of the partition. I often saw my mother crying, sitting in front of the only picture of him she still possessed, framed in a beautiful golden frame, placed in the middle of the table in the sitting room where she offered her prayers.

August 1970

When Mansoor and I met the first day after vacation, I approached him with a smile of recognition and acceptance. It caught him by surprise for a moment, and then I felt a wave of warmth approaching me.

He invited me to the cafeteria for a cup of tea and I said yes.

"How was your vacation?" he asked.

"Busy but rejuvenating."

"I went to Chittagong," he said.

"Chittagong?"

"Yes, my mother lives there. She is a professor in a college."

"What does she teach?"

"History."

"And your father?"

"He passed away a long time back—I was a child."

"Sorry to hear that."

"What did you do during vacation?"

"I went to Karachi, families of my parents live there."

"Did you enjoy your time there?"

"Yes, I went with my sister . . . do you have any siblings?"

"No, I am the only one . . . let me get tea for us." He left to go to the café counter.

I looked around, nobody was paying attention to us. Almost all the tables in the canteen were occupied. The two walls of the canteen, only three feet tall, were unable to hide the green pastures behind them. Sitting at my table I could see the history and political science departments through the branches of the eucalyptus trees that were swirling in the light showers.

I heard a shriek and I turned my head toward the owner of the excited voice. It belonged to the corner table where two groups of students were debating about the Bengali identity and military rule in Pakistan. One group was insisting that more than ninety percent of the army consisted of West Pakistanis and was predominantly Punjabi, therefore Bengal has no role in martial law and that the army would always oppress East Pakistan. The members of the other group belonged to West Pakistan and were insisting on calling the army the Pakistani Army, representative of the whole country. The second group was stressing the need for martial law due to the vacuum in the political arena, and due to the bickering of politicians. The two groups were as many miles apart as the two wings of the country, East Pakistan and West Pakistan—1500 miles to be precise. They agreed only on one point: The democracy was fragile, and its future would remain in jeopardy.

Mansoor brought tea, and I came back to my personal preoccupation, endeavoring to know about him. I asked a lot of questions about his family but he never asked anything about mine. I found him interested in me and my life, but he had nothing to ask about the backdrop in which I lived. When we were leaving the cafeteria I asked, "You have no interest in my family?"

"I have interest in you, the rest is irrelevant . . . but it does not mean that I wouldn't like to know about it."

I looked at him closely. His silky dark skin seemed to have a dialogue with his black eyes. Thick loops of his hair were intruding on his wide forehead, covering half of it.

He wanted to bicycle with me to the bus station. At that moment I realized we were miles apart culturally, despite being close physically. All his attitudes showed the fragrance of the liberal Bengali air. For him, cycling next to me to the bus stop was no problem, but for me, the notion that I could be seen walking with a boy on a cycle in the street was a troublesome one. I decided that if we had to reach anywhere together in life then he should know who I was, and where I was coming from. Before we would go any further, I should tell him.

In our next couple of meetings, I told him all about myself—to make him aware of the difficulties in our path—but he didn't show any retreat. He insisted that we were adults and only we could decide about our lives. I wish, Rehmatea, that the world we lived in was really that simple.

One day when I walked into the cafeteria to meet Mansoor, I saw a middle-aged woman in a white *sari* sitting next to him. I stopped in the corridor, not sure if it would be appropriate to approach them. He stood up and waved at me, I realized that the woman was his mother. My hesitation turned into reluctance. He

74

walked two steps toward me, and waved at me again. Fearing this interaction of ours would get the attention of the people in the cafeteria, I walked to their table.

"Hello Tara . . . meet my mother."

"*As-salāmu 'alaykum,*" I greeted her.

"*Wa-'alaykum-us-salām.*"

"I have heard a lot about you from Mansoor," she said.

I remained silent.

"How are your studies?"

"Very well, Auntie." I stared at Mansoor while responding to her.

"Don't be angry with him." She smiled. "I called him yesterday night about my visit to Dhaka . . . and when he told me about you, I couldn't resist meeting you."

"I am not angry, Auntie," I rushed to clarify. "It's just that I was not expecting you."

"She will take her revenge on me once you are gone, Mama," he said with a laugh.

"Go get some tea for us, Mansoor." She sent him away.

"What does your father do, *beta*?"

"He exports cotton and jute."

"I am glad to meet you."

"It's nice to meet you too, Auntie."

"I have only one child, and his wishes are very dear to me, and I like you very much but . . ." She hesitated.

I sat my eyes on her face.

"*Beta*, in the East marriages are between two families and not two people . . . I wonder if your family would be able to meet with us as equals, and if you would be happy in our small home. . . . It is very small, and very humble."

"I hesitated before putting my feet on this path—for dozens of reasons . . . but now I have come too far. I am afraid there is no turning back."

"Do your parents know about Mansoor?"

"No, not yet!"

"You need to tell them as soon as possible. If they are ready to receive me, let Mansoor know."

I remained silent. Mansoor was about to approach us. He placed the cups in front of us. After finishing her tea, she stood up. "I should be going. I am meeting Salma for lunch before catching the bus for Chittagong."

"How is Salma Auntie?" Mansoor asked.

"She is fine . . . she has asked about you so many times, but you never bother to call her or drop in, she lives just a few blocks from the university." She turned to me. "Salma is a very good friend of mine. . . . It's very nice to meet you, *beta*."

She tapped Mansoor's shoulder, who was about to stand up. "No, no, you sit here, I'll get a rickshaw on my own. . . . I'll call you in the evening after getting back home." She walked away from us.

"I am sure your magic is working on her too," he said.

"Shut up! Couldn't you tell me she was coming?"

"Oh my, *ma'am*, I did not know. She called me late in the evening."

"Do not call me ma'am—I have told you so many times."

He just laughed.

"I am afraid of the future Mansoor."

"Always remember that we are the decision makers, not anybody else," he said.

"You are a man, this is easy for you to say."

"Decision making is not about gender, it's about clarity . . . until women learn to make their own decisions it won't get any easier for them."

I looked at my watch. "It's time to go, or we'll be late for class."

He threw his book bag on his shoulder and walked along with me.

December 1970

On that day, almost all the students wore a strip of black cloth on their arms. On the surface it was the sign of their opposition to the ban on *Social History*, a book written by Qumruddin, but in reality it was rebellion against the army and its rule, and the supremacy of the West through the army and political machine of the martial law government.

In the book, the writer had connected Bengal's social roots to Kolkata, the other side of Bengal—part of India. *Social History* was an attempt to evaluate the cultural roots of the Bengali identity in terms of the role of fine arts and literature in the lives of people. In place of *Social History* the government was making *Waish au Kurushti (Land and its People)* part of the curriculum. This book stressed the ideological connections of West and East Pakistan, and implied that common religion strengthened these ideological ties. *Land and its People* seemed to ignore the role of culture in the lives of people.

Coming down the stairs of the department building, I saw Mansoor talking to a group of students. Above the pony wall of the canteen behind them, I could see the heads of students sitting around the wooden tables, engrossed in dialogue about everything under the sky. The branches of the papal tree next to the wall were enjoying the song of the wind at the dawn of the spring; their rollicking leaves were filling the environment with an uproar. Our eyes made contact, and he moved toward me with a smile.

"Why are you wearing this black strip? Are you becoming a revolutionary too?" I asked him in Urdu instead of Bengali or English so that our conversation remained confidential. Most of the Bengali students showed little enthusiasm for learning Urdu, the language of West Pakistan.

"You just need to order me to take it off and I will."

"Do not flirt with me like that. . . . Why did you wear it in the first place?"

"*Yar*, they tied it on their own, I let them do it just to make them happy. . . . My *ma'am* seems to be in a bad mood today."

"You called me *ma'am* again!"

"Well, we have no other choice but to call our masters from the other side *ma'ams* and *sahibs*," he could speak Urdu quite fluently, but he mimicked the Bengali accent.

I knew he was just teasing me, but an unknown fear gripped my heart. "Sometimes you scare me, Mansoor."

The change in my tone changed the expression on his face. "Come on, I was just joking. Let's have a cup of tea."

"No, I should get back home . . . Baba worries too much about me these days."

"That conservative father of yours, let him become my father-in-law, and then see what I'll do."

"Shut up!" I moved toward the street.

He rushed to get in my way. "I am sorry, I am sorry . . . I was just joking."

"You joke too much . . . it's impossible to talk to you seriously ever," I scolded him.

"I promise, I'll be serious now, but first tea."

"I'll stay only for fifteen minutes."

"All right."

I went to a table in the corner, and he went to get tea from the counter.

When he was coming back, he was stopped by a group of boys. Their gestures were making it quite obvious that the conversation was not pleasant. I looked above the pony wall of the canteen—a group of soldiers were watching the scene, ready to jump in if the conflict escalated. I took some deep breaths to calm myself down but they were in vain.

I saw Mansoor taking off his black strip, and throwing it on the floor. One of the boys stepped toward Mansoor, but another one in the group rushed to come between them. Mansoor picked up the tea mugs that he had placed on a nearby table, and walked toward me.

"What were they saying?" I asked him the moment he reached me.

"Nothing!"

"Tell me *na!*"

"The same old prattle." He was irritated.

"What?"

"Just drink your tea!"

"I am going." I stood up.

"No . . . please!"

"Then tell me!"

"They think that it's insulting to them that I am friendly to a girl from . . . from Punjab."

"Punjab?"

"They are just ignorant fools."

"I think I should be going." I stood up again, unnerved.

"Come on, at least drink your tea."

"No . . . I need to go."

"I'll come along with you to the bus stop," he said.

"No, you stay here . . . I'll be fine."

"What am I going to do here alone, I am leaving too."

The incident broke the spell of our companionship. My walk was touching the arena of running, and he was trying to move as fast as I was.

I was not sure what I was feeling, fear or anger or frustration. I stopped under a tree. "We should stop seeing each other."

"What?"

"We should stop seeing each other."

"You can't be serious."

"We are miles apart, socially, culturally and now politically. How long can we avoid this fact? Look around, all the violence in the city is communal and not just criminal, as the newspapers report thanks to the censors. What do you think all this will lead to?"

"I don't know. I just know that we are the decision makers in our lives . . . can you be a decision maker?"

I remained silent. Standing under the eucalyptus tree that was throwing soft shadows due to the overcast sky, I saw pure innocence in his eyes. I started to walk fast, he ran to catch me.

"You are very fond of worrying me!"

I stopped abruptly and turned to him. "I am fond of worrying you? Didn't you see the hate in their eyes toward me . . . if the army wasn't on the university grounds, I wouldn't be able to stay here even for a moment!"

"Everything will be all right after the coming elections, they will clear the air."

"I desperately hope to see you proven right."

A few drops of rain touched our foreheads to calm us down. He took out his umbrella from his bag and spread it over our heads. The loop of wet hair on his forehead was dropping down to his eyebrows. A thought grabbed my heart: Was it worth loving this man despite the awareness from the very beginning that there were strong chances of losing him? I couldn't decide.

A light shower usually turned into an onslaught of rain in Bengal. It was anyways monsoon season when a storm could sneak into the environment anytime to destroy the peace of our hearts. We walked to a nearby tree, and stood under it for a few moments.

"I am late, I should go." I took my umbrella from my bag.

"I am coming with you to the bus stop."

"Baba is adamant that I should go to the university only with our trusted driver, no more bus for me."

"I'll come with you to the car."

"No, I need to go alone."

"You don't want your driver to see me with you?"

I remained silent.

"Tara, you need to tell your parents now, we need to go to the next step."

"I am so afraid."

"The solution for your worries is to let it happen. Let them say whatever they want to say, let us reach a conclusion."

"And if they say no?"

"At least we will know where we stand."

"Let's wait till the elections. . . . My father is very worried these days due to all these brawls. It has affected his business, too. It will be easier to talk to him if we will have peace after the elections. At this moment talking to him on this issue would be like pestering a lion in his den."

"I think you are right."

"*Allah Hafiz.*"

"*Allah Hafiz* . . . I'll see you tomorrow."

I went out of the refuge of the tree. The angry rain of Bengal started thumping my umbrella, covered with a blue floral design. It seemed to punish me for drifting the man of Bengal away from the devotion to freedom of its land. I looked up into the dark clouds for a solution, but there was no answer. God forgot us, the humans, a long time back . . . after giving us a crooked free will. I moved fast to get to the main road to reach the car.

January 1971

On the night of the elections, all the members of our house sat in the living room in front of the television to see the incoming results of different federal and financial assembly seats. The two Bengali women and their two children—a boy and a girl of twelve and fourteen—who worked inside the house, sat on the carpet and eagerly watched the news. The special programming for the night was thrown into the telecast in between the results. It was an amalgam of comic skits, famous plays, real-life events in the polling stations and the results of the elections. Quite early in the evening it was clear that East Pakistan decided to come under the umbrella of the one-party Awami League, led by Mujeeb-ur-Rehman. On the other side in West Pakistan, Zulfikar Ali Bhutto's

Peoples' Party, was gaining prominence, and won most of the seats of the parliament in the west on its slogan, *Rotti, Kapprra aur Makan* (food, clothing, and shelter for all). Awami League was in a clear position to create the next government by the help of its alliance with many of the minor parties in either of the wings.

A sense of relief appeared all over the east wing when the date of the session of the new assembly, March 3, was heard. All the unrest from the streets went into the halls of politics.

The following Friday, I did not go to the university. Once my father left for his office, I talked to *Ammi*, my sweet mother, about Mansoor. She was perturbed. She knew she could not go far in convincing my father of something she herself had serious reservations about. I implored her to convince him to meet the mother and the son. She promised to take the matter that far for me, but made it clear that ultimately my father would be the decision maker, and she would not go against his wishes in this case.

In the evening, when my father came back home, instead of one of the maids, I saw my mother taking his tea to the living room. I came out of my room and went down the stairs to hear their exchange. Sumaira, who was sitting in the corridor by the window outside our rooms, ogled at me, reproaching me for my actions. I ignored her, and kept moving down the stairs.

"I was against sending her to the university. I very well know co-ed always brings some sort of trouble to girls. I am sweating to get her a suitable match in the community, and she is asking for a Bengali to be her husband. This is all because of your encouragement to her. . . . Don't you see what is happening outside? Separation, separation . . . it's on every Bengali's tongue, and this girl wants to marry into them. They will kick her out within a few days, if, God forbid, separation becomes a reality. Instead of reprimanding her and making her feel bad about her stupidity you are—"

"Calm down, Farooq. Since the elections nothing has happened in the city . . . and I hope everything will be all right once the democratic government takes over."

"Hope? Things don't run on hope."

"I am not convinced of this either, but there's no harm in meeting them . . . once they propose formally we will investigate their background, and think about everything carefully. If we aren't satisfied, we will say no. It will at least give her the satisfaction that we have done our best to accommodate her wishes."

"And why do I need to accommodate every idiotic wish of your daughter? Why can't she be like Sumaira? Sumaira stayed home after BA, accepted a husband I have chosen for her, learned how to handle household chores . . . there seems to be a problem with your daughter every step of the way."

"She is your daughter too."

"But she is just like you: rebellious and stubborn."

"Mohammed Farooq, times have changed. It's not like when we got married, twenty-five years ago . . . we cannot just walk over the choices of our children. There is no harm in meeting them."

"You have spoiled her completely! If I had a son I wouldn't—"

"You have always blamed me for everything negative in our lives, and you always will, but this is not about me, this is about our daughter. Put aside your animosity toward me, and just meet them."

"No matter what you say, Zubaida, I won't let this happen. A poor Bengali will not become my son-in-law."

"Poor? How do you know that?"

"A son of a college teacher? Yes, he must be a millionaire!" My father's sarcastic remark cut the whole environment like a sharp knife cuts a stick of butter. "You don't even know what his father did."

"He died a long time back . . . what difference does it make now what he did?

"It does, it sure does!"

"Let's just meet them . . . please."

A roaring silence hovered for a few moments.

"I'll meet them on one condition: Once that meeting is over, you will leave with your daughters to Karachi."

"Karachi?"

"Yes." I heard a sharp crinkling of the newspaper as if he was hitting it to take his revenge for the trouble I brought him. "I don't think that the Awami League will get the chance to make a government; the army won't let that happen. Once they—"

"But they have already announced the session of the assembly and—"

"Just listen to me . . . if the Awami League won't get the chance to make a government there will be chaos and plunder all over Bengal . . . Shehzad also came to the office, he has already sent his mother and sister to Karachi. He has heard that the session of the assembly may be cancelled."

"Is the military not going to protect us?

"West Pakistan is 2000 miles away; even a small number of soldiers from there to here take a day to arrive . . . there will be a fierce struggle between army and the rebels—and West Pakistanis will become the target. You stay at home and send your daughter out, but you don't know how bad the situation is . . . I talk to my brothers in Karachi daily, every paper in West Pakistan is saying that Awami League won't be able to get the chance to govern. The army has become a business enterprise that is making more and more money, it won't go to barracks. And Mr. Bhutto has started talking in terms of *this side and that side,* the peace you see now is an artificial one."

"But there is the matter of her studies."

"Her studies may go to hell . . . she can go to Karachi University, and complete it there . . . I will anyway call you back once the real peace returns."

"But—"

"No buts, this is the condition. Sooner or later you will have to go to Karachi if things get worse. I am asking my brother to rent an apartment for you, you will be fine, my brother will take care of everything."

Silence ruled the atmosphere once again. What needed to be said was said, and now the two adversaries had no reason to stay in the same location. My mother went to the kitchen, and I went back to my room.

I didn't go down the stairs to the dining table for dinner. I couldn't face my father. After dinner, *Ammi* came with a plate of food to my room. I was in bed, watching *Get Smart*. In the title of this American TV series the comical hero who was a spy went through one door after another to reach a telephone to contact his superior. Looking at his clumsy but careful stance I felt I was that telephone and those doors were the traditions of the society. *Ammi* placed the plate on the side table of my bed. I turned off the television.

"I have very little hope but I have convinced him to meet them. If it suits them they can visit us on the coming Sunday."

On Saturday, during classes, I told Mansoor what had happened at home on Friday. I also told him that my father was already very hostile toward this idea and that he had a capability to be rude and insulting when things did not go his way, and therefore, we should drop this idea of meeting my parents all together. But he insisted that we needed to take the risk, and give it our best try to convince him to change his mind.

On Sunday morning, through the window of my room I saw a sky whose horizon was covered with dark clouds. They seemed to be running toward me, eager to punish me for daring to challenge the status quo of the social structure of that society. The scent of the Jasmine next to the main door of the house ruled the front yard, showing off its strength to the second floor on the impetus of wind. I saw *Ammi* stepping down the three steps of the porch to receive the guests in the passage where their cycle rickshaw had stopped. It looked small and insignificant, sitting behind the three parked cars. Thinking about the outcome of this meeting, my mind was swirling.

A few minutes later, Sumaira came to my room. *Ammi* was

calling me to the drawing room. I went down the stairs into the living room. Shenaz Begum, Mansoor's mother, was sitting next to *Ammi* on the three-seat sofa and Mansoor was sitting on the chair next to his mother. The maid was serving snacks and tea. I sat on the chair next to *Ammi*. That day the red tones of the carpet and upholstery were increasing the palpitations of my heart. I was reluctant to make eye contact with Mansoor but my furtive glances toward him told me that he was calm. The maid took the tray that had meat *somosas* and chutney to him. He took one and put some chutney on his plate. My mother was asking indirect questions about Shenaz Begum's work and her family background.

Ammi left us twice to call my father, but he did not appear. During her absence I tried to engage Shenaz Begum in conversation to maintain the social graces but my mind was entrapped in the whirlpool of the negative outcome of this meeting and our conversation travelled on a bumpy ride. When my mother left the room the third time, she brought him with her. He came into the drawing room but did not sit down. Standing behind the sofa on which *Ammi* and I were sitting, he said to Shenaz Begum, Mansoor's mother, "Madam, our families have very different backgrounds. They are children, and do not know the way of the world. We cannot be receptive to the unreasonable demands of our children."

I turned around and looked at him. I was sure he had not even glanced at Mansoor.

Shenaz Begum set the cup of tea she was holding on the plate. "I don't think they are children, they are adults and have the right to decide about their lives . . . I am aware of the difference you are referring to, and I told Tara that we have very humble means to live our lives."

"I have told you what I intended, too," he said.

I looked at Mansoor; I could see that he was both embarrassed and offended.

"Baba please!"

"You need to be quiet . . . go in."

I was frozen.

"Go in!"

I went behind the door in the hallway.

"Wouldn't it be better if you think about it before you decide . . . I am sure Tara's happiness is dear to you," Shenaz Begum said.

"I do not need to think. The decision, I have already made."

"Why did you ask us to visit your house? To insult us?" she asked.

He came out of the room without responding to her and passed by me without looking at me.

"I am sorry for the unpleasant behavior of my husband. Things that are happening outside have an influence on his mind," I heard *Ammi* say.

"I was reluctant to visit your house . . . I wish I would have listened to my inner voice," Shenaz Begum said.

I looked into the room. They were going toward the door, and my mother was following them.

A few minutes later, I heard my mother from Baba's office, which was next to their room. "Having some money doesn't mean that we lose all decency. You could call them afterwards to say no to them. Nobody treats their guests like this."

"Don't lecture me. If you can't see that this is just their way to pull themselves up from their class then I don't have anything to explain to you."

"Mohammed Farooq, your pride will take you down. Look back and remember your past too."

"Stop this prattle of yours and get out of here!" He was using all the muscles of his throat, yelling as loud as he could. "You just had the responsibility of taking care of your two daughters, and you couldn't even do that."

I saw my mother coming out of his office. Our eye contact told me that nothing further could be done. I went back to my room.

The next day, my mother told me that we were leaving for

Karachi sometime next month, and that I would be able to complete my master's in Karachi. She also told me that I wasn't allowed to go to the university anymore.

Sitting at home, trying to immerse myself in books, radio, and television, giving effort to cooking, going out with my sister and mother for shopping—I failed to defeat the agony in my heart.

One morning Sumaira came to my room. "Mansoor is on the line; I am keeping my mouth shut this time, but if I receive his call again, I am telling *Ammi.*"

I picked up the extension in the hallway outside my room without responding to her. He wanted me to elope with him, and get married; I refused to be part of any such plan. I asked him not to call again. We had no future, it was no use torturing ourselves. He said that he had heard from Shukuntala that I was leaving Dhaka, and that he would come to Karachi to meet me. He thought I would feel stronger in Karachi to go along with his plan. I made it clear to him that I couldn't promise anything.

When I came back to my room I found Sumaira waiting for me. "*Baji,* this needs to stop."

"You need to mind your own business."

"We women have to follow the parameters set by our parents, they are for our own good. In this divisive society we need these protections, you wouldn't get anything by rebelling against them."

"I am sorry I cannot accept everything that is imposed on me, like you can, but I am not rebelling against anything either. It's over, are you happy? Now leave me alone."

We were flying to Karachi on February 15. Sumaira's fiancé, Shehzad, came to meet us a week before our departure. He was a handsome man. His tall stature and broad shoulders gave his uniform a very strong stance. The very first time I thought about the decision of his people, choosing Sumaira for him instead of me—was she better looking than me? Or did they have the same thoughts about me as my father? "Rebellious and stubborn."

The same day, Shukuntala called. She wanted to throw a tea

party for me to meet the girls of the department before I left for Karachi. Before giving her a positive signal, I asked my mother, who willingly permitted me to go to Shukuntala's house.

Two days later, during the hustle and bustle of the party, Shukuntala took me to the hallway next to the living room of her house and handed over the telephone receiver. I thought it would be someone from home but it was Mansoor. We went through the same motions except that this time I found him more aggressive, and found myself more firm in refusing to commit myself to his propositions.

Around five in the evening I came out of Shukuntala's house and crossed the street to get to the car. In the spur of a moment, my life was hijacked and destroyed.

Before I could go to the next page, I heard the key rolling in the door. I pushed the diary and the photograph under my comforter. Bayfazal opened the door. "It's two o'clock in the morning, what are you doing up so late?"

"I couldn't sleep," I said.

"We only have two hours left." He turned off the light and said, "Get some sleep."

He closed the door and left me in the dark with thoughts that were like serpents devouring my brain, thoughts that gave birth to questions that might never be answered.

* * *

Ahmed opened the door at four in the morning and helped me to pack my things in the sack he'd brought for me. He took me downstairs to the hall where we had learned to read the holy book. Some breakfast was laid out on a plastic sheet and the *talibs* were sitting around it waiting for Bayfazal.

He came a few minutes later and we ate. The younger ones who were staying behind brought tea for us. When Bayfazal stood up we came out of the room to do *wazu* — a sequence of cleaning the hands, face, and feet — to get ready for the Morning Prayer. After the prayers we picked up our sacks and went to the gate of the *madrassah*. Bayfazal embraced his students before they got into the van that was taking us to the train station. I was like a stone in his arms. While pulling away from me he whispered, "War will fix you."

I was told to sit next to Jallad, who was going with us to the border. Bayfazal wanted to make sure that I would make it all the way beyond the mountains, into the hell called Afghanistan.

IX

The Training

There were eighteen people on the train, including the two men responsible for handing us over, lambs to fuel a war.

When the train stopped at Quetta Cantt in the evening, two men with *chitrali* hats met us and took us to two vans waiting outside the station.

Through the window of the van I saw the world waking up in the spring air, wildflowers sneaking out of the rugged lands to witness the ferocity of life. Every few miles were settlements of mud huts and barns belonging to the poor people of the Bugti tribe, whose rich leaders dominated the province of Balochistan.

Once the sun had set and darkness engulfed the earth, perhaps ninety minutes later, the vans stopped at a big house. It had two floors, and was made of red bricks, with dozens of rooms all jumbled together. We were taken upstairs and told to divide into groups of three or four. Ahmed, Rehman, and I were in the same group.

Each group was given a room. In our room, scraps of blue paint flaked off the white emulsion and fell to the dusty wood floor. There was no furniture except an old armoire in one corner and three bare mattresses on the floor. A small reading lamp sat on top of the armoire.

I opened the window to let in some fresh air. The cool wind had nothing to block it for miles and miles. It hit my face with all its primal strength, spoiling the peace of the room. I closed one of the panels of the window and let the other rest close to the window frame, forcing the wind to sneak through the small slot.

An hour later, one of the men called us downstairs into the big hall where food was served.

While we ate, a tall man with a black turban and thick pleated, loose trousers stood up and said, "I am Farhat Khan."

I looked around—and so did many of the others—and it didn't seem as though anyone had ever seen this man before.

"Forget the comforts of city life," he said with a dry, humorless smile. I had no idea where he got the notion of this comfortable "city life" we had been living. "You will be the soldiers who will bring the laws of *Shariah* to Afghanistan, the common ground upon which the people of Afghanistan will live. We need to support this new force, the Taliban. It is rising fast on the horizon of Afghanistan to bring peace to the country."

At that moment I saw that none of the so-called "soldiers," even the eager ones, had any idea what this "Taliban" was.

"Stability in Afghanistan will allow the refugees on Pakistani soil to go back to their homes, and with them will go the heroin problem in our cities."

Trying not to laugh or smile, I pushed my rebellious thoughts deep into the pit of my stomach.

"Finish your meal," he said, "then go back to your rooms. Rest! The trial of your lives awaits you tomorrow."

Once back in our little room, Ahmed and Rehman took the mattresses closer to the door, and I went to the one near the closet.

I took down the old desk lamp and plugged it in. I was surprised to see that it actually worked, and let out a sigh of relief when it threw a stream of light on my mattress.

I opened my sack and took out the diary.

February 1971

I fought with all my strength but it was meager in front of the brute force of those hoodlums. The driver had been pushed to the front passenger seat, and was under the two pistols from the back, he had no way to resist them.

I had no idea where they were taking us. Contracting my body so that it did not touch the two men on my sides, breathing unevenly with a sinking heart and a dizzy mind, I cried and begged for mercy, but they just laughed at me.

In the outskirts of the city, at a deserted spot, the man at the steering wheel stopped the car, came around, pulled the driver out of the passenger seat, and pushed him toward the cluster of trees on the side of the road, keeping the barrel of his pistol over the head of the driver. The driver was begging for mercy but I knew they had no mercy to offer. Taking advantage of the diversion, I attempted to escape from the clutches of the two men sitting next to me, but instead of freedom I got a few more slaps and a torrent of obscenity.

A couple minutes later, I heard a shot, and my last connection with the outside world escaped his body.

A few minutes later, my father's big car stopped outside a small cottage in the middle of the woods. I was dragged into the house and turned into a victim of their venomous hate. The sour breaths and brutal pressure of their bodies crushed me. My struggles made my hands bleed and my face turned red from slaps and punches. I kept shouting, scratching, and trying to escape but I was a deer under the attack of a pack of wolves—no, a deer is luckier, he dies, but I remained alive and beasts roamed free until they left behind a damaged body, a ruined life, and a torn soul.

I lay there for hours. I could not find any energy or any reason to drag my naked body out of the bed. How could he do that? How could he give me up to these beasts? I was his *ma'am*. I was his friend, his consort; how could he . . . No! This was not his fault. He could not do this to me—life could not be so cruel to me.

But it happened, and nobody could change that.

At dawn, I ran through the rooms and hallways to find a way out of that empty house, but all the doors were locked, and all the windows had iron bars. I was their toy, they were not ready to let me slip away any time soon.

My mind was a maze. It went from one dead end to the other, unable to find a way out. I was unable to peer into the future to find out what sort of life or what sort of death was laid out for me. Everything was calm in the city, what made them do this to me? Did he orchestrate all this? I kept thinking and then refuting my own conclusions.

When this cat-and-mouse game was finished, they would kill me. Why should I wait for them to kill me? Why shouldn't I end the game?

I ran around the house to look for a soul through any of the windows. The woods around the house were full of squirrels and monkeys running through the trees, but I couldn't see a single human face or hear any voices.

In the afternoon, rain started whipping its zillions of heads on the asbestos roof of the house, on the sidewalk outside, on the leaves of the trees—and on my fate—but it couldn't clean any of them, it couldn't clean any of me.

In the evening the hunger of my tired body won, and I ate some food from the kitchen.

The third day was worse—at least for my psyche. Time was a scorpion whose stings had the capacity to bite a thousand-fold. It refused to pass, and appeared to come back at me with its stings again and again. Every second seemed a century, and every minute seemed another blow to my sanity.

They came back in the afternoon. I ran into the bedroom and locked the door. A couple of minutes later, I heard the iron rod sliding into its socket on the other side of the door.

This time they had a new man with them. He said, "You have the full support of Delhi, but I advise you to spend your energies on your task and not on these . . . extracurricular activities."

Somebody laughed.

I assumed I was the "extracurricular activity."

"What are the chances of an attack from your side to seal the deal," one of them asked the man from across the border.

"Yasin, only Prime Minister Indira Gandhi can decide such things. I'm just an agency worker."

The rumor that India was supporting Mukhti Bahani, the violent wing of Awami League, was news to me.

In the evening, somebody slid the rod away from its socket, and my cage was extended to the rest of the house again.

The next day, I saw the headline of an English newspaper that was lying on the kitchen floor. *Assembly Session Cancelled—Mujeeb-ur-Rehman Imprisoned.* It was dated February 28, 1971, the day I was snatched away from my life.

Now I realized the source of their anger and vengeance. I was the symbol of the people who had cheated them. Had Mansoor anything to do with it? Did I know him so little? I had been so proud of my ability to read character. Was I naïve or was he clever enough to dupe me? Or was he innocent? My head started spinning, but the questions in my heart refused to renounce their scowls.

In the afternoon, I thought I heard a knock. I heard it loud and clear the second time. I ran to the door and looked outside through the black bars of the window. An old man was standing in front of the door.

"Is Yasin here?"

"One of them is called Yasin," I said.

"Who are you?"

I remained silent.

He looked carefully at my face before saying, "This ridiculous politics can go to hell. They have ruined a whole generation . . . every young man is busy with plunder. I have only one son, and I have lost him to this godforsaken Mukhti Bahani. They are clever when it comes to leading a young man astray."

"Why are they doing this? What has happened?" I wanted any confirmation of what was happening—the words I'd read still seemed unreal.

"It all started after they cancelled the assembly session."

"*Baba*, help me, take me out of here."

He thought for a few moments. "The windows have these bars

and this door is impossible to break. . . . Do you know a weak point in this house?"

"There is a door at the back of the house, it's weak at its hinges."

I saw him going toward the back of the house. I ran toward the back door.

"I am looking for something to break the hinges." He knew I was nearby.

The door started creaking under his blows. The screws lost their hold and the door fell down.

I went to the room I was locked in, and took off the sheet from the bed and wrapped it around me to cover my tattered clothes. When I came back, he asked me, "Where will you go?"

"Home!" I felt as if I had named an alien planet.

"Where is that?"

"Gulshan."

He was silent.

"Can you take me there?"

"Probably not. Gulshan was plundered the most in the last week, despite curfew and army presence, they won't let me go in . . . I can leave you at the post outside the neighborhood, the soldiers there can take you to your home."

The old man, whose name was Bashir, drove me back to the city in his cycle rickshaw. He earned his living by dragging people around the streets of Dhaka. He lamented his son Yasin's fall after getting involved in politics at the university. He provided Yasin's education through hard labor on the streets in the hope that his son would have a better life than his. But the son had different aspirations. A better job and a good house was not enough for him.

The streets were mostly deserted. I saw a few man, all Bengalis, comfortable, walking the streets in their dark skin—streets that were sacrificial altars for outsiders. Those outsiders were running away to West Pakistan, or to different camps in Bengal, or were just imprisoned in their homes waiting for their fate to be decided. We were stopped at one of the army posts outside the neighborhood. I asked some soldiers for help getting to my home, and they decided to take me there in one of their jeeps. I thanked Bashir. He turned his rickshaw around and left.

Throughout my journey home I passed houses that had been burned down to ashes. I prayed for mine, and for my family, but those days none of my prayers seemed to reach heaven.

All that was left of my home were the ashes of my comfortable life. The beautiful ochre pillars, part of the facade of the house, which had glimmered in the sunset, were black. Most of the roof of the house was sitting on the ground. I moved toward the part of the house where my room had been. There was nothing that could tell of the life I had lived but a burned copy of *Pride and Prejudice*.

I was living proof of Bengali pride and prejudice.

Only the last three steps of the stairs were still intact, the rest of the stairs along with the second floor were part of the rubble that lay around me like a dead ogre. The house was not only plundered but it seemed to have exploded from inside. Sitting at the broken front stairs, feeling intense pain in my stomach, looking at the ruins that were my home just a week back, I wanted to die, to be done with this life once and for all.

"It's getting dark. We should go back," one of the soldiers said to me. "We will send you to the barracks. Many refugees are living there. You will be safe there."

They took me to an office in the building just after the main gate of the cantonment. They checked the records but no refugee by any of the names of my family members were there. Did they all catch the flight on time and leave? And if they had left, could I blame them? After writing my name and address in a register, they took me to a house where women who had no family at the camp were living. Most of them were girls from the university hostel, and other women's colleges. They escaped from their hostels to save their honor and lives. They couldn't rely on the security at the hostels to protect them, as the men there were neither equipped to defend them nor could they be trusted. The house was full. Some of the women slept in the kitchen, they made some space for me at night.

I went to the office daily and asked them to look for my family, but I never received any news. After two weeks I came to the conclusion that they had left on time, on the flight my father had reserved. They might have left with an empty seat next to them, probably the very last reminder of Tara Farooq.

I could imagine the beautifully trimmed lawn, carefully fashioned pastures, and clean paths and sidewalks of the cantonment before the cascade of refugees. And now nothing was in place and nobody cared about these delicacies.

The frustration, the suffocation, the despair—they had all made a home in my heart and were controlling my mind, which kept looking into the future to find some light, even a glimmer, but always ended up finding a void, the nothingness that exhausted it within a few seconds.

A few days back I had lived in a house that was too big for the family of four, and now I had to move from one room to the other in a small house to find a place large enough to rest my exhausted body. But that body refused to sleep, and often refused to eat the food for which it had to stand in line half an hour and sometimes more to get—food usually devoid of any taste.

One day I asked the office about Shehzad. They told me that he had gone to Pahartali Thana, a town south of Dhaka, near Chittagong, a month before I came to the cantonment. They didn't know when he would return. They promised me that they would let me know if there was any word of his getting back to Dhaka.

The refugee population in the cantonment increased every day, and the breathing spaces in the houses, in the tents, in the bathrooms and kitchens, and in the lines for food, became more and more unbearable. And the air became more and more toxic, hygienically and emotionally. There were not only more and more people living in small spaces, but they were also living with their dilemmas, spilling their frustrations and sorrows to everyone around them. Women were crying and lamenting day and night, children were unnerved and confused, and men were bursting with anger in frustration, a hell was loose on earth, and that cantonment was its vortex.

March-December 1971

I heard the blasts in the city. I heard journalists lying and blaming everyone in the world except their own government and army. I heard the shrieks and sighs of camp dwellers. But in this matrix of sounds, there was a voice inside me that was becoming overwhelming. The more I tried to negate its presence, the louder it would turn. My calamities had no end.

A soul was busy making a home in my womb.

There was a war outside my body between Mukhti Bahani and the Pakistani military, and there was a war within my body between me and the soul that wanted to be born into this insane world through a woman who lived under a borrowed roof and relied on charity for food. I tried everything I could in that environment, where one could smell even the emotions of the next person, to kill it. But it clasped the walls of my womb more fiercely at every rebound. And it won.

Many eyes lifted up to look at my face when my body started to advertise my secret. Some were accusing, some sympathizing, and the rest indifferent.

My depression and the lack of nutrition brought the day unexpectedly. When my water broke, death appeared imminent and the thought of it did not seem threatening. Two refugee women who had worked as nurses threw me back to life once again—a life of depravity and scarcity. The weakling also lived despite my animosity toward him.

I couldn't make myself think of a name for him. Every day he reminded me of the time I had been snatched away from life. I kept asking: Who was the father among the three? It was a fruitless exercise. What difference would it make even if I knew? What would be the future of this child who was the result of a kidnapping and gang rape? Where would life take me with him? My thoughts spun in a vicious circle, kept throwing me back into a sea of catastrophic outcomes. I was ashamed and broken.

Two months after his birth, on December 3, 1971, the daily skirmishes with India at the borders turned into a war. All the forces of both the east and west wings of Pakistan were dragged into the conflict. The next day, we were moved to a school near the cantonment, and defending the new refuge fell on the shoulders of the men of the camp. The soldiers had a war to lose.

It was probably the shortest war in history. It lasted only thirteen days. Despite the fact that the war started at a point where the demise of the united Pakistan was imminent, Pakistani generals, the cronies of a military dictatorship climbing on the weak shoulders of the corrupt media, kept bragging about their strength and power.

Once the Indian army swept East Pakistan, and the trucks loaded with goods went across the border to Kolkata, the division of the Indian subcontinent completed another of its steps. When the prisoners of war were counted and dispatched across the borders, the men and crippled soldiers sent to refugee camps of Dhaka, and the raped women and lost children sent to their sojourns next to the dwellings of the men, the first Bangladeshi government took its oath.

"What are you reading?" Ahmed was still awake.

"Nothing."

"Go to sleep. Who knows what we're in for tomorrow."

The unfinished story told me all. No other secret in it could shake me after what I had already read. With a trembling hand I turned off the lamp.

Not only my life, but also my birth, was a fruit of repression. How could there be any love in it? I stared in the dark till dawn, when Ahmed turned on the light to wake us up for *fajir* prayer. For the very first time, I had nothing to thank God for in that prayer

After breakfast I saw Jallad talking to Farhat Khan and pointing to me. After a couple minutes Jallad came to me and said, "I am leaving. If you want to stay in one piece, you better behave. You are not in *madrassah* anymore. These guys don't have time to put up with your bullshit, they just shoot."

I remained silent.

He poked two fingers like the barrel of a pistol into my ribs then smacked me on the back of my head.

All throughout that day, Ahmed, finding me distracted, hustled me from one chore to the other. During the evening meal he said, "What's wrong with you?"

"Nothing."

"Please don't start some other new fuck-up."

I looked at him angrily but remained silent.

When we came into the room, I took out the diary.

"Since when have you become so fond of reading?" Ahmed said, taking off his shirt to go to bed. "Show it to me."

"No, never."

He was surprised by my response. "Is it something in there that's bothering you?"

I remained silent.

"Stop reading it," he said. "You already have more than enough problems in your life." He threw himself on the mattress.

A minute later Rehman came in, smiled at me, and lay down.

I couldn't open the diary for long. I hated its rusty brown cover, embossed year 1970, and its torn edges. But at the end of my struggle I concluded that it could not hurt me anymore than it had already done.

There was nothing to lose if I started reading again.

1972-1974

Our new refugee camp was called Geneva. Somebody chose the name to laugh at us, the foreigners, no longer the citizens of that land.

The new country under the shadow of the Indian government was allowed to be called independent. Change of name, change of government, new alliances and new triumphs for those who ruled, and further dislocation and new frustrations for those who were ruled.

Geneva was a big ground with asbestos sheds where we were left to shiver, scorch, and get wet. The north and east sides were occupied by families; the south side, where the main entrance was located, by men who had no families; and the west side by women who had no men to turn them into families, though many had children. Bathrooms that were located in the corners on each side usually stunk like sewers, particularly the men's side. Food was distributed three times a day: 7:00 a.m., noon, and 7:00 p.m. There were big lines, widespread chaos, and a few fights each time food was distributed.

Sometimes affluent Bengali women brought food for babies out of pity, sometimes Bengali politicians brought clothes and blankets to procure the opportunity to advertise their philanthropies in the newspapers, and there were times when Bengali industrialists and businessmen visited us with articles of daily use. They gave their precious time to our camps because the depravity of Punjabis, West Pakistanis, exploiters—or whatever they called us—made them realize the security they had now in their land, politics, and entrepreneurship. But those visits, whatever the motivations of the visitors were, brought us at least some necessities.

Once a woman asked me the name of the child, my silence made her realize that I had given no thought to his name. "Let's call him Raza," she said.

I nodded.

Children cried all around me, but Raza kept himself quiet. He not only showed a lot of resilience to the depravity and scarcity around him, but also a lot of empathy for his mother, the miserable mother who was sometimes unable to show the same empathy for him. But I slowly warmed up to my child.

One day when I was in the line to get a meal, I saw a man on a wheelchair a few feet away near the men's shed. In the dim light of the setting sun, I couldn't see his face clearly, but something in me was urging me to find out who he was. My gaze went to his direction many times but I was unable to make up my mind. I wasn't ready to accept that the face from the window of the past—proud and handsome—was the face of the man sitting in that wheelchair, ashamed and scruffy. Despite the urge to confirm my suspicion once for all, I couldn't take a step toward him.

I brought my meal but couldn't eat it. I wanted to sleep but sleep remained a stranger to me. And when I finally dozed off, nightmares with ogres looking down at me appeared from the deep receptacles of my mind. They were laughing and pointing at my haggard appearance and sunken eyes.

The next morning, instead of going to the line to get the cup of tea, I went to the men's side. He was dozing in the warmth of the rising sun, unaware of my presence. The fear that kept me hungry and awake all throughout the night was now the reality of the day.

"Shehzad?"

He opened his eyes and looked at me with a listless stare, unable to recognize me.

"Shehzad. Is it you?"

I heard a voice that seemed to be coming from the depth of a well, weak and deflated. "Tara . . ."

That man who was engaged to my sister, and who I knew very little about, brought a glimpse of comfort in that hell.

When the storm of emotions settled down, he told me, "When your disappearance dawned on your parents, they went everywhere to find you. Your father wanted to keep it quiet, but your mother called me two days after your disappearance and begged me to use my influence in the forces and look for you. She did not want to be on that flight to Karachi, but your father forced her to leave with Sumaira. He stayed behind to look for you."

"But I went to the house. It was burned down. Did he. . . ?"

"No, no . . . he went to the Hotel Agrabad. It was safer there."

"Why was the hotel safe?"

"Some of the staff of the American embassy lived there, and Mukhti Bahani did not want to offend America in any way. They knew they would need recognition and support for the future Bangladeshi government. Your father left on the last flight operated between the two wings of Pakistan."

We remained silent for a few seconds, then he said, "I . . . I also went to . . . your friend's house."

"You mean Shukuntala?"

"I went to Shukuntala's house many times to get information, but I meant Mansoor."

"I don't want to hear his name."

"He died the same evening you were kidnapped."

"Died?"

"Yes, he was murdered that evening."

I did not know what feeling of mine was stronger—loss or relief. The news of his death shook me up, but the proof of his innocence relieved me from the agony of nailing the miseries of my life to the one I had loved. I turned around and left Shehzad. I could be alone with all those women but I could not be alone with him. He knew all my secrets.

War is the enemy of both men and women, it kills men's pride and shatters women's dignity. I wanted to share his pain but the news of Mansoor's demise brought memories of the past, and the ashes of lost love made my heart sick. I didn't go back to Shehzad all day.

The next morning, before the distribution of tea and bread, I went to the men's side of the camp. He was sleeping. I sat near him. When he woke up I started helping him to brush his teeth and wash his face. He kept resisting my help, and I kept ignoring his resistance. Two men helped him to get on his chair, and I wheeled it to the line. Men and women were supposed to be in separate lines but I remained behind his wheelchair in the men's line. The people responsible for the distribution of food gave us our tea and bread without any objection. He held our cups, and I wheeled him back to his place.

While we were drinking tea, I asked, "What happened to you?"

"Isn't it obvious? What's in the details?"

"We have ample time to go into details."

"Every soldier knows that disability and death are in the wings of the final stage of war . . . they knew that death would be preferable to me so they decided to cut my legs to inflict as much pain as they could."

"Where did it happen?"

"They sent us to Pahartali Thana where two hundred West Pakistanis were executed in a football ground. When we took care of the business there, they sent my regiment to Khulna District to confront Indian attacks at the border. On our way, Mukhti Bahani attacked us from all sides in the jungles of Sundarban, near Barisal. Most of my men died."

Just a few months back, that man was full of energy, proud of his badges and uniform, handsome and intelligent. I felt as if my heart was melting.

"I have heard that Red Cross representatives are coming to the camp to find people that have been separated from their families," he said. "They may have a list of individuals they are looking for, and they will also talk to everybody in the camp. You should take advantage of this opportunity to find your way to your family."

This information numbed my body. "I can't."

"Why?"

"I . . . I didn't tell you. I am a mother."

Silence ruled us for a while.

"Is it Mansoor's?"

"Mansoor's? Do you really think that I would let him touch me before getting married to him? Is that the impression you have about me?"

"No, no, please don't go," he said when I shot to my feet. "I am sorry. I just wanted to be sure."

"Sure of what?"

He did not reply.

"That child is a symbol of repression . . . I have made myself love him after a long struggle." I sat down again on the stone near his wheelchair.

He remained silent for a while. "I think you should take advantage of their visit. You will have a better life there than in this godforsaken camp."

"And you?"

"This camp is my home now . . . I can't go there to become a burden on my mother and sister. It may already be very difficult for them to survive. I can't take my frustrations to them. But you have a child. You have to look to his future, and there will be none here."

"And Sumaira?"

"I have nothing to offer her." The convulsions in his voice told me of his tearing heart.

I went behind his wheelchair and took a firm grip on his shoulders. "I know how you feel." Our tears tore away the distance.

"You should go," he said after a few moments.

"I can't. I won't. Who will accept this child in that narrow-minded, chauvinistic society? They will always call him *harami*, illegitimate of a Bengali. Their hate will make him crippled. You have released your claim on Sumaira but who will marry a girl whose sister has given birth to a *harami*? I was lost when I was picked up by them but I died for my family when I gave birth to him, could you understand this? Why am I angry at you? I am so angry, I am just angry at everything."

He patted my hand, which was still on his shoulder. Not facing each other helped us spill out our frustrations. Eye contact has a capacity to facilitate shame and reinforce loss.

On that day I made him my responsibility. After waking up each morning I would hand over Raza to the women who were friendly with me, and go to the other side of the camp to the men's side to help him with his chores, to wheel him to get tea, and then to put his space in order. Then I would go back and get Raza to stay with him. In the afternoon I would give Raza back to the women again, and take Shehzad to the line to get our lunch, and then in the evening to get our last meal. He would say that he was not my responsibility, sometimes politely, and sometimes with frustration, but I would maintain the routine. I knew he was not my responsibility, my weak connection with him was destroyed when he gave up his association with my sister, but taking care of him gave me strength and purpose.

One day, people from all the four sides of the camp were sent to the middle of the ground, one side at a time. They wanted to spread DDT all over the camp to get rid of the zillions of bugs that nested in the camp, and the rotten smell that hovered all over it. They needed to prove to the visitors from the Red Cross that they were taking care of us in the best possible way, and overwhelming the stench in the camp with the toxic odor of DDT was their solution.

The next day, two individuals from some Western country, a man and a woman, along with two Bengali officials, visited us. We were told that all of us would go back to Pakistan in groups but at that moment they were looking for people whose families had requested they find their relatives. They had received information about people that were in our camp from the Bangladeshi government, and they wanted to talk to each person or family separately to confirm the information they had. They started in the male side of the camp.

A few minutes later I heard a commotion. "I am not Shehzad, I can't go, I won't go." I ran to his side, but I couldn't get through the crowd of men surrounding the scene.

"Sir, all the people in this camp have to go to Pakistan sooner or later, it's just that the people who have families there are going first," the male visitor said.

I wanted to persist to find my way to reach him, but a thought froze my feet at the edge of the crowd. If they could find that I am related to him, they would send me too. What if they had a request for me too? I decided not to show my connection to him, I went back where I came from.

When they came to our side, they called the names of each of us, and then checked it against the list they had for any request for that person. There were no requests for me. I sighed with relief.

When I went to Shehzad before the evening meal, I found him dozing in the setting sun. Due to the abundance of DDT on the campgrounds, flies kept themselves over the furniture, attacking its inhabitants fiercely. They would glide on him from one place to the other after his every attempt to scatter them.

"I am not hungry. Don't push me there," he said without opening his eyes. "Get your meal, I have to talk to you."

"I can't eat anything in this smell," I said.

He opened his eyes. "They will soon send me to Karachi. I haven't said anything about you to them, but I know that the second group will consist of women and children who have no men with them, and they will include you in that."

I remained silent.

"I hate to become a burden on the two women of my family, and you are afraid to go to Karachi because of Raza. I can . . . I can become Raza's protection," he said.

"I am not sure what you mean."

"Have *nikah* with me. After our vows, Raza will be our child. I have nothing to offer you except a name for Raza. I am damaged. This body is useless. If you are ready to live with me to protect your father's name and your child's, we can call some people tomorrow from the camp, and ask a *maulana* to marry us."

"You are asking me to save the name of men in my life by sacrificing myself."

"You don't want to save their names? You don't need to tell me right away."

I nodded and went back to Raza.

The memory of the day my mother confided that she had been thrown into the lap of my father during the insanity of the partition knocked at my consciousness, many times. Their home never became their heaven. I very well remembered that she had rushed to conclude that no matter what might happen between the two of them, our father would do everything to secure our safety and future. She probably wanted to throw water on the fire she had ignited by telling me about her painful relationship with my father.

Turning left and right on my comforter all night, thinking about past, present, and future, feeling sharp stings in my heart, I was unable to decide for a long time, but dawn brought the decision. At every catastrophe in the stream of history, men revive sooner or later, but women crippled by the norms of society lose their stance if they aren't crushed in the torrent. I couldn't do it. I couldn't accept him. Now when I look back, I find my decision naïve, Rehmatea, and his proposal very realistic. I was angry and wasn't thinking clearly, and now guilt lives with me just as this ailment lives with me.

The next day I didn't say anything to him, and he did not ask me anything. We went through the day like any other day. After the evening meal I picked up Raza, and said good night.

In the middle of the night I came out of the nightmare in which ogres were eating my flesh. I couldn't breathe. My swarming chest was struggling to get some shreds of oxygen but its muscles were defeated at every gasp. Somebody shook me awake. I heard someone asking me repeatedly to breathe. I saw a woman bending over me, and another one trying to calm Raza, who was crying his heart out.

Gradually I came out of the terror of the nightmare and overcame the protesting body that was like a lamb under the sharp knife of the ghosts of the mind. I took Raza from the woman, and apologized for disturbing their sleep. I stood up to rock Raza. The full moon was hanging low in the sky. Under the silence of the night, ogres of the mind were visiting many occupants of that camp. On that summer night where people were sleeping outside their sheds, the camp looked like a graveyard in which death sneaked out on the surface from the belly of the ground. A few moments later, Raza settled down and fell asleep.

I turned to go to my comforter but something was urging me to check on Shehzad. I started walking to the other side of the camp, carefully taking steps so that I wouldn't disturb the men sleeping in the open. The view in front of me sank my heart. His upper body was twisted, facing downward on the ground. His hands were clasped tightly in fists, showing his agony in his last moments. He took advantage of the available DDT and escaped from life to avoid seeing the defeat in the eyes of his people.

A few months later, those of us who had no family, or whose kin had the courage to sit back and not claim their damaged loved ones, were sent to this slum of Karachi, a larger camp in the new Pakistan, where the formulae of division has a bright future.

December 1975

Just a few minutes back, when I finished my story, my new friend and consort in pain, Rehmatea, looked at me with pity in her eyes. The pity I had hated in the eyes of the women of the refugee camp in Dhaka did not bother me. It has become a part of my life, the landscape from which I hope I will be released soon.

She insisted that I should try to find my parents. She said that a lot of water has passed under the bridge and that seeing my situation, my father will forgive me. She clearly hasn't understood him through my story.

Now when I have spat out my story it seems frivolous in the misery that is scattered around me. They all have a story—tales of suffering and survival, fables of friends and foes, descriptions of past affluence and present poverty. All their stories have catastrophes that shame the happenings in my life.

The agony of the mind, no matter how frivolous it seems to me at this moment, is agonizing when it revisits and increases the pain in the body. I bless this pain because without it, I would be locked completely in the agony of mind. This pain is like a waterfall. It collects itself at the peak of the mountain, increasing its intensity at each moment, relieving me from the agony of the mind but tearing down the body with its steady pressure, then releasing itself, moving down the mountain, giving its host some relief—the relief that always come with the agony of mind.

Raza is sitting at the doorway of my shack, curiously watching passersby in a sewage-ridden alley. He will never know that he is the fruit of rape and not love, and that his existence has brought his mother down to nothingness where she could not even place herself in a nightmare a few years ago. But what will happen to him after me? Thoughts of his bleak future multiply the sickness of my heart a thousand-fold.

I put away the diary and turned off the lamp knowing I had another sleepless night ahead of me.

X

Into the Mountains

We would wake up early every morning and do some exercises: push-ups and weight lifting. At 7:30 everyone would receive a *paratha*, an oily wheat bread, with a cup of tea. After our tea we would take our textbooks and notebooks out from the cupboard, place them in the corner, and sit in rows to be ready for the teacher. He would appear a few minutes after 8:00 to teach us Pashto. He was a tall man with a long beard, quite polite in comparison to Bayfazal. He would teach until noon. Five Pashto-speaking students would work as tutors to help us learn the language. My roommate, Rehman, was one of them.

Around 12:30 we would get our lunch—usually beef curry with some vegetables and nan—which was much better than what we received at *madrassah*. On Fridays they also served rice pudding. In the afternoons we recited the Quran. In the evening we would go in the courtyard and mingle with the caretakers: the teacher and four other men. The courtyard was a large space with tall redbrick walls that had flower beds along with them. Trees in these beds helped to hide our presence.

One evening when Ahmed and I were sitting on a bench in the courtyard, the teacher approached us and asked, "How are you two?"

"Very well, sir," Ahmed said.

"Do you think you are ready to go to the front?"

He was addressing me but Ahmed saved me by responding, "We need training, *Sahib*, but we are ready to do whatever it takes."

"How about you?"

The tree with long pointed leaves over my head shuddered in the wind and lost some leaves, which came spiraling down. One came to rest on my head, and as I brushed it off, I said with all the enthusiasm I could show: "Yes, *Sahib*, I am ready."

"Ready for what?"

"Ready . . . ready to fight for *Shariah* in Afghanistan."

"Good . . . that's what I wanted to hear. I know you are Fazal Khan's students. You will make all of us proud."

Ahmed smiled and I attempted one of my own. The teacher went away and joined another group of students.

"I wonder if that was a test," I whispered.

"Well, you need to polish your hypocrisy skills . . . I won't be able to defend you forever."

"Why are you so mad at me lately?"

"I am not mad." He took a deep breath. "But I am afraid you will do something foolish and get in trouble again."

"You mean I get into trouble on purpose."

"I have been with you since we were what? Nine or ten years old? And every year or so you invent some new way to get into trouble. I have been on buddy-watch for you almost all my life, and I have put bandages on you several times."

"I am thankful for everything you have done for me."

He turned his head and looked at me for a few seconds, trying to judge the sincerity of my gratitude. "I waited for that 'thank you' a long time."

"I know you don't want to go to war like these other morons." I looked around to make sure nobody had heard me. "I can't go back. They are hunting for me everywhere. But you can. Why don't you sneak out?"

"I can't . . . I have never left the *madrassah* all my life . . . I have nowhere to go and nobody expects me, I just have to keep going wherever life takes me."

At that moment I felt more fortunate than him. I had some memory of my mother, and then the precious slice of life with Perveen, and the proud heart of a father-to-be, even though I might never see my child. But Ahmed had been thrown into the *madrassah* by a relative after his parents' demise. He had nobody.

He *was* nobody. I placed my arm around his shoulders and pulled him a little closer to me.

"What do you think you're doing?"

I loosened my grip. Whenever I felt close to him he pushed me away.

"You are angry," I said, "but I am not the enemy."

"I know. . . . If you were my enemy I wouldn't have saved your ass so many times."

Farhat Khan whistled for us to go in. We walked inside in silence. Each day two students helped the man who cooked for us, and two served the meal.

That day it was our turn to serve dinner, so we went to the kitchen right away.

* * *

I tried my best to fit in. When I altered my speech and behavior, Museabate's words resonated in my head: "You are rebellious like your mother."

It made me proud, but at the same time afraid. I was not one of them, but I had to live with them, and that was like walking on a rope over an abyss. Though I was reluctant to accept what was impressed upon me, I had no clear idea of who I was and what I believed in. I had seen the exploitation of Bayfazal, the mediator of Allah, and I had seen the manipulation of society through Shahbaz Khan and the government, who were throwing us into the fire of war to achieve their ends. But I didn't know the world that was possible for me without these exploiters. I couldn't imagine a world in which I could make a single decision about my life.

We stayed in that house for fifteen days. On the last day of our stay, they gave us a black sheet of cloth and taught us how to use it as a turban. They told us that after leaving that place we should consider ourselves part of the brotherhood, and be ready for martyrdom.

* * *

From Quetta we were taken to Chaman, a small town at the border of the two countries. At Chaman we spent the night in a small house. Early in the morning we put our bags on our shoulders and followed our caretakers. We walked through the passageways in the mountains during the day and made a camp at night. They told us to make a fire and open cans of beans to cook. We sat around the fire and two *madrassah* students served us the meal. They cut the dried beef the caretaker brought into pieces and gave it to us with the beans on a *nan*.

"Have you ever been to the front?" one of the younger ones asked the men.

"Many years, against different people . . . they have given us this job because of our experience," Farhat Khan said.

"Who did you fight against?

"When the Russians came, all the young men of my village went up into the mountains and fought against the Russians. When they left I thought the war would come to an end, too, and Mohammed Zahir Shah would come back, but that didn't happen. I didn't know what to do. I didn't want to be part of a war in which Afghani was fighting Afghani, but there was no escape. Everybody in the village said we are Pashtuns and we need to fight for Pashtuns, but I didn't think that way. I left the village and went to a refugee camp outside Peshawar. All throughout those years in the camp I heard about different Afghani groups fighting with each other and got tired of the bickering of the leaders of these groups, but when I came to know the success stories of the Taliban, I knew they will be the ones who will unite Afghanistan."

Everybody was silent, we could only hear the crackling of the wood in the fire.

Our eyes rested on the man next to him. "I fought with many . . . I was with Dostum in the north. He changed his alliances and went to Rabbani. I fought with the forces of Rabbani and then with Hikmatyar. When Dostum made an alliance with the Taliban, I fought with them, and when he decided to leave them, I didn't. Dostum is interested in gaining temporary advantages by his alliances, but I am looking for unity and lasting peace."

We sat around the fire a few more minutes, then the leader said, "It's time to get some sleep. We need to leave early to get there before evening."

We took out our sleeping bags and lay them on the ground. Farhat Khan threw more wood into the fire.

The stars, watching the drama of life on the earth, probably felt better about their deserted planets, shining with ice.

Since the day I had received that diary sleep had been a stranger to me. I had already been at the lowest rung of the ladder, why did God have to push me down a few more notches? I wished that Museabate hadn't given me that diary. The nameless, aimless Raza was much better than the Raza who came into being by violence and chaos.

I sat down and looked around. Farhat Khan was smoking a cigarette, sitting on a large stone at the edge of the circle of sleeping bodies. He was probably on watch for some portion of the night. He looked at me but didn't say anything. I came out of my sleeping bag and took the diary out of my sack. The envelopes and the photograph fell on the ground. I picked them up and put them back in my sack and then threw the diary into the fire. The flames quickly devoured the old, dried-up pages, happy to reduce my secrets to ashes.

I looked at Farhat Khan, expecting questions, but he didn't say a thing. I went back into my sleeping bag to wait for the stranger: sleep.

* * *

The next evening we reached two cottages a few feet away from each other in a valley. They took us into one of them where we were received by three men, our new caretakers. The men who came with us said their farewells, and the new caretakers let us rest for the day.

They woke us at 5:00 a.m. the next morning. It was spring, and looking up to the mountain I took in the vast patch of the valley full of yellow wildflowers in front of our cottages. We cleaned our teeth with the provided *manjan*—a rough powder made of herbs and spices—using our forefingers, and then washed our faces in big buckets of water. Fifteen or twenty minutes later, one of them called us back.

I saw two men bringing *nans* in a cane basket, a big kettle, and a tray of mugs from the other cottage that was probably a kitchen. The other four followed. One of them told us to sit on the grass in a row in front of them. They gave a *nan* and a cup of tea to each of us. While we were finishing the food, they started asking us questions in Pashto to judge our language skills. Very few of us understood their questions.

"My name is Qasim Khan and I will be the one who is responsible for your training," one of the men said. "These men with me are Salman Khan, Wazir Khan, and Mehtab Khan. I am very disappointed with your language skills. Your evenings will be spent in learning Pashto," he said in Urdu. "I personally know your teacher Fazal Khan. He used to teach us in the refugee camps, and it was a privilege to be his student, as I am proud to train you. I will make sure that you get all the skills you need to go to the front and I will keep you on your feet twenty-four hours a day if I have to to achieve this goal.

"Now, some ground rules. . . . All of you need to get up at 5:00 and get ready for training by 6:00. Any slacking on your part will be severely punished. Nobody can leave the valley and nobody should step out of those rooms without one of us. If we find anybody alone in the valley without our permission, he will be severely punished. Even for the call of nature, you need to tell us first before going out.

"I am also going to form groups of three to clean that cottage and the kitchen, and to cook, and to bring water from the well in the valley. The groups will not join their training on these days. There are sixteen of you, so each group will have a turn every four days. We are also expecting two more groups in the next few days from other *madrassahs*, so you will have to make space for them. Some of you may have to sleep on the kitchen floor. It's cold out here at night so we all have to remain inside. When the other two groups meet us, your turns for cleaning and cooking may come every ten to fifteen days."

One of the other men, Wazir Khan, interpreted Qasim Khan's account in Brahavi.

"Are there any questions?" Qasim Khan asked us.

"Can we form groups with our friends?" Rehman, our Pashto tutor, who was one of the younger ones in our group asked. His whiskers were just about to sneak out and he seemed to be struggling in his efforts to appear a man. He was the same boy who had once complained about Bayfazal to his parents, and received severe punishment.

"Yes, you can."

"After we finish training, where will we go?" asked Karim, a boy I always disliked in the *madrassah* for his ingratiating behavior toward Bayfazal.

"Nobody knows that . . . Allah has mysterious ways . . . maybe by that time our brothers will be in Kabul and we will join them there. But wherever and whenever you will join your brothers, you will feel proud to be a part of people who are bringing *Shariah* law to Afghanistan."

"How long will our training take?" Ahmed asked.

"We don't know yet. We'll see how fast you learn the skills you need. We're not going to let you go until you're ready."

"How long did the other groups take?" Ahmed asked.

"It always varies . . ." Qasim Khan replied with an irritated shrug. "Don't worry so much about time. We will send those who learn fast. The others will stay behind until they're ready."

"Why are you in such a hurry?" I whispered to Ahmed.

"I want to get out of the sight of these morons, and go in there to live or die."

"After Bayfazal they seem like angels to me."

"Wait for the training," Ahmed scoffed. "They'll screw you up enough to change your mind."

"You two young men," Qasim Khan said, pointing at us. "What could be more important than what I am telling you?"

We remained silent.

"Come up front and do thirty push-ups."

"We were just talking about—"

"*Fifty* push-ups."

Ahmed remained silent this time. We stood up and went to the front. Ahmed looked at me angrily, his eyes blaming me for getting him in trouble.

And he was right. They were not nice. They didn't even wait for the training to begin to change my mind about them.

While we were doing our push-ups, counted off by one of the men, the leader started speaking again. "The battlefield gives you no chance to slack. If you don't listen to your leader on the front, you will lose your life. These two may be grateful some time for the lesson I am giving them today."

A few minutes later, when our arms were numb, our palms had distinct marks of the grass and cobbles, and our feet shook, the training started.

XI

Arshad

I was completely exhausted when I reached the Islamabad Marriott Hotel after travelling more than thirty hours, four of which was a layover in Istanbul. I found the repetition of the pattern of white arches in the somber facade of the hotel. Two young men in black uniforms with yellow stripes running around their collars and the fronts of their shirts came out of the lobby and approached the cab. The driver opened the trunk and the young men took out my bags. When I gave the driver a tip of a hundred rupees—less than three dollars—he smiled widely and left happy.

At the reception, one of the staff members gave me a welcoming note from one of the connections my paper had given me, Arshad, promising he would call the next afternoon to arrange a meeting.

After a warm shower I went to bed, but jetlag kept me up. My mind swam with thoughts both comforting and disturbing, about my marriage and my departure to Afghanistan. Was I sacrificing my marriage for my ambitions? Did I love my husband when I married him or was he just the guy at the right place at the right time? Was he just a rebound guy after Peter? I couldn't marry a rebound guy. I must have seen something in him to say yes to him. He was warm, polite, considerate, and . . . it was surprising that I couldn't find any more adjectives for my husband and the three I found had the same flavor, any one of them could comprise the other two. And that godforsaken country I was going to was pure hell, particularly for women. What if this was my last trip? Any trip could be the last in a war zone.

I think I fell asleep around three that morning.

I woke up at eleven and got ready to meet Arshad. Around one in the afternoon he called me and apologized for not being there, he was forced to sub in for another reporter for some assignment.

He told me he would meet me by five in the evening.

I hired a cab and roamed around the twin cities of Islamabad and Rawalpindi. Islamabad, built in the 1960s to replace Karachi as the capital of Pakistan, had a somewhat cold feel. Its new buildings seemed distant, as if they were angry at the newcomers for disturbing them from their slumber. Its twin city was much more congested and loud, a very stark contrast in the two, seldom found in any other type of twins.

I came down to the lobby a few minutes before 5:00 and found a comfortable sofa in the east corner of the lobby, far from the hustle and bustle of the reception desk and entrance. My reporter's mind noted little details in the notebook that rarely left my hands: the light maroon color of the sofa but with dark brown cushions, a square table in front of it, the small vase on the table had pink flowers with large petals. The sunlight showered its last rays on that part of the earth before moving to the other side—from where I had come from. Even the sun seemed to support the dichotomy between east and west. When it lit one side, it wrapped the other in darkness.

Around 5:30, I saw the young lady at the reception desk talking to a man. She pointed at me. I watched him approach, a short man whose athletic body could have hid his age a little longer if he wasn't losing his hair. His thin moustache was a good combination with the French-cut beard. He wore a vermillion shirt that gave his brown skin a softer tone.

"Is it Rachael?" he said in his British-accented English.

"Yes, please have a seat. Arshad?"

He warmly shook my hand and sat on the leg of the L-shaped sofa. "So what's the plan?"

"Interviewing Mullah Omar."

"You have a very difficult task in mind," he said, though not dismissively. "Not only the mullah but none of the leadership of the Taliban allow female journalists to interview them."

"That's why I need your help."

"You want me to interview him for you?"

"No, I want you to convince him to meet me," I said. "I was told you've interviewed him . . . I can wear a *burqa* if he wants me to."

"They are not the negotiating types," he said with a grim smile. "I can give it a try, but I don't think he'll cooperate." After a brief pause he added, "Is this the only thing for which you need my help?"

I nodded and said, "Once I get that interview you can head back to Islamabad if you want to. I have to cover Afghanistan for a while."

I could tell he was surprised by that but tried hard not to let it show. "Where is your photographer?" he asked.

"I travel alone."

"Your paper doesn't want—"

"I'm a pretty good photographer," I interrupted, blushing with embarrassment at being impolite. "I get the images I need on my own."

"Good," he said and his smile and nod showed he forgave my interruption.

I invited him to dinner, and he accepted. We went to one of the restaurants in the hotel, the Royal Elephant, which offered Thai cuisine. I found the Topaz-colored chairs against the backdrop of the shiny wooden floors of the restaurant soothing. Arshad and I talked about politics, both regional and global, over dinner. We had opposing views about almost everything we discussed, and the differences of opinions kept our discussion alive for longer than I expected.

As we stood to leave, Arshad told me, "I've arranged for us to visit the Afghan refugee camp a few miles from Peshawar tomorrow." As I nodded he said, "And we'll be flying the day after next to Kabul."

The smile felt stiff on my face. I swallowed.

* * *

The next morning I found Arshad, along with an officer of the Interior Ministry of Pakistan, in the hotel lobby at the appointed time. After some cursory greetings, Arshad and I climbed into the back seat of a black SUV. The officer gave the notebook in my hand a sidelong glance then sat next to the driver.

The Interior Ministry officer was a tall man with a big moustache and thick black hair that fell on his forehead and shone with some oil or gel. I asked his name and wrote it down: Syed Choudhry Jamal Khan. As the SUV bounced along, the government man talked and talked, hardly pausing for a breath as he prattled on, aimlessly covering the culture, politics, history, and who-knows-what of both Pakistan and Afghanistan. He repeatedly mentioned the partition of the subcontinent and the hostilities between India and Pakistan, as if everything happening now sprang from that one event.

I wished that he would shut up so I could talk to Arshad. I kept nodding politely without responding to him but he never got the message. It took us two hours to get to the city of Peshawar and another half an hour to get to the camp. Syed Choudhry Jamal Khan only interrupted his history lesson to occasionally give irrelevant directions to the unresponsive driver.

The paved road gave way to the dirt-road entrance to the camp: a large, flat patch of dusty ground full of tents. The wide dirt road separated the camp between the tents of the aid workers and the more densely packed tents of the refugees themselves. The first tent on the left side was marked Office, and the next two were clinics into which long lines of refugees slowly streamed.

No one formally greeted us and though the government man in the SUV kept talking, I went directly into one of the clinics. A lady doctor was talking with the help of an interpreter to a woman with a child maybe six or seven years old in her lap. Two children with IVs lay on beds in the far corner, looking curiously at me. Their eyes were so dark they seemed black in the dimly lit tent. One of them wore a T-shirt with one of my own son's favorite cartoon characters on it. It was torn and dirty, the colors muted as though the cartoon was from decades ago, in a darker, less colorful time.

Next to the beds were three cupboards with open doors, scattered with different medical instruments. Behind the doctor were narrow shelves of medicines, running along the wall of the big tent, and going into the corner. A nurse sorted through the medicines, putting them on a little metal table on their related prescriptions.

"Could you give me a couple of minutes of your time, Doctor . . . ?" I asked.

"Be brief please," she answered, barely sparing me a glance.

"Your name?" I prompted, showing her my notebook. "For the record?"

"Axel," she said, "Isabelle Axel." Then, showing she'd talked to a reporter before, she spelled her last name for me.

Her accent was vaguely European. She wore Pakistani clothes but without a *duppatta*, the piece of cloth most of the women wore around their necks. The sleeves of her long purple shirt were rolled up to the elbows. Her unkempt hair was tied at the back of her head.

"Do you have all the facilities you need?" I asked.

"We have all the medicines, but few doctors. And the camp is full of cholera, diarrhea . . . dozens of other diseases."

"Is there anything you need?" I asked. "I'm a journalist. I could get the word out."

"Doctors, restrooms, tents . . ." she said, simply dictating a list. "Large families are sharing a small tent, and many families are sharing one toilet and they are all getting sick, particularly the children."

"How about the water? Is it safe to drink?"

Dr. Axel looked at the water bottles peeping out of my bag. "Probably not." Her answer was short and its implication was clear: I was expected to go away, taking my bottles of American water and leaving her with her patients.

"Thank you for your time," I said with a smile she ignored, then I stepped out of the clinic tent.

Arshad was talking to Syed Choudhry Jamal Khan, whose back was to the clinic. I took advantage of that opportunity and crossed the dirt road to walk between the tents. Children were playing and women were cooking on archaic little stoves outside the tents. The women's long hair was in beads, and their colorful dresses would have been charming if they were at all clean.

I stopped to watch the two girls who were making good use of stones they'd found. They played a game in which they would throw some small, somewhat round stones on the ground in front of them then they would throw a bit larger stone in the air and tried to pick up as many stones as possible while catching the larger one in the air before it hit the ground.

Jacks, I thought. From found objects.

I came out of the alley into an open space between tents. There was a big blue tent with a white flag over it. I moved around it to get to the front of it, which was on the other side, facing east. It was full of boys reading the Quran. It was a mosque.

A man with a white scarf over his shoulders sat at the back of the makeshift place of worship. He looked at his watch and stood up. He went to the microphone in the front of the tent, not very far from me. After fixing the microphone to the desired position he started reciting *azan*, the call for prayer. His voice was husky, struggling with the rhythm of the Arabic words. The boys folded their holy books, put them away in a box in the corner, and started straightening the rugs on the floor.

I felt a presence behind me. I turned around, and it was Arshad, waving at me to move on. He was clearly uncomfortable with my standing outside the tent, watching men now gathering for prayer. I started walking toward the other side of the open space. But before I made it to the path between the tents, I heard my name— not from Arshad, but from somebody whose voice belonged to the past. I turned around and saw Peter White coming toward me, a cameraman and a woman with red hair following him.

"Hey, Rachael! What are you hunting?"

"Not you, that's for sure," I said through a grin I didn't bother trying to hide.

He laughed and bent down to embrace me. He was about six feet tall with blue eyes and blond hair. The embrace was friendly, and it felt good.

"What are you doing here?" I asked.

"Covering this goddamn country," he replied. Pointing to his crew he said, "Edward Allen . . ." but I didn't catch the name of the redheaded woman.

I turned around to find Arshad. He was near the mosque, talking to the man who'd delivered *azan*.

"This is just a quick stop for me," I said.

My eyes flicked back and forth between Peter and Arshad when he asked, "Where are you going from here?"

"Kabul, and then probably Kandahar."

The look on his face drew my attention back to Peter. "Be careful there."

"My host, Arshad Khan"—I tipped my chin at Arshad—"will be with me the whole time."

"Be careful with Arsssshad too."

"Your sense of humor hasn't lost its edge."

"Sorry," he said with a twinkle in his eye. "I guess I'm not for everybody."

"There's no reason to be sorry anymore," I thought I had to say.

There was a silence filled with the ever-present din of the camp. All I could smell was dust.

"I kind of like to think there is," Peter said finally.

I remained silent, but wrote quickly in my notebook: smell of dust. Peter.

Arshad approached us with a smile.

"Peter White," I said as the two men shook hands. "A colleague from America." I swallowed, having forgotten the name of Peter's cameraman and the woman with them, but Arshad just nodded at them. The cameraman nodded back and the woman looked away, her eyes darting around the camp from tent to tent, person to person, as if expecting the worse.

"Me and my camera are frying in this heat," the cameraman said to Peter. Then he reached out a hand and took the redhead by the arm. "We'll be in the van."

Peter tossed his long hair off of his forehead, a twitch of his I'd almost forgotten. "Well, I'll be in Kabul too sometime in the next few days, maybe we'll bump into each other again."

"Maybe."

Peter followed his crew into the sea of dusty tents. I didn't watch him go, didn't want Arshad to think . . . what?

We were a thing in college, Peter White and I. Later, when I was a struggling journalist in New York, we both ended up at the same paper. Like bees to honey, we ended up in each other's arms. And like bees, we eventually buzzed over to other flowers. I opened my notebook to write that down but laughed at myself and closed it.

It wasn't a metaphor worth remembering — sort of like those days together that slipped into routine then boredom and all the while an unhealthy competition. Peter was moving up the ladder fast then — he had that ability, almost like a superpower. I broke up with him and he just seemed relieved.

XII

Commander Masud

We flew from Islamabad to Kabul, which had been under attack by the Taliban since President Rabbani and his militia leader Masud took it over. The year before, in October 1995, a Red Cross plane was barely missed by a Taliban rocket attack. Very few passenger planes flew to Kabul in the last ten months, since the Taliban siege began, but there was no other way to get to Kabul. Bagram Air Base, twenty-seven miles north of Kabul, received UN convoys for humanitarian aid, and military assistance for President Rabbani from Iran and Russia, but the base was never used for regular passenger flights, even when Kabul International Airport was under constant attack by the various factions that desperately wanted to get hold of Kabul.

Half of the PIA plane was empty and the other half seemed to be made up of mostly journalists. When we came down the stairs from the plane, a bus took us to Immigration. There were very few people around, and everyone seemed on edge—they looked exactly how I felt.

The staff at the airport just seemed exhausted, and this manifested as a general apathy. The man at the desk stamped our passports without asking us even the simplest of questions. He probably assumed that anyone flying into the middle of a war zone were either journalists or crazies, and he didn't care either way.

When I commented on the lack of security at the airport, Arshad said, "Commander Masud has only twenty-five thousand troops. He needs to keep as many as he can at the battlefront to keep the city in the hands of the Rabbani government. Police and the other paramilitary forces dissipated a long time back. Those men are now fighting with different warlords."

When we came out of the airport, a few men approached

various arriving passengers. None of them were cab drivers, per se, but in this war-ravaged country this was a way people could make a little money. Getting paid in dollars was the best part, and they could charge just about anything they wanted for the long trip from the airport to the two major hotels of Kabul, where most of the foreign journalists stayed. I let Arshad talk to one of the men and settle the fare to the hotel.

The dark, deserted streets lined with sagging buildings seemed like the set of a Hollywood movie, a postapocalyptic ghost town fading away in the feeble light of the sunset. As we careened for the hotel, the whoosh and thunder of rockets grew louder and louder. Camped south of Kabul, the Taliban were bombarding the city mercilessly. I saw a few men walking fast to get to their destinations. To me they seemed afraid of the city itself, as though Kabul was plotting to arrange their deaths by rockets from above or muggers from the shadows, either content to leave them buried in the rubble, as anonymous and forgotten as the city itself.

It took us an hour to get to the hotel but I was glad we got there before dark.

* * *

Though the night was fairly calm in comparison to the evening, I still couldn't sleep. After getting tired of turning east and west, stretching my legs and then curling them like a baby to soothe myself, I got out of bed and slid back the heavy curtains to see the lawns of the Hotel Serena lying outside. Only one light near the boundary wall was on, unsuccessfully fighting the darkness. The Taliban didn't have the capacity to fly over the city, otherwise even this light would be throttled to escape the merciless bombardment. I picked up one of the books I had bought in Islamabad, which I'd placed on the table next to my chair. It was a translation of a collection of poems by Faiz Ahmed Faiz, a well-known Pakistani poet, with a distinct socialist slant to his poetry.

Don't ask me the love I had for you my dear
I thought that
You were the shining beacon of my life
Your anguish makes the agonies of the world irrelevant
Your face sustains the spring in the universe
There is nothing of value in this world besides your eyes
I would command the destiny when you would be mine
I wished all this to be real but it wasn't
There are sufferings other than the sufferings of love
There are blessings other than the blessings of meeting the love

Woven in satin and silk
Humans are sold in streets and squares
Immersed in dust and drenched in blood
Pus dripping from the putrid sores
No matter how much I resist my eyes slip to them
I am still enthralled by your beauty but
There are sufferings other than the suffering of love
There are blessings other than meeting the love

Some time during the night, the book fell from my lap and I slept fitfully.

* * *

I woke up around 5:30, got dressed, and went downstairs to the hotel restaurant. I was desperately in need of coffee. When I walked into the dining room I saw a man in Afghani clothes with a white turban reading *Daily Dawn*, an English Pakistani newspaper, from two days ago. I put my book and key on a table covered with white linen. A continental breakfast was flanked by two nervous-looking waiters in crisp white clothes. I left my table to pour myself a cup of coffee, and a wave of shock came over me when I turned around to come back.

The man was sitting at my table.

I grabbed my keys from the table quickly, my hand shaking enough to spill a little coffee.

"Do I look so different in these clothes?" Arshad said, laughing. A sigh left my lungs with a *whoosh* and I blinked in relief. "You do," I said, smiling and blushing. "I might still think you're a stranger if you start speaking Pashto."

"*Sahar di nabkamargha, Zamad adlanah bankha . . .* you still doubt?" he said without hesitation, then laughed.

"I didn't know you could speak Pashto," I said, sitting at the table across from him.

"I speak a little."

I took a sip of coffee, my hand still shaking a little. I saw him notice that, and an embarrassed look came over his face. Before he could apologize, I changed the subject. "Do they bother journalists too much on the way north?"

"You never know," he answered, apparently relieved the moment had passed. "Besides the inflexible Taliban, Afghanistan is full of warlords these days, big and small. Sometimes, it's easier to deal with them if you portray yourself as a civilian and at other times as a journalist." He finished his coffee then added, "I equip myself both ways."

I nodded and asked, "When should I expect you back from Kandahar?"

"I'll be back within a week . . . you, anyway, have lots of things to do in Kabul."

I nodded again.

A man appeared in the hallway leading to the main entrance and waved at Arshad.

"He is my ride. I'll see you later."

"*Khudda-hafiz,*" I said, exercising the Urdu farewell I'd learned in Islamabad.

Arshad was going Kandahar to meet someone who was close to Mullah Omar, in an effort to find a way for me to not only get there safely but to meet the elusive Mullah Omar. I wasn't happy having to hire another journalist to do part of my job, but my editor insisted. I was not only new to the customs of this ancient country but also intruding in the middle of a civil war.

The rest of the day I spent writing down my observations so far, just to have something to send to the paper and start work on my book.

The sound of rockets kept intruding on my peace, but somehow it became less and less disturbing, as though I was tuning into the aura of Kabul, where war had been part of life for the last eighteen years.

Most of the hotel was occupied by journalists, and as the day wore on I saw many familiar faces. Besides American journalists, there were many from Europe and Asia, from independent and not-so-independent papers. This was the time just before corporate news, and investigative journalism was still alive, though already dying.

I joined a few fellow journalists for breakfast the next day then we all went to the UN building in the eastern part of Kabul for a press conference. The German diplomat Norbert Holl was visiting Kabul as a United Nations mediator.

Every street our van passed through showed signs of damage. Many buildings were less than half intact. Walls tired of bearing the insults of bullets seemed to surrender their roofs to the ground. Children played in these ruins and begged in the streets, sometimes along with their mothers. A society that had been in the clutches of tribal rifts and had lived a few centuries behind the modern world had lost a cultural grace that included hospitality, pride in its heritage, and perseverance in the face of the problems of everyday life. The people of Kabul were being crushed under their own poverty like their houses were being crushed under their own roofs.

The van stopped in front of a compound in which a set of intact buildings stood like some last redoubt against the end of the world. We were guided into one of these fortified buildings and past a reception desk into a large room lit by fluorescent lights. A few cameras sporting familiar logos waited to roll. We settled down for a ten-minute wait and I looked around.

Most of the journalists were men. My first few encounters with Afghan society was driving home the reality that had been somewhat clear to me at home: It was easier for men than women to move around, let alone extract news in Afghanistan, particularly from the Taliban.

A reporter I knew from the *Chicago Tribune* sat next to me and smiled. "Is there any hope for this peace mission?"

"John Orwell," I said as we shook hands. "It seems the Taliban have to go to a point of no return before they'll accept any agreement."

"Can I quote you on that?" he asked with a wink.

"Anonymous source close to the negotiations?" I winked back.

"You are in the third row," he chuckled. But he was serious again when he said, "It'll probably take them a few more years to reach that point. At the moment, they seem to be getting stronger. Thanks to the Pakistanis."

"Well, they want their puppet government in Kabul to have safe passage to the resources of the Russian satellite states. They've been planning on that pipeline through western Afghanistan for how long? But every time they get close to a deal some warlord spoils their best-laid plans."

"The Taliban listens to the Pakistanis when they want to and ignores them every other time," a German journalist sitting next to John said. Reporters jump into conversations. "They seemed to me the central character of Goethe's poem, *Der Zauberlehrling,* falling victim to the forces he had blithely liberated, he couldn't control them."

"So you don't believe in Benazir Bhutto's denial in Manila a few days back?" I asked, really just teasing him.

Both John and the German laughed.

"Come on, who's she kidding," the *Tribune* man said.

A hustle and bustle in the front caught our attention. Mr. Holl appeared with his two aides, and sat behind the large table in front of us. He was a tall man, whose hair was thinning more on the left side creating a wave that fell away on the right. The most prominent feature on his face, a high nose, gave him an air of authority.

"I'll be glad to answer your questions," he began, "but before I do that I want to express my disappointment on the attitude of the Taliban. Their rockets keep striking different areas of Kabul, and many of them have fallen close to the UN compounds. This is no way to treat a peace emissary, by shooting at him. It demonstrates a sort of contempt for my mission. Their behavior gives me no hope, and through you I want to send the message to them that if they are serious about peace then they should create an environment for the success of this mission."

The questions for Mr. Holl centered on his views of the future of Afghanistan. In his diplomatic way, he showed optimism despite his anger toward the Taliban leadership. But I knew every reporter in the room knew how little could be done in that environment of severe ethnic divide.

As children of the Jihad, the Taliban emerged from the deep disillusionment with the factionalism and corruption of the Mujahedeen that had fought the Russians. They saw themselves as the last hope of a decaying social system. Their uncompromising attitude signaled all along that they would crush everything around them, wherever they went, to make their interpretation of Islamic law the only law in Afghanistan, if not beyond into the rest of the Muslim world.

* * *

The night was considerably more calm, except for the beating of the rain that fell on the hotel lawns, over the trampled buildings of

Kabul, on Commander Masud's soldiers, and on the enemy camps outside the southern edge of the city.

The next day as I sat near the window in the hotel restaurant, having breakfast, I watched the sun emerge from its hiding place in the clouds.

I waved at two journalists who sat at a table next to mine. Arnaud Grosset of FFAP and Ben Baldwin from Reuters were planning to go south, where regular skirmishes with the Taliban were the order of the day. I had planned to go into the city and talk to some of the ordinary people of Kabul, but I changed my mind and decided to join Arnaud and Ben.

There was a jeep waiting for us outside the hotel. The driver wound through different parts of the city, avoiding the more chaotic districts. The closer we got to our destination, the louder the sound of rockets grew.

We were stopped by Masud's troops a couple miles outside the city. It was a sort of gateway between rocky hills, leading to the battlefront. Trucks full of ammunition disappeared behind the hills.

The driver, who had been provided by the hotel, interpreted for us. In response to our questions about Masud, one of the soldiers went to the nearby tent and came back with a tall man, whose hefty cap gave the delicate features of his face an air of strength and resilience. His large, bright eyes observed us keenly. He smiled at us while sliding his right hand over his neatly trimmed beard.

"That's Masud," Baldwin, sitting next to me in the jeep, said.

"*Salut. Ça me fair plaisir de vous voir,* " Masud said in unexpectedly flawless French. He had studied at the Lycee Istaqlal in Kabul.

"*Vous aussi,* " Arnaud replied.

To be polite, this time he directed his question in English. "What are your intentions today?"

"We want to see the front," I said.

"I can lead you to a hill that is fairly safe, but you will need your binoculars."

Masud climbed into a jeep standing on the other side of the dirt road and waived at us to follow him. After ten minutes we stopped at the foot of a hill, got out, and started climbing. The rain-swept hill was slippery, but we carefully followed the commander, helping each other on the way. A few soldiers followed behind us. Masud disappeared over the top of the hill while we were only halfway up, struggling to keep our balance with shoes now covered with mud. When we arrived at the top, we found him looking toward the south. Trucks with fresh troops and ammunition rolled up the adjacent hills, through the mud. The occasional shouted command echoed up to our vantage point, riding a wind thick with the smell of tar and gunpowder despite the continuous rain.

When we looked through our binoculars, we found dozens of Taliban in pickups trying to break through Masud's lines in the valley below, under the cover of their artillery barrage. In return, Masud's Russian-made D-30 howitzers pounded the hidden Taliban artillery. The thud of shells shook the mountains, deafening our ears and making me sway at the knees. One of the pickups stopped and the three others turned around and went back. I focused my binoculars on the stopped truck. The windshield was broken and blood gushed out of the driver's chest. The men in the bed of the pickup jumped down and ran behind it to use it as cover. There was another artillery assault from the Taliban to provide the cover for their men. Four of them ran away from the pickup. One fell to the ground under a rain of shells from our side, and the rest disappeared behind the hills.

"The Taliban have large supplies of ammunition and they shoot off thousands of shells, but their gunners are very inaccurate. They are making better use of their tanks and pickups," Masud said. "They rely on frontal assaults and there seems to be no effective chain of command."

It was obvious that despite enough firepower the Taliban were unsuccessful in achieving a breakthrough to enter the city. Masud broke up their formations every time they tried. Though he could hold the lines around Kabul, he didn't have the forces to carry out an offensive that could push the Taliban farther south.

* * *

I spent the next few days exploring the complexity of Afghan society and checking the facts I had collected at home with the reality on the ground. I met people from the Rabbani government and ordinary Afghani men and women.

In Afghanistan, each ethnic group had a name and identity of its own—the dominating Pashtun to which the Taliban belonged, then Hazara, Uzbek, Tajik, Turkmen, Nooristani, Mogul, Kirghizi, and so on. But more than fifty percent of the population of the country—the women—had no name and no identity. Most of them were covered, day and night, which is why they came to be known as "*Siya Ser,*" black heads.

Kabul, which had been equipped with all the modern amenities before the Soviet invasion, had been transformed into a sort of island where women could be seen in Western dress—skirts and blouses—at least in the university. But the rest of the southern part of the country was trapped in suspended animation, in the times of tribal identification and norms, where women were treated as property.

In the north of the country, Hazaras and Uzbeks were comparatively liberal, not only toward women but also toward the practice of religion. But they never had a chance to rule the country and therefore, never had an opportunity to bring their liberal values to the front of Afghan society.

Uzbeks, who were the descendants of Genghis Khan, could be vicious, and were often seen as womanizers. When the forces of Genghis Khan attacked in 1420 and took over northern Afghanistan, the local Tajik were forced to share their genes with the invaders and their progeny began the strain that was now called Hazaras. One of the reasons for Pashtun animosity toward Hazaras was their mixed blood. In that tribal society, not having a clean line of racial ties with the past was contemptible. And then there was the Taliban's militant animosity toward Shias in particular, to which Hazara belonged, and toward art and literature in general, which were essential components of Hazara life.

I wanted to interview Rabbani, but the Presidential Palace always turned down my request. They had the same excuse for every journalist who approached them: "He is busy defending the nation."

* * *

When Arshad came back, he told me that Mullah Omar was not interested in meeting any journalists at this time, and he didn't meet with female journalists at all, so I had no chance of interviewing him. I suggested that we go to Kandahar and meet *any* of the leadership of the Taliban that was willing to meet me. I also wanted to meet some of their members at the lowest echelon to find out what they thought about their leadership and the future of Afghanistan in general.

But Arshad insisted that we should remain in Kabul for a while. When I pressed him he said, "When I reached Kandahar, hundreds of mullahs from central and southwest Afghanistan were arriving. Their discussions were all held in extreme secrecy, but my sources told me that their meeting ended with a declaration of *jihad* against the Rabbani regime."

"But they haven't been able to enter Kabul in the last ten months, why are you so sure that they can do it now?"

"My source has told me that hundreds of armed Taliban supporters from Afghan refugee camps in Pakistan are moving across the borders to Jalalabad. The Taliban is planning to take hold of the areas around Kabul to attack the city from two or three sides."

"Do you think they can do that?"

"The eastern provinces will be easy to take," he replied with a shrug. "There are few troops to defend them . . . but we need to wait and see."

"Don't you think you should tell the government about their plans?"

He frowned and said, "You are a journalist. You know we are not supposed to expose our sources. It's quite possible that the Rabbani government already knows what's coming. There are spies everywhere from both sides. Anyway, I cannot spy on one for the other. They will hunt me down. My job is to find stories and be there at the right time when they are playing out."

I remained silent. He was right. He was not a snitch, nor a spy, nor a mediator. Moreover his sources could be wrong and even if they were right, there was little President Rabbani and Commander Masud could do, except leave the city.

If the Taliban was planning to attack Kabul soon, it wouldn't be necessary to leave the city. The news was actually coming to us.

XIII

Kandahar

They kept telling us that those who weren't ready would continue their training at the camp, but they ended up sending all of us to Kandahar on the first call, without any discussion or reprimand for those who were falling behind.

We started walking through the rocky brown mountains the way we had first come to the camp. At times the passages were only wide enough for a single man to slip through at a time. Wazir Khan was the first to step on the rocky path, Mehtab Khan was the last. We had been told before we left the camp that if we were interested in getting to Kandahar in one piece we'd need to keep our ears open for the directions of the two men. Any deviation from their commands could send us falling a couple of thousand feet, or at least would bring the wrath of the older, more experienced men. But our journey started to get easier after an hour or so. We began to move down more and more, and only had to climb sporadically.

By midafternoon we reached a dirt road where some jeeps were waiting for us. We were fifty-three including the sixteen students from my *madrassah*.

We came onto a paved road after a few minutes' drive, and after a couple of hours the jeeps started driving on dirt paths once again, then we came onto the road again.

This pattern kept repeating itself. Every patch of dirt road would shake our insides and made our bones chuckle. The open spaces made me nervous and dust from the road sometimes irritated my eyes, but after the congested slums of Pakistan, a few breaths of fresh air did me good.

There were signs of the ravishes of war everywhere, but it was impossible to differentiate between the destruction from the war against the Russians and the scars of the war among different

Afghani factions. War, apparently, did not ask who was destroying the country—insiders or outsiders.

The buildings along the road almost all had roofs on the ground and walls leaning on each other. When the jeep ran over the rubble spread out from one of these ruins, it would produce an unexpected jolt and an unpleasant crunch, as if a huge bug was crushed under the weight. Leafless trees stood like ghosts, sensing the low vibration of the human drama with exasperation and contempt. The thirsty fields around us seemed to have long since surrendered any hope of growing anything again.

Whenever we stopped for the call of nature or to eat, we were warned to be careful, as there were landmines everywhere. Our training at the camp in that regard was already in practical use.

Some of my fellow students, who now knew how to fire a gun and do a few other tricks of war, appeared foolishly overconfident, as if they were going to play a game. They cracked jokes and teased each other in the jeep, oblivious to the destruction around them.

Ahmed sat next to me in the jeep immersed in thought. He had played many roles in my life—snitch, messenger, healer, protector, and sometimes a friend—but I wasn't sure which of those roles he would play in the war. All throughout our training I found him protective at some times, and at others distant, as if he hadn't yet decided whether to provide his shield for me or let me suffer the results of my own failings.

In the evening we reached Kandahar. The driver, whose name was Shirazi—a talkative man with a high nose, wearing a *Chitrali* hat—kept pointing at different buildings to impress us with their significance. We were too tired to pay attention to the bragging of a native Kandahari, but he stopped in the city center and demanded our attention, pointing to a round building with a big green dome surrounded by a few minarets of the same color. "This is the 'Shrine of the Cloak.' Prophet Mohammed, peace be upon him, wore the cloak that is kept in there. And then Amir-al Muminin, Mullah Omar, wore it when he took the responsibility of leading the Islamic Ummah. Remember you are the soldiers of the prophet and Amir is the vehicle that guides you." He'd skipped the whole history of the cloak from the prophet to Mullah Omar in a single breath.

"Can we see the cloak some time?" Rehman asked.

"No, the cloak is locked away. It's too precious to be looked at by us," Shirazi said politely.

We went through the narrow streets of Kandahar, stopping at every corner and every junction when a vehicle would appear as if from nowhere to block our way, and after an exchange of a few bursts of horns and sometimes heated words we would move on to our destination. Our ride became much smoother once we left the city.

An hour later we stopped in front of a big iron gate and Shirazi talked to the two men standing outside it. I looked around, but I couldn't see any of the other vehicles that had been behind and in front of us. A couple of minutes later, the men opened the gate and Shirazi drove into a big compound. He parked the jeep in front of a sign, written on a big piece of wood, that said OFFICE. Shirazi told us to wait for him before going in.

The compound was surrounded on three sides by three-storey buildings. A veranda with a four-foot wall ran in front of the rooms on the second and third floors, and doors opened onto the veranda. The fourth side, with the gate through which we had entered the compound, was a twelve-foot cinderblock wall.

Shirazi came out of the office after a couple minutes, holding a sheet of paper. The seven of us went with the driver to the second floor, where he pointed to the two rooms on the east corner of the veranda, opposite the main gate.

"These are your rooms . . . food will be served at seven, go down the stairs and turn left to go into the hall." With that, Shirazi turned around and left us.

We went into the first room, then the second. They were the same. Ahmed, Rehman, and I took the first one, and the other four took the second.

In our room there was a large mirror with a dresser under it, two beds in the middle of the room, and a small table with two drawers next to each bed.

The turban I was forced to wear was killing me in the dry summer heat. I opened the drawer of the table closest to me to rest my turban over it. There was an envelope in the drawer. I took out the envelope and opened it. It contained two letters, both written in Pashto. The writer had written every letter with such care that each word looked like a piece of calligraphy done by an artist. I figured out some parts of the letter but most of it was beyond my skill in the language. At the end of the letter there were marks made by lips that had worn lipstick. I shoved them back in the envelope fast, then stuffed the envelope far into the back of the drawer.

Through the window I could see the signboard outside the gate, written in black letters in Pashto, over which somebody had painted a red cross.

"You can take one of the beds if you want to," I said to Rehman who was placing his sleeping bag on the floor.

"*Brother,*" he said in Pashto, "*I have slept all my life on the floor, why use the comfort of a bed now?*"

"*You helped me a lot in learning Pashto,*" I replied.

"*No problem, brother.*"

"I can't read that one though." I pointed to the board outside the large gate. "What does it say under the red paint?"

"Girls' Hostel, Kandahar University."

"I figured out 'girls' but couldn't figure out 'hostel'," I said.

"You are going to learn fast now, you are living with Pashtuns," he said while taking his things out of his satchel.

I remained silent.

* * *

In Kandahar, with those turbans and loose *shalwar qameez*, we looked very much like every other member of the notorious brotherhood. It was difficult to figure out how many of them came from across the border, but it was quite evident that *talibs* were arriving regularly, and all the public buildings including the university and school buildings were used to lodge them.

After two days we were collected outside in the compound. There were other students of different *madrassahs*. Though most of them were Afghanis, and quite possibly Pashtuns, all of them probably came from the refugee camps across the border.

A few minutes later a man with broad shoulders and a pudgy look stepped on the stairs and called for our attention. "My name is Rustam Khan, and I am your commander. All of you live in this building, this is your chance to get to know each other and your *jamat*. I do not know when we will leave but I can tell you that there is a very important task ahead, and knowing each other well will help you on the front. If I am not around then follow Suhrab Khan." He pointed to a tall man whose heavy facial hair, including huge eyebrows, seemed to push his eyes deep into their sockets. "You will be challenged soon. Allah is merciful, and success in this venture will take us far in our mission."

* * *

A few days later, when Ahmed and I came back from the lunchroom, I saw a group of boys on the veranda in front of our room, struggling to snatch the letters from Rehman's hands. He would pull them away long enough to read a phrase, but then would have to move them away again to escape from the grasp of his friends. By the time we reached them the two letters ended up in different sets of hands and two sets of laughs shot into the air.

"Don't giggle like girls!" I said. "Give them to me."

"Why? They aren't yours." One of the boys waved a letter in his hand, stretching his arm up to keep it away from his friends.

"Give them to me!" I insisted. "I found them first."

"No, not you, *he* found them," another boy said, pointing at Rehman.

"No," I said. "I didn't tell him because I was afraid he would do exactly what he's doing now."

"What is this about?" Ahmed said.

"Brother Ahmed, I found them in our room," Rehman said.

"I found them first," I said, trying to snatch the letter away from the boys. "How would I know what they are if I hadn't seen them before you."

"What are these letters about?" Ahmed asked.

"They are a girl's love letters," Rehman laughed.

"What is going on up there?" the stern voice of Suhrab Khan rose from the street.

Rehman replied to him in Pashto and was answered in a commanding tone from Suhrab Khan something I couldn't figure out. Rehman took both of the letters from the boys, made a loose ball of them, bent down over the railing, and threw them away. The paper swirled in the wind in front of us before rolling down, and sinking toward the ground along with my heart.

Suhrab Khan caught the letters in the air, spread out the paper, and glanced at the writing. He turned his head up, covered his eyes from the direct light of the sun, and shouted, "Come down!"

We looked at each other and moved to the stairs one by one. On the stairs Ahmed whispered to me in Urdu, "Are they Perveen's?"

I shook my head.

Suhrab Khan rested his elbow on top of the side wall of the stairs, brushing his long beard with his fingers. "Who found this?"

"He did," Rehman said, pointing his forefinger at me, though a few moments ago he refused to believe I had.

"They were in the room when we got here," I said.

"Do you know who they belong to?" Suhrab Khan asked.

"No," I answered truthfully.

"Were they sent to someone in your *jamat*?"

We remained silent.

"Answer me!" he yapped.

"They were there when the room was given to us," I said.

"All right," he said, waving the letters at us dismissively. "Go to mosque, you are getting late for *zuhur* prayers."

While going through the familiar motions of the *zuhur* prayers, I kept asking Allah to save the girl who had written those letters to someone she loved, and kept cursing myself for not tearing them to shreds when I first found them.

When I left the mosque I found Ahmed waiting for me. His wide forehead with a mole in the middle had many folds.

"Yes," I said, "give me one of your long lectures, prove to me that I am an idiot. You have another chance to prove yourself cleverer than me."

"I have never called you an idiot."

I ogled him.

"At least . . . I have never meant it."

I remained silent.

"You should have destroyed them the moment you found them," he said.

"I thought that after the war the same girl may come back and find her letters."

"You *are* an idiot!" he said, raising his voice. "I don't care what you think. Do you think this war is about to be over? It won't be over in our lifetimes."

"Why do you always tell me what to do after something bad happens?"

"Because you never tell me your foolish ideas before acting on them," he said, a little more quietly. "If you told me you were about to elope, I'd . . . I'd . . ."

In the spur of that moment, in which he was unable to find words to express himself, a thought overwhelmed me: There was more than a friendly concern for Perveen in his heart. He seemed more annoyed with me since the day I met him in Karachi in the alley, looking for refuge. Before I ran away with Perveen he was stern but protective but since my return to *madrassah* I found him bitter and abrasive. He shared my affection for her. I felt so close to him at that moment that I had the urge to step forward and embrace him. But I stayed where I was.

"I wish I could go back in time to when you gave me her note," I admitted. "I would refuse to meet her. She never deserved any of this."

Ahmed shushed me and whispered, "They are coming. Let's go." He grabbed my arm and pulled me softly toward the hostel. We walked fast to get away from the crowd coming out of the mosque.

* * *

Early the next morning, someone knocked loudly on the door. Ahmed, whose bed was closest to the door, opened it with his half-opened eyes. Shirazi stood outside.

"You all need to be in the courtyard at eight, so get ready," he said.

"Yes, brother," Ahmed replied.

Shirazi moved on to the next door.

Ahmed came back into the room and said, "Wake up you two. Get ready."

He went into the bathroom. I got out of the bed and woke up Rehman, who was still in his sleeping bag on the floor.

We came down the stairs a few minutes later. Two men in the compound, by the stairs, were telling *talibs* that breakfast would be provided afterward. Shirazi was waiting for us, and we followed him. He told us to stand on the left side of the big table. The friends of Rehman that were involved in the letter-snatching game were already there. *Talibs* were gathering all around us, men with long beards and young men with comparatively smaller beards, all with black turbans, loose trousers and shirts, and eyes that lacked empathy. After a few moments I saw three men bringing a woman in a white *burqa* and a man walked close to her. They were told to stand on the right side of the table. A few minutes later Rustam Khan and Suhrab Khan, with two old men probably in their seventies, appeared and sat behind the table.

One of the old men behind the table stood up after consulting his consorts for a couple of minutes. He started talking to the audience in Pashto. I figured out some portions of his speech. It was full of words like *Shariah*, traditions, and heritage but I was sure that none of the words matched with the notions of sympathy, pity, or love.

The old man waved the two letters in the air and added a few more sentences to his speech. I could easily understand what he was conveying without understanding the words.

"These *mujahids* found this letter in room number twenty-nine. Did you live in that room, sister?" Rustam Khan pointed his fingers toward us while addressing the woman.

"I don't remember, brother."

"Did you live in this hostel?" Rustam Khan continued his cross-examination.

She remained silent.

"Answer me, woman!"

"Long time back."

I ruined another life. I was a magnet for sad outcomes. A ball in my throat was expanding as if somebody was throttling me from the inside.

"Are these your letters, sister?"

"I don't know . . . I can't see them."

Suhrab Khan gave them to a *talib* standing near him, who gave them to the man standing next to her, the husband.

"It can't be hers, I know her writing," the husband said.

"Give the letters to the woman," Rustam Khan said.

The husband reluctantly handed the letters to the woman. She brought them close to the net that was in front of her eyes, attached to the *burqa*. She looked around at the crowd but did not say anything.

"Are these letters yours?" Rustam Khan asked the woman again.

No sound came out of the *burqa*.

"Woman! Do not test my patience."

"Brothers, I wrote them a long time back... to my husband... but I never mailed them."

"But he was not your husband at that time."

She was silent again.

"What difference does it make?" The husband took off his cap and dried the perspiration on his forehead with it. "She never mailed them."

"But she wrote them, which shows the corruption of her mind," Rustam Khan said.

"This is why we don't believe in the education of girls, their minds become the home of Satan," the old man sitting close to Suhrab Khan said.

"There is nothing wrong in writing poetry, we have had many famous poets in our history."

"They were *men*," Rustam Khan said.

"Many were women," the husband insisted.

"This is a new era. All those fallacies of mind cannot be tolerated anymore. The Quran and *Shariah* are clear regarding this."

"No, they are . . ." the man started, but his wife pulled his shirt at the elbow.

"Woman!" Rustam Khan pointed his finger at the woman furiously. "Do not ever stop a man from speaking."

Silence ruled the crowd for a few moments.

The old men talked to each other for a minute and then one of them said something to Suhrab Khan, who was sitting next to him. Suhrab Khan conveyed the message to Rustam Khan.

"Evidence shows that this woman has committed adultery of the mind, and therefore she is sent to jail for ten years according to the laws of *Shariah*," Rustam Khan said, addressing the audience.

"You can't do this!" the husband shouted. "She has children. Who will take care of them? What kind of justice is this? Where in *Shariah* is written ten years of sentence?"

"Shut his mouth," Rustam Khan commanded.

One of the men standing behind the man him hit him with the butt of a Kalashnikov. The husband's cap jumped away from him and he fell down. The woman rushed for him and was about to sit near him when another man started hitting her with a stick. She turned away to cover herself with her arms and hands. But the man didn't stop. She stood up and turned away.

"Take her away," Rustam Khan said.

The man pushed her with the tip of his stick. The crowd parted to give her way and she went out of my sight.

The heavy ball in my throat was now on my heart.

* * *

The day passed but the night seemed eternal, I couldn't sleep. I turned and turned in bed for a long time. When I got tired of that I got out of bed then left the room to stand on the veranda and get some fresh air. It was dark. Two lights, one on each side of the gate, fought unsuccessfully against the dark.

I tried to picture the cell in Karachi where Perveen was breathing, her valor providing breaths to our child. What was she thinking right now? Was she cursing me and the child inside her? My miserable heart made my eyes moist. The door behind me opened and Ahmed came out.

"Couldn't sleep?" he whispered.

"No."

He stood next to me and rested his elbows on the railing on top of the veranda wall.

"Do you think there is any hope for her?" I asked him.

"No, they will not let her out before her ten years are up."

"No, no, I meant Perveen."

He thought for a moment then said, "They have never put any woman to death under *Hudood* law. . . . Her life in jail may become tougher after the birth of the child, but . . ."

"I hope it will be a girl," I said. "A boy . . . a boy may end up with Bayfazal."

He made eye contact to convey that he understood my fears. "Leave the past behind . . . it will just give you pain."

"I will never be free from heartache." I tried to look into his eyes in the dark. "Did you love Perveen?"

"Have you gone mad?" he said, looking away from me toward the gate of the compound.

"Why did she trust you?" I pressed. "Why did she choose you to give the message for me? That message could have brought a lot of trouble for her if it had ended up in somebody's hands."

"Are you accusing me of something?"

"No, I am not, but . . ."

"I don't know why she trusted me."

"You can tell me, Ahmed."

"I never thought she belonged to me," he said.

We stood there between the black sky and the black earth, I trying to gauge his feelings for her, and he attempting to gauge my reaction to his confession.

Finally, Ahmed stepped back from the railing and said, "Go to bed. Who knows what tomorrow will bring." He turned and went back into the room.

Two days later we were collected again in the courtyard and Rustam Khan told us that the very next day we would leave for Kabul.

XIV

Taliban in Kabul

On the twenty-sixth of September 1996, when the Taliban were expected to enter the city, I took all the Eastern clothes I'd bought in Peshawar out of my bag and hanged them in the closet, and took all my Western clothes from the closet and put them in the bag.

The three eastern provinces had fallen to the Taliban fast and they made major headway in the north, taking over Bagram Air Base. When they started making advances toward Kabul, Masud decided to leave the city. It was not possible for him to defend the city from three sides with only twenty-five thousand troops, and his resistance would just be the cause of more bloodshed among the civilian population of the city. President Rabbani left a couple days earlier than Masud.

In the early afternoon I got dressed, took my bag that had my camera, and went into the deserted streets. No children played in the ruins, and no beggars and no cars moved along the streets except a few families I found near the Presidential Palace. They were Hazara and Uzbek civilians and they were right to leave the city. They were usually the first targets of Taliban atrocities. I took a few photographs of the families, and a few more of the city, and came back to the hotel.

When I got out of the elevator on the second floor to go to my room I saw Arshad waiting to get in.

"Streets are deserted, where are you going?" I asked.

"A friend of mine is in Peshawar, but his family is still in Kabul," he said. "They live across town, and I am just going to check on them."

"Would you mind if I come with you?"

He shrugged and said, "I will stay there for an hour or so . . . it would be better to get back before dark. *They* will be here some time in the late evening."

I got back in the elevator with him.

We came out of the hotel and got into his rented car. Arshad knew the city quite well. He had been covering Afghanistan since the beginning of the Soviet invasion. We drove by the UN compound and the Presidential Palace and then entered the neighborhood of Ghazi Stadium. He turned off the main avenue into a side street and parked his car in front of a two-story house. We stepped down from the car and Arshad pressed the bell next to the gate.

A young man in jeans and a black shirt appeared and greeted Arshad in Pashto. He had a wide forehead with thick eyebrows. Arshad shook his hand and said something to the young man, pointing to me.

"Good evening, please come in," the young man greeted me in passable English.

I pulled the *chadur*, the sheet I was wearing, over my head and went in. He led us through a small lawn and opened the door to let us in. I scanned the living room with a reporter's eye: a brown sofa along the wall and two chairs on each side. The big center table had a small, carved wooden panel behind its glass with a vine tracing a complex floral pattern. Over the table there was a big bowl decorated with a floral design, parts of which were metal stripes cut into leaves, pasted on the pattern of the bowl. The wall behind the sofa had an embroidered landscape, and the other walls had landscape paintings, two stuffed heads of deer, and a few embroidered floral patterns.

We sat on the sofa and the young man went into the house. A couple minutes later a middle-aged woman appeared. She wore a long shirt with a purple and green floral pattern, and loose green *shalwar* trousers matching the pattern of the shirt, and a thin *duppatta* to cover her head.

"*As-salāmu 'alaykum,*" she greeted.

"*wa-'alaykum-us-salām* . . . How are you?" Arshad finished in

English.

She replied in Pashto or Urdu. I was still struggling to differentiate the sounds of the two languages.

Arshad said something to her and then introduced me in English, "This is Rachael Brown. She is a journalist, covering Afghanistan like me."

"Nice to meet you," the woman spoke English with only a slight accent.

"Razia teach in Kabul University," Arshad said.

"Taught," Razia corrected before turning to me. "Soon they will close the university, I am sure."

"That will be a disappointment for you."

"Yes, definitely."

The young man came back in to stand behind his mother.

Arshad turned to him and said with frown, "You need to wear your traditional clothes, Jamal. Look at me, you need to live like Romans in Rome." Arshad pointed to his long, loose shirt and loose trousers.

Jamal replied in Pashto, and it was clear that neither Arshad or Razia liked the answer.

"Please put some sense into him," Razia said to Arshad. "I am tired of arguing with him."

Looking sternly at Jamal, Arshad said in English, "You are young and I really respect your desire to be who you are, but we are not dealing with reasonable people here. Your father has called me from Peshawar several times to see how you and your family are doing. He is very worried. Do you think it would be good that they harm your family just because you don't want to change your clothes?" Arshad seemed to be prepared for this conversation. "Don't do it for yourself, do it for your mother and sister."

Jamal remained silent but it seemed that Arshad's words sank in.

"Nasir said that he is calling you for the last two weeks but couldn't get through," Arshad said to Razia.

"Arshad *bhai*, the phones of the whole area are out of order for quite some time, nobody is coming for repairs and once they are here it may never be fixed."

"I'll let him know when he will call me at night," Arshad said.

"Let him know that we are fine. He doesn't have to worry about us and he shouldn't rush to Kabul until it is safe." She turned to me and said, "I am sorry, I didn't even ask if you would like to have tea or something cold."

"No, I am fine. Just water will be good," I replied.

"Sure, but please have some tea," she said, and then said something to her son in Pashto, who went back into the house.

"What do you teach?" I asked her.

"English literature. . . . How is your stay in Kabul up till now?"

"Pretty good."

"You look beautiful in Afghani clothes."

"Thank you," I said. "Are you native to Kabul?"

"Yes and no . . . my father migrated to Peshawar when he was young, where he married his cousin and settled down, and when I grew up I got married and came to Kabul with my husband. He has a hand-knotted carpet factory in the city."

Jamal came in with a jug of water and a few glasses on a tray. Razia poured the water in a glass and handed it over to me. I was distracted by the sound of a girl's voice coming from somewhere in the house. I looked at Razia, who smiled and said, "It's all right, Amina, come in. It's just your Arshad Uncle."

A young girl of fourteen or fifteen, covered in a *chadur*, brought a tray with a teakettle and cups.

"*As-salāmu 'alaykum*, Arshad Uncle," the girl said, her voice soft, hesitant.

"*Wa-'alaykum-us-salām, Beta.*"

She put the tray on the center table and started talking to Arshad, probably asking about her father.

Razia started pouring tea. "Milk?"

"No, thank you."

Razia handed the cup of tea to me, and placed the sugar pot in front of me.

"Would you mind if I ask you some questions about women in Afghanistan?"

"You can ask me anything as long as you don't mention my name anywhere."

"No, I won't. I'm just collecting material to write a comprehensive article about the plight of women in Afghanistan. We all know the severe laws the Taliban impose on women, but I would like to know your views on the status of women before all this chaos."

With a wan smile Razia said, "Women usually end up as property in the tribal systems, but wherever we've been allowed an education, like in the cities, our situation has been different. But at the same time I don't believe we need to copy the West to be free. We need to find freedom in the context of our own society."

I nodded, though I wasn't quite sure I understood where that line was drawn. "But if the society is tribal, how would you find freedom in its context?" I asked.

Razia sat back in her chair and really seemed to consider the question for a moment. "It may be that 'context' is not the right word here. . . . What I meant was that freedom should be an attitude and not the superficial aspects of appearances. Some societies, and some people here, too, have decided that if women copy the West and start wearing skirts and jeans, they will find freedom, or if they are allowed to go out of their homes to work they will find freedom, but a woman in jeans can be beaten as much as a woman in a *burqa*. And forcing a woman to take off her *hijab* is as much a form of oppression as to force her to wear one. We see quite often in the West that a woman is beaten or harassed, and she is harassed here too, so what's the difference? But I am not talking about the severe laws of the Taliban against women, I am talking about the general Afghan society."

"I guess the difference is that in the West a woman can find help if she is beaten, as you say, or harassed."

"Right," Razia said, nodding and leaning forward toward me, "that's exactly what I wanted to say. The protection comes from the laws at the highest level and these laws are made when a society matures by the right kind of education . . . modernism should be about freedom and the status of women in the society, it should be about the right kind of attitudes and not about appearances. In the case of Afghanistan, this maturity of attitude was interrupted by more than eighteen years of war, and unluckily, a group of foreigners help put the society in reverse. We have fourteen women professors at this moment in Kabul University. There was a time there were none. Change was happening but it has been sabotaged by war and extremism."

I smiled and nodded enthusiastically, my practiced journalistic cool defeated by the exhilaration of talking to an educated Afghan woman without the filter of an interpreter.

"What do you think lies in the future for Afghanistan?" I asked.

"It's difficult to say . . . if the Taliban takes over then there is no future, even for the men, let alone the women. If more liberal forces take over, the future will take a better course. But the change had better be indigenous and not be forced on us by political forces outside the country."

"Why do you think it's wrong to get the help of forces outside the country . . . I mean, what's wrong with the outside forces if they help to bring about the right change?"

She gave me a wry smile, clearly happy to explain, "The problem is that the other factions get help from other outside forces for their agenda once we get help, and then there is no end to this . . . the foreign forces start dictating a lot more in the agenda of different groups than the forces inside the country." Then a hard transition to: "More tea?"

"No, thank you."

"We should be going," Arshad cut in. "It's getting dark, and it's better if we don't have to go across town while they are entering the city."

"Okay," I said, and stood up. I wanted to stay much longer and talk at greater length with this fascinating woman, and maybe get her daughter's perspective as well, but I knew Arshad wasn't just being overly cautious about being caught on the streets when the Taliban marched into the city. I offered Razia my hand and said, "It was very nice to meet you."

She stood, shook my hand, and replied, "Nice to meet you too." She came with us to the door.

The crescent moon in the west seemed lonely, giving depth to the darkness of the night. There were no lights in the windows of the surrounding houses, their residents seemed to be hibernating, away from the surface of the earth where beasts roamed. There wasn't a single vehicle on the streets except ours. Here and there I saw passersby, all men, walking fast to get to their destinations.

It took us half an hour to get to the neighborhood of the hotel. We heard gunshots near the UN compound. Arshad turned off the car's headlights and kept moving, though very slowly. He parked the car across from the UN compound.

"Something is going on in the compound," he said in a hushed but nervous voice.

"Should we go in?" I asked.

"No," he said then paused a few breaths to think. "I don't think it would be a good idea. . . . Let's wait here."

When I took the camera out of my bag, Arshad whispered, "Don't use a flash, it will attract attention."

I nodded and whispered back, "High speed film . . ."

We didn't have to wait long. We saw a group of men with turbans pushing two men without turbans out of the compound. When the two men fell on the sidewalk, a torrent of kicks and fists were thrown at them. Two of the men in turbans tore the clothes off the unconscious men, bending down over the bodies.

"What are they doing?"

"What is the epitome of insult to a man?" Arshad asked.

I opened my mouth to reply but decided against it. I wanted to look away when the unconscious men were dragged to a pickup truck parked a few yards away. The men in turbans tied their victims' heads to the bumper of the truck, feet down on the street. Then they got in the truck and I closed my eyes and tipped my head down. The engine started, but I couldn't watch as the two men were dragged away behind the pickup.

Arshad started the car once they were far enough away.

"Where are you . . . ?" I started to ask, but had to choke back a sob.

"You should not look," he advised. My face flushed, embarrassed, feeling weak, but I didn't look up. "I want to follow them."

I nodded and asked, "Who were those two men? Any ideas?"

"One of them was definitely ex-president Najibullah."

"The communist?" I said, my voice sounding way too loud in the dark interior of the car. I looked up and then away as fast as I could at a glance of twisted bodies—things that couldn't once have been human. "Why didn't he leave Kabul?" I asked, trying to think away what I had seen. "What mercy could he expect from the Taliban?"

"I heard that Masud offered Najibullah help but he refused to go with him. He probably did not want to alienate his people, the Pashtuns, by leaving the city with Uzbeks. He had been asking for help from Norbert Holl, who is now in the UN headquarters in Islamabad, but I think the help he was expecting never came."

The pickups stopped in front of the Presidential Palace, and Arshad stopped the car a few feet away. We heard two thuds, one after the other: the skulls of the victims hitting the street when the knots were untied. Then they shot the two men, making sure neither of them remained alive. I wanted to get out of the car and scream, to run away, but I forced myself to just sit there.

A couple minutes later we saw two men hop into the pickup, carrying heavy ropes. They threw a loop over the traffic signal under which their pickup was parked. Then they tied a few knots to prepare a noose. The two on the street grabbed one of the bodies from the torso and pushed it to the men on the pickup. One of the men held the body from the underarms and the other squeezed the head in through the noose. They repeated the same motions for the other one.

The floor of the pickup was now a scaffold, supporting the weight of the bodies. They started the pickup and moved away with a screech, jolting the corpses forward, leaving them to swing in a pendulum motion.

I held my hands over my mouth and closed my eyes again. I might have been crying. I'm not even sure.

Arshad started the car and turned into the nearest side street to get away from the palace.

XV

Interviews

I was sure the bodies would be brought down by morning.

The act was heinous even by the Taliban's standards, and with such a big international press presence in Kabul they couldn't possibly gain anything from that display. The Taliban put themselves forward as peacemakers, as enforcers of law, as the best alternative to the chaos of tribal warfare.

I wanted to get news of this atrocity out to my paper as soon as possible. I went to the little table in my hotel room and wrote down the details of what I had seen, ending with a note that I would be sending the photographs as soon as I could. I went downstairs to the business center and faxed the single sheet to my editor-in-chief.

When I went out the next day, all my expectations were proved wrong. The bodies still hung there. Someone had wedged cigarettes between their fingers and shoved sheets of paper into their pockets—probably all covered with derogatory remarks. A crowd of journalists stood around the bodies, writing notes of the hideous sight. No photographs were allowed.

A few feet away, at the corner of the next street, two Taliban men stopped passersby and by their body language, gesturing to their own beards, and slapping the terrified faces of the innocent bystanders, they seemed to be warning men to grow their beards.

One passerby said something back to them, his brow furrowed, his tone heated. One of the turbaned Taliban fighters hit the man in the stomach with the butt of his AK-47 and the other pulled the writhing man into a waiting pickup truck.

I looked away, the poetry of Rudyard Kipling and the novels of George MacDonald Fraser appearing in my mind: wild, heavily armed tribesmen holding back the forces of modernity with ferocious zeal.

I started walking back to the hotel. When I passed in front of Pashtunistan Square, a few feet away from my hotel, I saw a group of them standing outside their pickups, talking to each other. One of them stopped me and said something to me in Pashto. He probably thought that I was an Afghan woman without a *burqa*. My hand shaking under his withering stare, I took my newspaper ID out of my bag and showed it to him. He smirked, and waved me away.

* * *

I stayed in the hotel the next several days, telling myself I wasn't hiding, but I knew I was.

Finally unable to stand my own company any longer, I ended up having breakfast with Ben Baldwin, who grilled me a little too forcefully at first about what I had seen in the car with Arshad. When he finally realized I was getting rattled, he patted my hand on the table and sat back, taking a sip of what by then must have been cold coffee.

"Najibullah's execution was the first symbolic brutal act by the Taliban in Kabul," he said as if dictating a story to his editor at Reuters. "It was a targeted killing to terrorize a population that had taken a liberal approach toward life, women, and religion. The very next day, they imposed the severest laws I've ever heard of, anywhere in the world. All women banned from working . . ."

"No consideration to the fact that one quarter of Kabul's civil service, the entire elementary education system, and much of the health system are run by women," I said.

"I talked to my driver yesterday," Baldwin said, "He said there's a growing fear that thousands of families headed by woman, like the families of war widows, are going to be left to just starve."

I had heard the same thing. Each new day brought fresh pronouncements from the Taliban through Radio Kabul, which had been renamed Radio Shariat.

"Thieves will have their hands and feet amputated, adulterers will be stoned to death, and those taking liquor will be lashed," I recited from a broadcast Arshad had translated for me.

"How many are affected by the girls' schools and colleges being closed, I wonder?" Baldwin asked, shaking his head. "Seventy? Eighty thousand?"

"Take your pick," I replied with a shrug, knowing that I had already quoted seventy-five thousand to my own editor. "And this dress code: head to toe veils for women? TV, video, satellite dishes, music, and all games banned? What are they trying to accomplish with this?"

"The religious training of the Taliban is heavily influenced by the Deobandi school, which preaches a form of conservative orthodoxy in which evil can be defined in terms of departure from rituals," Baldwin explained. He didn't look at me, just stared down into his half-empty coffee cup.

"Have they imported this Deobandi approach from the Makkah?"

"You mean Saudi Arabia?"

"Yes."

"No. Saudi Arabia is the pit of Wahabis. It is true that the Wahabi establishment lent support to the Taliban. The Afghan puritans emerged from the Indian Deobandi movement, which later spread to Pakistan after the partition of the Indian subcontinent and then gained momentum in Zia's time, who as we know used Islam to sustain his dictatorship."

I had done the reading too. The Taliban's incipient structure was the religious police force that was responsible for the Promotion of Virtue and Suppression of Vice, an agency we quickly realized was fond of executions and life sentences.

"I've been hearing this word a lot . . . *wahshat?*" Baldwin asked.

"The man at the reception desk said that," I replied. "It meant 'terror.' That's what the Kabulis feel Taliban rule has brought them." And I felt the same way.

163

Like narcissists, the Taliban were self-destructive. Detention and intimidation of Emma Bonino, European Union Commissioner for Humanitarian Affairs, and distinguished journalists William Shawcross and Christiane Amanpour on the grounds that members of their groups had taken photographs, served no purpose except to antagonize the international community.

My breakfast companion set his coffee cup down on the table and sighed. Now it was my turn to pat his hand. I forced a smile onto my face.

"I was one of the pundits who dismissed fears that this student movement would ever be able to take the capital," he said through another long sigh, as if confessing his sins. "I guess I failed to consider the fact that Afghanistan, after being the battleground of two superpowers, has now become the battleground between countries like Saudi Arabia, Pakistan, and Iran—using Afghanis for their vested interests, providing financial support to one or another allied group."

I nodded. He was right.

The result of this new battle was the pronounced ethnic and sectarian divide and polarization of the region.

"I wonder . . ." I said, pushing my own empty coffee cup a little away from me. "Would another foreign enemy bring these Afghan factions closer, or would it be the end of Afghanistan all together?"

* * *

Finally, unable to hide in the hotel any longer, I asked Arshad to help me interview some lower-echelon Taliban fighters. I wanted to know what lives they lived, what future they aspired to, and how much they agreed with the strict measures their leaders were taking.

Arshad's broken Pashto, and excellent Urdu and English, would help us to talk to all kinds of Taliban, those who were native Afghans and those who came across the border from Pakistan.

Arshad told me they were using Ghazi Stadium for their kind of entertainment: executions. "It might be a good place to talk to them if we get there early," he said. "The leadership has instructed their cadets at all levels to be at the stadium. This is their tactic, to intimidate their own people to show them the fate of deserters."

Quietly terrified of witnessing another murder, I nodded and followed him to his car.

We reached Ghazi Stadium two hours earlier than the scheduled time of the executions. It was a middle-class neighborhood, but the doors and windows of the houses and shops were tightly shut. Most of the locals had probably left the neighborhood. We found groups of men heading for the stadium, but none of them were ready to stop and talk to us, so we followed them in.

It was a large stadium, full of men with turbans. Cement seats with crumbling edges surrounded a field that had long since dried up. Devoid of even weeds, it showed the neglect not of months but years.

My jaw trembling, my knees and hands shaking, I looked around for suitable candidates to interview. Arshad would talk to the men I pointed out and once they agreed to talk he would convey my questions to them, which I recorded on my portable tape recorder to be translated later. This didn't allow for follow-up questions, but Arshad asked some.

One man stood out. When I asked for his full name, he said, "I am just Raza, there is nothing after it."

"Arshad has told me that you have come from the other side of the border," I asked him. "Did you live in a *madrassah*?"

"We all lived in *madrassah*."

"Are your parents all right with your coming here?"

He looked at me as if I were an alien from another world. "I have no parents."

"Do you like this life . . . I mean coming here to fight with them?"

"It was not my decision."

"You mean somebody forced you to come to Afghanistan?"

Another young man, sitting next to Raza, said, "He means that he did not want to come to Kabul, the City of Sin."

Raza looked at the other young man but remained silent. I saw they were protecting each other, and didn't want to say anything that could bring trouble for them.

To be sure of their stance I adopted another strategy. "So you are happy fighting with the Taliban?"

Raza remained silent but the other young man said after a pause, "Yes, of course we are."

Despite being sure they were lying, I silently saluted the resistance of their hearts to the life they were forced to live. I knew there were exceptions to the rule among the young Taliban fighters.

They wandered off with their comrades in arms and Arshad shook his head, whispering to me, "A shame, these boys . . ."

"They wouldn't like to hear you call them boys," I warned him—but he knew that well enough.

"They are boys walking in men's shoes," he said, quietly enough that only I could hear. "I doubt a single one of them has seen life outside their *madrassahs* or the refugee camps. Manhood comes with experience and self-knowledge that they couldn't acquire in the seclusion imposed on them by their ignorant mullahs."

I took a deep breath, worried that he would be overheard, but anxious to know what he thought of these young warriors.

"In the camps and the *madrassahs*, they studied the basics of the Deobandi school, as interpreted by their teachers who have never read anything besides the Quran and have no exposure to math, science, or history. These boys have never witnessed peace, have no memories of their tribes, their elders, their neighbors . . . I doubt most of them even have memories of their parents and siblings. These boys are the unfortunate generation that has lost almost all connection with the values of the past. Rootless, jobless, hopeless, they are not even trained for the occupations of their forefathers— farming, herding, carpet weaving, and—"

He stopped when a young man in a dirty white turban bumped into his shoulder, jostling him. The young man glared back with eyes so cold they made my skin crawl, and I could tell he had the same effect on Arshad.

When I saw more of the young fighters had noticed us, I whispered, "We should go."

Arshad drove me back to the hotel in silence. He had been more upset by what we saw at the stadium than me—and we had not seen anything but young men with turbans and rifles . . . and eyes full of resignation and agitated excitement, a brewing violence that scared me and seemed to disappoint Arshad.

Watching these boys, Karl Marx would call them Afghanistan's *lumpen proletariat*.

I wondered if any of them had ever known the company of women. They had either lived in the strict parameters of *madrassahs* or in the segregated refugee camps where they had little or no interaction with the opposite sex.

* * *

One day when I was sitting in the lobby, working on an article, I saw guards yelling at a *burqa*-clad woman who was trying to enter the hotel. She kept repeating the same sentence in Pashto and kept searching the lobby as if she were looking for someone.

When I heard my name coming from behind the *burqa*, I realized it was Razia.

"Guards!" I called out. "Let her come in."

They stepped aside.

"I need to see Arshad," she said without greeting.

"I haven't seen him for the last few days, what's wrong?"

I saw her eyes turning left and right and then coming in the front again under the masking net of her *burqa*. "They took my son Jamal."

Though I'd never really spoken to Jamal, my blood ran cold at the unspoken implication behind that simple statement. I felt the eyes of the Taliban guards that had been permanently posted to the hotel boring into us both.

"Come with me to my room," I said. "We will be able to talk freely."

We went upstairs to my room where she took off her *burqa* and sat in the chair I offered her.

"I don't know what they will do to him," she said, then started crying. "I thought Arshad would be able to do something."

"I'm calling Islamabad," I said, the phone already in my hand. "He was upset the last time I saw him. Maybe he went back to Pakistan."

I made the call but he was not there. His editor told me that he was in Surobi, a small town a few miles from Kabul, chasing after a story, but he had no way to contact him there.

"When you hear from him, please have him get in touch with me right away," I said. "It's Rachael Brown, calling on behalf of Razia, in Kabul."

Something in the way the man on the other end of the line responded made me doubt he was even listening, then he hung up. I didn't need to explain what I'd learned to Razia.

"The telephones in our area are still out of order," she said, her voice quavering. "I need to call my husband in Peshawar. I should let him know." She started crying again.

"Sure."

She moved to sit on the bed, dialed the number, and talked for a few minutes in Pashto, crying her heart out to her husband.

When she hung up, I poured a glass of water and gave it to her.

"I'll keep calling his paper," I promised her. "He'll check in with them soon, I'm sure."

"Thank you," she said as she stood up and started putting her *burqa* back on.

"How did you get here?"

"I walked," she said, and must have seen my surprise. "I had

168

no choice, there are no rickshaws on the roads."

"Why don't you rest for a while, have a cup of tea?"

"No, my daughter is alone at home." She started crying again.

"Don't worry, Arshad will sort this out . . . I have a rented car, I'll take you home."

I called the car rental shop and told them that I needed a car and I would be downstairs in fifteen minutes.

By the time I finished my call Razia had managed to compose herself. She adjusted her *burqa* and I put on my *chadur*, covered my chest, shoulders and head properly with it, and we went downstairs. The vehicle was waiting in front of the entrance, and driving carefully over streets not yet cleared of debris, I took her home.

I had dinner that evening in the hotel with Ben Baldwin and Arnaud Grosset. A member of the hotel staff interrupted us with Arshad's call. At the reception desk I quietly told him what was happening and after a painful silence he said, "I will be back in Kabul early in the morning."

* * *

I was trapped in a cage made of golden bars.

I saw my husband a few feet away from me calling an infant to run to him. The infant stood perfectly between us, turning his head toward him and then me. I realized this was my child and my husband was going to take him away from me. I started calling the child in despair. The child divided in two; one part ran toward him and the other toward me. He took the part that came to him and disappeared into the mist, but the part that came to me started growing and became a complete child again but the two sides of him were different. He had two different eyes, one blue the other brown, half his head had red hair but the other half had black. I was crying, screaming, and struggling to get out of the cage to hold the child.

I woke up with perspiration all over my body despite the air conditioning. I turned on the lamp next to my bed and changed my clothes. I knew I wouldn't be able to go back to sleep, so I decided to make coffee. The instant coffee the hotel provided was awful, but at that moment it seemed precious.

I turned on the radio and tuned in to the BBC. I heard Tim McGirk, a well-known British journalist, calling the reaction of the Clinton administration "unseemly haste." He said they "rushed to give support to the Taliban." He was referring to the promises of US officials for early talks with Taliban leaders and even discussed re-opening the US embassy in Kabul.

I couldn't focus on my work. The dream and the latest news that my country was wandering into an alliance with the most brutal regime on Earth merged into a sort of half-waking nightmare. All at once I decided to call my husband, even though we hadn't talked for quite some time.

"Hello, it's me," I said, almost whispering into the hiss of the international line. "How are you?"

"I'm good," he said, and I could tell by his voice that he was more than just surprised to be hearing from me. "Is everything all right?"

"Yeah, everything's all right, I couldn't sleep so I thought it's the right time to catch you . . . it's . . ." I squinted at my watch in the dark room, "eight in the morning there, right?"

"Yeah . . . I was getting ready to go to work."

"Can you talk?" I tried not to plead.

"Yeah, sure, I have some time."

"Is your mother with you?" I could hear his native language somewhere in the background.

"She came with my sisters."

"Were you expecting them?"

"No, they flew in yesterday to spend the long weekend."

The whole clan was there. I wondered what they were cooking, but didn't ask.

"When are you planning to come back?" he said after I let the conversation hang there too long.

"Things are . . ." I replied, blindly searching for words, "too, um . . . interesting here . . . for me to come back."

"I wish I could be that interesting to you, too," he said, and the worry seemed to have gone from his voice all at once.

I said what I always said, the routine at once comforting and degrading to us both. "Don't start."

"I've got to go," he said. "I need to get ready."

"Okay, bye for now."

There was a pause, both of us not sure we should really just leave it there.

Finally he said, "Bye," and hung up the phone.

The call turned the uneasiness of the dream into anxiety. His mother never liked me. In fact, everyone in his family had reservations about me, and their presence in my absence felt like some sort of conspiracy.

* * *

I found Arshad in the lobby the next evening and without preamble asked, "Any luck?"

He nodded and replied, "I talked to an official I know in the Pakistani Embassy. Head of the Kabul Shura, Mullah Mohammad Rabbani, accepted my request after a few assurances. Jamal is free."

I put my hand on his shoulder and sighed. Then I quickly realized I shouldn't do that, and he moved slightly away. Covering, I asked, "Why did they take him?"

"He didn't have a beard," Arshad replied. "And then he got into an argument when they warned him. . . . He is young, very well protected by his mother, and sometimes does not understand the way of the world."

"Well, his father will be here soon," I said. "I guess that will

171

help."

"No, I told him not to come. He is Hazara. Taliban hate Hazaras the most. They are the most educated and liberal community in Afghanistan. He would just complicate things."

"Did they know that Jamal is —?"

"No, his mother is Pashtun. It's usually not very obvious until he identifies with one or the other . . . I am taking them to Peshawar in a couple of days. My friend wants them in Peshawar as soon as possible."

"Why does he stay in Peshawar?"

"He sells most of his carpets to the vendors in Peshawar, Islamabad, and Karachi. Due to the war there is no export of rugs from here, he can only make any money by selling them across the border where there is a local market and a considerable export. He stays in Pakistan a couple of months every time he goes there to collect money and to get orders. It's a different market, often you need to be face-to-face to sort things out."

"Another poor family displaced . . ." I sighed.

"Yes, but they are in a much better position than the poor Afghani on the street . . . I am worried about all these women who can't go to work and there is no staff in the UN compound anymore so no handouts. These women are either widowers of soldiers or wives of handicapped men. Kabul will be a hell soon . . ."

I tipped my head to a couple of empty chairs off to the side of the hotel lobby and we sat down across from each other. He took a deep breath and I couldn't help but think this was the first deep breath he'd had in hours.

"I will be moving into their house," he said. "Razia wants me to stay in the house when I am in Kabul. These days, people just take over the empty houses."

"What do you think?" I asked. "What will their next step be after Kabul?"

"They will sooner or later move to the north. They will want to bring down the rest of the country to its knees to finalize their control."

I nodded and said, "And from what I've read most of the agricultural resources and eighty percent of the industry and mineral wealth of the country is in the north . . . wealth that's the key for the survival of Kabul, no matter who rules it."

"Yes, no doubt about it."

"We'll have to witness more brutality, won't we?" I asked, already knowing the answer.

"Well, we have chosen the glamorous job of journalism, what do you expect?" He laughed.

"When I was a student, I had such high ideals," I confessed. "Ideals about the role of journalism in society . . . whatever. . . . Now I think we're just nosy neighbors constantly chattering away about what's happening to the people around them . . ."

I saw my reflection in the mirror behind his chair. The thirty-five-year-old woman with brown hair, pale skin, and a few wrinkles under the eyes was very different from the young girl so determined to get her degree in journalism, who thought she would be a part of a world that brought clarity to people by discussing vital issues and reporting essential news.

"My friend you met in the refugee camp," I said, "used to call me an idealist."

With a dismissive shrug Arshad said, "We probably all are when we are young . . ." He sat in silence for a moment then said, "I am tired. I ran around a lot today. I'll see you later."

"Good night," I said, trying and failing to smile.

"Good night," he said, not even bothering to try to smile.

XVI

Mazar-i-Sharif

One evening when I was sitting in the hotel restaurant organizing my notes, I heard, "I've been admiring you from my table across the restaurant for quite some time." It was Peter.

"So you are in Kabul."

"I sure am," he replied with a grin. "How are you doing?" He took a pack of cigarettes from his pants pocket, opened it, and slid it across the table to me.

I shook my head and told him, "I quit. My husband doesn't like it."

Peter made a show of looking around the room, then said, "He's not here."

"I know, but it's a promise I made."

He lit one and sat down. "I'm going north to Mazar-i-Sharif in a couple of days."

"In the company van?"

"Oh, no, that would be dangerous . . . I'll go with an Uzbek family that's fleeing Kabul." He tried to wave the smoke away from me.

"They won't attack north before spring, why are you in such a hurry?"

"It's better to leave before snowfall, otherwise it'll be difficult to get through. Anyway, there's nothing in Kabul but black turbans and their idiotic laws . . . the news is in the north now."

He looked good in the dim light of the restaurant. Trying to keep it all business, I asked, "Do you think the north has the guts to stand against them?"

"I don't know," he answered with a shrug, "but they can give the Taliban a hard time if they remain united . . . you never know who fights with who here."

I looked down at my notes, a collection of sad stories of sad times in a sad city, and without being conscious of coming to the decision I asked, "Can I come along?"

"Sure," he replied without hesitation. "I've been to Mazar-i-Sharif before. I stay with friends there—it's cozier for me than a hotel. You can stay with us."

"No, no," I said, crossing my arms and grabbing my shoulders. "I'll find a hotel."

"It's a big house," he prodded, leaning in and smiling. "I have three big rooms on the second floor all to myself."

I looked at him and had no choice but to return his smile. "I guess . . ." I said, blushing at having given in so quickly, not at the prospect of staying in the same house with him. "But only if I can share the expenses."

He smiled and shrugged, and so did I.

* * *

Two days later, early in the morning, a pickup appeared at the hotel entrance. The bed of the trucks had a makeshift roof made of steel pipes and some heavy cloth. A wooden bench ran along each side. Two women and two children sat on one side and an old man sat on the other. The women were covered in white *burqas*. A man was sitting in the cab next to the driver, who didn't seem to be part of the family. He didn't share their Uzbek-Mongolian features. We put our bags in the aisle between the seats. I sat with the women and Peter and his cameraman, Edward, sat next to the old man.

The younger woman next to me smiled and said something to me that I couldn't understand. In response to the confusion on my face, she repeated the question in broken English.

"I'm fine," I said with a smile.

Once the pickup left the outskirts of Kabul, the women threw back the front of their *burqas*. They wore the required long dresses that came to their ankles. The woman next to me was enveloped in a colorful pattern of flowers of blue and pink whereas the old women next to her was wearing a white dress with blue stripes coming together around the front.

Peter was talking to Edward about the book the cameraman was holding. I bent down a little to read the title *The Gods of Eden*.

"What's it about?" I asked Edward.

"The writer thinks we have wars because it's profitable to certain sections of our society, and that our history is guided by extraterrestrials."

"Guided by extraterrestrials?" I asked, smirking. "In a malevolent or benevolent way?"

"According to him, most of it's malevolent."

I sighed and sat back. "Men . . . humans in general . . . we love war—just *love* it, really, but we're so reluctant to accept that's part of who we are we end up looking for some supernatural cause for it . . ." I shook my head. "Look around. Nature is brutal. It's either hunter or hunted. . . . What did Tennyson say? 'Nature, red in tooth and claw'?"

Peter glanced at the old man, who didn't seem to be paying any attention—most likely didn't even understand English, then asked me, "What are you trying to say? Do we fight wars to feed ourselves?"

"Well," I said, shrugging and looking up at the makeshift tent as we rattled across the primitive road, "this need for war may not be as immediate, as day-to-day as a lion kills for food, but—"

"We fight wars for money, plain and simple," Peter interrupted.

"Come on, Peter," I said, shaking my head. "It's not that simple."

"Well, enlighten me then."

"But what Peter is saying makes . . ." Edward started to say, but then he bent down to look through the gap between the front seats. His worried look made us all focus our attention to the front.

Four men with Kalashnikovs were waiving at the pickup to stop.

The women quickly brought forward the front of their *burqas*, and went back into hiding. When the pickup stopped, one of the men approached the driver and started asking questions. After a heated back and forth, the driver searched for something under his seat and took out a bag of brown paper and handed it over to the man. The armed man opened the bag, looked into it, then took out a small knife from his pocket and dipped it in the bag. It came out with some white powder, which he tasted. He folded the top of the bag and handed over the bag to the man next to him.

"*Pindkawi,*" he said.

The pickup rattled on.

I started to ask, "Did he just. . . ?"

"Yes," Peter said, his smile gone. "This is how it works. At every checkpoint the driver will have to give up something to pay for our passage."

"We are part of drug trafficking?" I had to ask.

Edward shrugged and wouldn't look at me, but Peter said, "There's no other way to get through."

I looked at him and shook my head slowly. "And you are sharing in all these expenses?"

"All of it, the family is just a camouflage," he said, and I could tell that fact didn't make him at all happy. "But of course, not from my own pocket."

The women threw back the front of their *burqas* again. A few minutes later, the younger woman woke up the children. She took out *nans*, wheat bread, from the cane basket and put some mutton over it from a pot. She took a piece of cheese, put it on some *nan*, and offered it to me.

"No, thank you," I said.

She offered it to Peter and Edward, but they didn't accept it either. She gave the *nan* to the old man and started preparing another one. She gave a *nan* to each member of her family and then asked the two men, her husband and the driver, if they wanted food. The truck rumbled to a stop at the side of the dirt road, and the young woman's husband came around to the back to get his food. She prepared two *nans* and gave them to him on the lid of one of the pots.

Peter and Edward hopped down off the pickup to smoke, and I started walking along the patchy, dry grass along the side of the road to stretch my legs.

"Darawem! Darawem!"

The driver seemed to be shouting at me but I had no idea what he was saying.

"Stop! Stop . . . mines," the husband of the young woman said, realizing I had no clue what had been said to me.

I froze where I was.

Peter and Edward came toward me, walking on the edge of the road.

The driver went behind the pickup and slid an old metal detector out from under the bench I'd been sitting on. He came right across to me, turned on the instrument, and started carefully moving closer to me. He stopped a foot away from me and checked the ground between our feet then he beckoned me to follow his footsteps.

"Are you all right?" Peter asked the moment my feet were on the road.

"I'm okay . . ." I huffed out then leaned forward, unable to say more just then.

The driver scowled at me as he slid the metal detector back under the bench.

"Thank you," I said, but that only seemed to make him more angry. He started talking to the husband in a fast, clipped, high-pitched voice.

That didn't last too long, though, and once the men finished their meals the driver motioned for us to get back into the pickup and we moved on.

We were stopped a few more times. Peter was right. Money or drugs were offered at every checkpoint, but still, heated exchanges often took place. The driver seemed to be experienced in these kinds of negotiations.

We entered Mazar-i-Sharif in the late evening. I put my skill in identifying the major ethnic groups to the test and concluded that even if I was wrong half the time, it was evident that this was a diverse city, predominantly Hazara and then Uzbek, but with a large mix of other racial groups including Pashtuns.

The streets were fairly clean and traffic was behaving much better than in the Kabul of the Taliban.

The pickup stopped when we entered the outskirts of the city and the driver came to the back. "Address . . . address," he repeated. It sounded as if he was stressing the *d*s more than twice. He looked exhausted after the eight-hour drive.

Peter took a piece of paper from his shirt pocket and gave it to him. The driver took the paper and went back behind the wheel.

He dropped us at a two-story house, its facade was a combination of stone and concrete. We were barely out of the seats before the pickup roared off, leaving us in a cloud of black exhaust. Coughing, Peter pressed the bell next to the black gate.

A man with a high nose and somewhat tan skin in comparison to the Pashtun population of Kabul, appeared. He didn't have Mongolian features, leading me to conclude that he was probably Hazara and not Uzbek. He shook hands with Peter and Edward, and reluctantly held my hand when I put it forward, shaking his head politely.

"I take it." He pointed at the bag on my shoulder.

"Thank you." I handed over one of the bags to him.

He took us up the steps next to an open garage to the second floor. A narrow hallway led us to a large room from which opened the doors to three bedrooms and a kitchen. The living room had one three-seat sofa, and two easy chairs, ochre in color, with a large wooden table in the middle on which sat a vase with some artificial roses. The red carpet under the furniture had black patterns of inverted squares.

He placed my bag on the sofa and opened the doors of the bedrooms.

"Tell me what you need," he said, his English clear despite a heavy accent.

"Thank you," I said, though I wasn't sure exactly what to say next.

Peter and Edward placed their bags on the floor.

"Take whichever one you want," Peter said to me.

"I'll take whichever one you guys didn't stay in before," I said.

Edward laughed and asked, "What . . . have we *soiled* them somehow?"

"I think it would be better if you take that one," Peter said, pointing to the room next to the kitchen. "One of its windows opens onto their backyard and last time I may have startled our host's wife . . . but she won't mind you there." I nodded and Peter said to the man, "Thank you Nehal."

Nehal placed my bags in the room next to the kitchen, bowed, and left us.

I went into the room and closed the door behind me. After the long drive I hoped I could take a shower, and maybe even lay down for at least a few minutes. There was a bed in the middle of the room and a closet in the east corner. On the other side of the bed was a table and a chair. A lamp was on the table. I put my bags in the corner and lay down on the bed—comfortable enough. Then the doorbell rang.

"Oh, you didn't have to do this," I heard Peter say.

"No problem, sir," Nehal's voice responded. "I told wife use little spices, you like it."

"Thank you."

"You want breakfast."

"Yes, Nehal, that would be good . . . and could you bring the bag I left with you?"

The door closed again.

Then came a knock on the door of my room. "There is food

here," Peter said. "You must be hungry."

"I'll eat after I take a shower."

"Okay."

I stood up, hung my clothes in the closet, and took one of the best cold showers I've ever had. It felt as if a full inch of dust fell off my skin.

When I dried off and changed I went out into the living room. An old bag sat open on the floor. A French press coffeemaker had been left on the table along with a tray of food. Both men must have gone to their rooms—the doors were closed.

The food was delicious. There was a vegetable dish—potatoes, peas, eggplant, and beans in a tomato curry—chicken that was probably baked in an oven after it had been soaked in spices, and rice with cumin seeds. There were some *nans* in a folded piece of cloth. I ate and went back to my room.

I slid open the curtains and opened the wooden panels of both windows. The first window opened onto an alley, and the other to the backyard of the house. A boy and a girl were playing in the yard. They both looked up and the girl waved at me, her younger brother followed. I waved back. The girl said something, looking down at the ground floor of the house. I heard a woman's voice respond.

The girl waved at me again, shyly, and went back to running after her brother.

The sun was setting in front of me. Its weak rays desperate to travel to the other side of the world, where I had come from, to find their lost strength. A couple of minutes later I heard *Azan* coming not far from the house. A mosque was nearby.

I took out my pens and pads and brought them to the table to write down the experiences of that long day.

* * *

The next day I went shopping with Peter. Mazar-i-Sharif's bazaars were full of imported products, including Russian vodka and French perfumes.

"For the Uzbek troops," Peter told me with a wink.

Mazar-i-Sharif, once a bustling stop on the ancient Silk Road, was now a major hub for smuggling goods from neighboring Iran and the Russian satellite states, the bulk of which would end up in Pakistan.

I saw a group of girls in skirts and high heels in a boutique. A pad and pen in my hands, I put on my reporter's cool smile and struck up a conversation. They were students of Balkh University in Mazar-i-Sharif, the only still-operational university in the country. In many shops I saw posters advertising performances of singers and dancers from Kabul—artists who couldn't perform in Kabul anymore and had moved to Mazar-i-Sharif to survive.

Mazar-i-Sharif, under the leadership of Abdul Rashid Dostum, was not only the refuge of progressives, students, and artists but also an indispensable trading partner for the neighboring states of Iran, Uzbekistan, and Russia, who now saw Dostum as the only man standing in the face of Pashtun fundamentalism in the form of the Taliban. The financial support of these states contributed to the stability of Mazar-i-Sharif. Their support of Dostum was not only based on his ethnicity but because of his consistent opposition to the fundamentalism of the Pashtun factions, even before the rise of the Taliban.

My preoccupation in those first days was to get to know the city and its people. Unfortunately, calm Mazar-i-Sharif wasn't really where the news was, and I had to wait for the conflict to spread there. And for that I probably had a couple of months' wait. The Taliban wouldn't move to the north until spring. There was no way they could have launched a successful invasion in the winter. I took advantage of the time on my hands to work on my book.

One morning, when I was standing in the window of my room to get some fresh air after finishing the first draft of a chapter of the book, I saw a woman in a long red shirt with mirror-work on the chest, hanging freshly washed clothes on the line in the yard. She felt my presence and looked up.

"Hello!" she said.

"Hi."

"It's nice to see a woman up there," she said.

"It's nice to see a woman down there."

She laughed. "I am Laila."

"Rachael. . . . Nice to meet you."

"Nice to meet you," Laila replied. "I am coming to clean your house today. Are the men gone?"

"You don't have to do that."

"No, it's part of my job. We are paid for it . . . I cannot do it when they are in the house, so I wait."

"Nobody is home but me," I told her.

She pinned a white man's shirt on the line and said, "I will come soon."

I watched her hang her clothes for a little bit then went back to work.

A few minutes later I heard a key turning in the door.

"I am here," Laila called.

"Okay."

"I will clean your room in the end so I don't disturb you."

"Thank you."

An hour and a half later, I heard a gentle knock on the door of my room.

"Come in."

"I am ready for your room?"

I waved her in and said, "You speak very good English. Were you educated in Mazar-i-Sharif?"

"Yes, yes, I went to a very good school of the city," she said, blushing a little. "My father was once a mayor of the city. He always wanted me to finish school. I even went to the university but did not complete my bachelor."

"Why?"

"I got married."

"You were in love?" I asked.

"No, not really," she said with a casual shrug. "It was an arranged marriage."

"Why didn't you wait for the graduation?"

"I really didn't care . . . graduation or no graduation, my role was to stay home and look after a husband and children."

I made sure that my face didn't make me seem judgmental. Still, I had to ask, "Do parents consult their daughters when they're arranging their marriages?"

She thought about that for a moment, still standing in the doorway, but I think she was just translating in her head. Finally she shook her head, shrugged a little, and said, "It's different in every community. I haven't seen a girl who has protested . . . mothers usually know if their daughters are happy with the proposal. But Afghanistan is so diverse, from arranged to love marriages, everything is here."

The little boy—her son—ran into the living room and said something in Dari, a Persian dialect that sounded quite different from Pashto. She answered him and he ran back downstairs.

"My brother is here," Laila said. "Would you mind if I clean your room later?"

"No problem . . . it's not that bad anyway."

"No, I will clean it. My mother is ill, and I think my brother has brought news about her."

"It's really all right, Laila, go ahead and talk to your brother."

* * *

Peter came to Mazar-i-Sharif with some projects in mind, one of which was a documentary on the ancient city of Balkh, whose ruins lay a few miles away from Mazar-i-Sharif. I became fascinated by Balkh as he told me more and more of its history. With the city still in peace, I volunteered to help him with research. This led to my agreeing to write the narration for the documentary after getting back to the US.

But I couldn't find a library in the city that had any books in English, so I decided to try the library at Balkh University. Instead of waiting for the car I had leased and that I expected to get in the next couple days, I walked to the main road to catch a rickshaw. Quite a few of them, with different colorful panels on the sides of the passenger seats, stood at each intersection. I showed one of them the paper on which I had asked Nehal to write down in Dari the name of Balkh University.

The driver took the note and showed it to his friend. The friend read the note and the driver beckoned me to get into the rickshaw. He passed through many narrow streets and alleys and I kept wondering if he was really going in the right direction. But he knew what he was doing; I got to the university within half an hour.

Libraries always comforted me. My father was a librarian, and I loved visiting him in the library with my mother, after school. I went to the same school where my mother taught and spent many happy hours with my parents in that library. It closed early on Fridays and I stayed there till the end of the day, finishing my homework and reading books with my mother in the children's section. Then we would go out for dinner. We each took turns choosing a restaurant. Of course, as an eight-year-old, I always chose McDonald's. They never protested.

In this case, too, the lady behind the glass porthole, through which the students requested the books they were looking for, warmly welcomed me. She ushered me in beyond the locked door when I told her I was a journalist working to find material on the ancient city of Balkh for a documentary.

A bunch of notices and stickers attesting to the generosity of foreign donors were clustered on the notice board next to the door, their pale colors emanating an odor of philanthropy mingling with the dust and mildew of the books.

The librarian showed me where the books in English were, and I discovered that a large collection of the library consisted of a number of copies of expensive hardcover volumes on molecular biology, management dynamics, and other subjects, still in their plastic shrink wrap.

"These are sent by donor agencies," the librarian told me, "but they were quite useless to the departments at the university, as those subjects are not taught. Of course, donations of textbooks in Dari would be enthusiastically received."

I nodded and smiled, feeling a rush of guilt that I hadn't come there with a truckload of Dari textbooks.

Later, during my search for the books on Balkh I also found that the donor agencies, in their wisdom, had donated overviews of the culture of the American South, and guides to public speaking patently aimed at US politicians. They were not only irrelevant but probably beyond the English language skills of an average student at the university.

I spent a couple of days in the library the next week and went through as much information on Balkh as was available in English. I made a list of themes I thought would capture the essence of the city. And as the work went on my excitement for the project started to overshadow Peter's.

The Vedic name of the ancient city of Balkh, the oldest in today's Afghanistan, was Bhakri, which later became Bactra for the Greeks. It is considered to be the first city to which the Indo-Iranian tribes moved from north of the Amu Darya, approximately 2000 BCE.

We hired a van and two men who could carry our things and help us film the ruins. When we reached the area of the ruins we saw two edifices. One was the mausoleum of a distinguished theologian, built in the fifteenth century. The shrine consisted of a tall octagonal brick chamber, over which rested a fluted dome. The entire exterior was enveloped in a brilliant blue-tile mosaic, much of which was slowly peeling off the walls.

Across from the mausoleum stood a tall gateway with some decorative tilework, the leftovers of the impressive blue-tiled mosque built in the seventeenth century in the Timurid style: axial symmetry, double domes, and color-perfused exteriors.

It took us some time to discover the earlier monuments. A couple of nondescript mounds probably marked the site of the temple that Xuanzang, the Chinese scholar, had described as being "lustrous with precious gems." Despite the decay, the walls of the city were still sixty feet high in places. They enclosed a roughly circular field almost a mile across. Dry scrubs, low mounds of debris, and here and there potsherds and broken bricks seemed to call for attention.

The shards of the pottery that had been used by the citizens of Balkh more than two thousand years ago, and were now under my feet, created a connection for me to all those people who had given life to this city. A sublime current ran through my spine as I gazed out at a city that had seen its secular zenith two millennia ago.

Life can be very fragile, the life of people and the life of cities. This was the city Arabs called "the mother of all cities" when they invaded it in the seventh century. Here Zoroaster preached, three thousand years ago, and he might have stood right where I was standing. Somewhere in this city, Alexander the Great set up camp and talked about his strategies for the new battlefront—India. Inside these city walls, the Persian poet Rumi was born. And on these paths Buddhist monks walked in their robes and begged for their daily ration to keep themselves humble and empathetic. The city that was the center of civilization was now buried under dust. Crows sat on its decayed walls and rats scurried under them.

* * *

It was much easier to get an appointment to meet Mr. Dostum in Mazar-i-Sharif than to meet President Rabbani in Kabul. The day I reached Qala-i-Jangi, the Fort of War, it was Nowruz, the New

Year festival. Nowruz was later banned by the Taliban, who called it a pagan event.

There were bloodstains in the muddy courtyard. I asked the guards if a goat had been slaughtered for the festivities.

"Dostum, an hour ago," one of the guards replied, "punished a soldier for stealing." The simple, matter-of-fact way he said that made me shudder.

"Punished. . . . ?" I started to ask.

"Thief tied to the tracks of a tank—a Russia tank," the guard said, "which then was driven around courtyard."

I swallowed and asked no more questions as the soldiers led me through a passage in the fort.

Dostum stood at the door of a large room. He seemed to be a reincarnation of Genghis Khan—six feet tall with bulging biceps. He took my hand in his and shook it softly. I felt like a cat whose paw was in the grip of a bear.

After talking to him about his upbringing and earlier experiences, I asked him, "Despite changing alliances, what is the reason that you are still so revered?"

He looked straight at me as if to say, "How dare you be so blunt?" and didn't I know that even a gruff laugh of his frightened people? But he didn't say those things.

"I don't know about reverence," he started slowly. "But I am respected because this city had not been touched in the past eighteen years of war. Mazar-i-Sharif has never seen the shelling and the street battles that have destroyed other cities, including Kabul."

"You are accused of murdering the brother of your second-in-command"—I looked at my notes to be sure to properly pronounce the name—"General Abdul Malik Pahlawan. Is it true?"

"No," he said.

I paused, but when I realized that was all the answer he intended, I asked, "Do you trust Mr. Malik?"

"Yes." He thought for a moment, as if he wasn't satisfied with the effect of his short answer. "I am sure he will not do anything to put us in danger, he understands that we have to defend the six provinces we have till the last man falls, otherwise there is no hope for the people who are crushed under the fundamentalism of the Taliban."

XVII

The Real Battle

We had not seen the actual fighting in Kandahar or Kabul, we had only seen its by-product: executions and imprisonments. We were told that, through the grace of Allah, a major leader in the north had renounced his animosity toward the Taliban, and as such we would face no further difficulty in getting hold of the rest of the country.

This was true. We seized the two northern provinces without any resistance, and soon reached the city of Mazar-i-Sharif.

We were told to disarm all the men on the streets, and bring anyone who resisted to Rustam Khan.

There were nine of us, led by Shirazi, including Ahmed, Rehman, and his friends from the *madrassah*. They were all about Rehman's age, younger than Ahmed and I.

We faced no resistance at first, but when we came to the main square of the city, we found a group of Hazara men who refused to give up their arms. The argument turned into a brawl, and somebody started shooting and everything descended into an armed struggle. Men on both sides ran to find cover, firing madly at each other.

Then someone started firing mortar shells at us from behind the two-story building most of the men had disappeared into. That terrible high-pitched whine then the dull thud of an explosion had me pressing my hands against my ears. I looked wildly around, trying desperately to figure out where the next shell might land, when I realized they were coming not just from that one building but from at least three emplacements.

One of our party threw a grenade and few more of us followed suit, but these were all blind attempts at finding our attackers—none successful in stopping that chain of whine-thud-whine-thud-whine-thud. Debris piled up on the street.

Shirazi shouted, "Get into the truck!" I never thought someone could yell that loud.

Ahmed, who crouched next to me, still had to yell to be heard. "I will cover for you—go!" He stood, though not all the way, and fired over the low cinderblock wall we hid behind. I knew he didn't know where to aim—none of us did—but under his wild shooting, I ran for the pickup truck we'd come in, and behind which Shirazi crouched, his arm pinwheeling to urge us forward.

Under a hail of gunfire and a cloud of dust from the mortar explosions, we jumped into the pickup. Shirazi rolled into the driver's seat. I looked back at Ahmed, who had paused to reload.

"Get in!" I shouted at him, and Rehman called out the same thing.

Another blast went off and I ducked back behind the steel sides of the pickup, laying down with my AK-47 across my chest. The sky was full of black, sooty clouds—debris already raining back down around us.

"Ahmed!" I shouted as loudly as I could as the pickup rumbled to life.

I lifted my head, squinting in Ahmed's direction. He appeared in frenzy. It seemed as if some unknown force had taken control of his body and mind.

"You moron!" Shirazi yelled. "Get in!"

But Ahmed didn't seem to hear him and kept wildly firing into the impenetrable clouds of dust and smoke that filled the square.

Even under the onslaught of bullets hitting the side walls and doors of the pickup, I heard the sound of the fatal bullet. Still lying in the pickup, I heard the mortar shell whine through the air above me—even imagined I could see it—as it fell to its target. Something heavy fell on the hood of the pickup, and then a sound like a sharp knife scratching a metal plate ended in a thud. Ahmed's rifle had fallen on the hood and was dragged across it by the weight of his body before he hit the street. My heart sank.

Shirazi jammed the pickup into gear, but before he sped away, I jumped down. I took Ahmed by the arms and dragged him into a corner under the shattered sign of the closest shop as spurts of the bullets flew all around us.

"You idiot," I said in my anger, but this "idiot" had much more warmth in it than the word he'd used whenever he was angry with me. A bullet, or shrapnel from the mortar shell, had hit him in the chest. I took off my turban, which had fallen onto my shoulders, and put pressure on his chest.

A matrix of voices ran toward me from the end of the street.

I bent down and tried to listen to his heart, there was nothing.

I tried to sense his pulse, there was nothing.

My snitch, watch-buddy, protector, and partner in affection was dead.

I looked back at the pickup behind me. Shirazi, seeing a break in the onslaught of fire from the other side, came back for me. We couldn't see them in the smoke, but neither could they see us.

"Get back in!" Shirazi yelled.

I abandoned my friend on the street.

Shirazi turned the pickup around and even as I jumped and rolled into the back, the hands of my comrades tugging me into their center, he sped away.

Rolling onto my back again, I saw men running the length of the rooftops along the street, firing on the pickups in front of us. The men in our pickups fired back, but the men of Mazar-i-Sharif had the advantage of higher ground. Our bullets either ran above their heads or hit the walls of the houses. We couldn't use grenades— we were too close to our targets and it was just as likely a grenade would fall short and bounce off a wall and right back into our laps.

Shirazi turned onto a side street to escape the onslaught. None of us, including Shirazi, knew the city. We had no idea where we were heading, we were not even sure if we were moving away from the rest of our men or closer to them.

Then the narrow side street came to a dead end. Shirazi tried to turn the pickup around, but it seemed to take forever in the narrow street. Then a torrent of gunfire descended on us. Two of Rehman's friends were hit. I heard the dull, wet thud of the bullets going into their flesh and their equally wet grunts of surprise and pain, like a *tabla* played by inexperienced hands.

We started madly firing in all directions again, and again without any effect. I looked around and realized that Rehman and I were the only men left standing in the face of the attack. The rest were either gone or unconscious.

"Jump!" I shouted. "Get under!" I pushed Rehman to encourage him to jump off.

"But—"

"*Jump!*"

The moment he was on the street, I followed him, and we rolled under the pickup.

I closed my eyes and tried to remember to breathe. Until finally, a few minutes later, the gunfire stopped. I didn't really think it was safe, but how long could we lay there under the truck? I inched myself to the other side of the pickup and looked out. I saw no one on the nearby roofs or on the street.

"We can't hide here too long, they may come down to check the pickup," I whispered to Rehman.

"What should we do?"

I didn't know, but I was sure it wasn't a good idea to stay there too long. "When I say go, run. We will turn into the first street we find."

"There will be more in that street."

"Maybe, but they won't fire at us until they're sure we're Taliban. So don't run once we get away . . . and leave your rifle here."

He shook his head, his turban rubbing across the greasy undercarriage of the truck. "I can't do that."

"Do you think you have a chance with that one rifle of yours, when they're up there?"

He remained silent for a few moments.

"Are any of them still breathing?" he asked, pointing his forefinger at the bed of the pickup above us.

"I don't think so," I said, a part of me somehow wishing that were true. How could we drag half-dead, wounded men along with us? "They have all been hit . . . several times by now. . . . Do you know Dari?"

"Little."

"Well if we ever have to talk to any native, you'll have to do it." I looked out again, and again I saw no one on the roof of the houses or on the street.

As if to urge us on, the blood of our fellows began to drip down from the sides of the pickup, reminding us with all its ferocity that we were now officially a part of a war in which our roles would be minor, but our sacrifices would be major.

"Now *go!*" I said.

Without waiting for Rehman, I left my rifle on the ground and slid out from under the pickup and ran. A few steps away, I turned my head and saw Rehman—also unarmed—running after me. A few shots came our way, but they were too late to catch us. We turned onto the first street that came in our way.

This strange foreign city, nothing but a blur, I only stopped when we hit a main road. Rehman slid to a stop a few feet away from me, and bent down to catch his breath. I looked around for a place to hide.

There was an old house to our right. The grounds were two feet below street level, and stairs led down to a small passage and a door closed with a big lock in the hook of an old latch. The floor of the protruding veranda on the second floor covered the passage, making it a safe haven for us from shots from the roof—a chance to catch our erratic breath.

I grabbed Rehman's arm and went down the stairs. We huddled in a corner where I could see a small patch of the sky at the edge of the veranda, red with the light of the setting sun. That sun had seen a lot of blood and fury that day, and to me it seemed happy to leave this part of the world and not have to witness more of this brutal chapter in the history of Mazar-i-Sharif.

We came out of hiding once darkness had more fully descended. We walked to the main road as casually as we could with our knees shaking from fear, exhaustion, and dehydration.

A sudden burst of gunfire came from across the main road and hit the stairs and the side wall of the house. We turned back, ran into the street, and took the first right.

We hid ourselves whenever we suspected that there was a chance of an attack, and moved carefully in the deserted streets whenever we perceived that it was safe. We heard nearby gunfire a few more times, but always moved away from it.

In an hour or so we came across a dairy farm. Through the iron grills of a black iron gate we watched the cows absently chewing their cud, unaware of the hell that had come to the streets around them. On the left side of the gate was a shed with an asbestos roof. The walls were about five feet tall, and there was an open space of maybe two feet between the walls and the roof, which rested on wooden pillars in each corner.

I looked around. Nobody was on the street. I put my hands on the wall and lifted myself up to see if there was anyone in the shed. A young man with a bucket went from one side to the other.

A chain had been wrapped around the frame of the iron gate a few times before it was trapped in a big lock. I put one of my feet into the heart-shaped pattern of the grill, pulled myself up, and jumped over the gate. Rehman followed me.

The man in the shed must have heard us. He came out, and we stood in front of each other for a couple seconds before he ran into the compound. Rehman took a shovel that was leaning against the wall next to the door of the shed, and ran after the man. I took off in the other direction, to corner him from the other side. I searched the compound, looking behind the animals and in the pits in front of them full of their food, but couldn't find him.

A few minutes later, when I reached the other side of the compound, I sensed a commotion in the front and then heard a loud cry. I rushed to the gate. Rehman was hitting the man with a shovel again and again. His body lay awry near the gate, soaked in his own blood.

"That's enough . . ." I said, reaching out for Rehman. "He is gone."

Rehman ignored me and hit the man again. I stepped forward and caught the shovel handle when he brought it up again. I started pulling the shovel out of his hands.

"Are you crazy?"

He looked at me angrily for a few seconds and then let go of the shovel.

We stood over the dead man and caught our breaths, then we dragged the body into one of the animal feed pits.

We went into the shed. It was full of buckets, rags, and sackcloth used to cover the cattle in winter. There was an old mattress in the corner.

When it was dark, Rehman went out and milked a cow. That raw milk was our only meal that night.

Around 3:00 a.m., we came out of the compound and carefully slipped onto the street. We moved as fast as we could, keeping our tired bodies in the shadows, our ears on the sounds of the night. It was dawn before we saw a few of our men in a pickup, and they took us to the camp outside the city.

Before we were able to pause for a much-needed breath, we were told that we needed to go back to the city and join our brothers. They still had no plan to either capture the city by force, or to negotiate with the people to gain control of it peacefully.

In ten weeks of fighting, most of our men had either been killed or taken prisoner. Only two were left of the sixteen people that had been sent from the hell of Bayfazal to the hell of war: Rehman and me.

When it became evident that the city was an endless pit that sucked in more and more of our men every day, our leaders decided to leave Mazar-i-Sharif and move to the province of Hazarajat in central Afghanistan, where the people had rebelled seeing the success of resistance in Mazar-i-Sharif.

Near the city of Bamyan I fired at the head and groin of the giant Buddha, and turned it as ugly as our lives were, full of violence and coercion. The war was making the blood of my veins dark, and my mind devoid of empathy.

XVIII

End of Us, Beginning of We

My optimism in regard to Dostum lasted less than a month. Malik, who was stationed in Faryab Province, betrayed Dostum and went to the Taliban with three other senior Uzbek generals. With the help of this unlikely alliance the Taliban moved swiftly from Herat and Kabul. Dostum fled with his confidants to Uzbekistan.

Heavily armed Taliban troops flooded into Mazar-i-Sharif in their pickups. They started disarming the Uzbek and Hazara troops, and took over Shiite mosques and used them to declare the imposition of Shariah law—entirely Sunni in its essence. They shut down schools and the university, and drove women off the streets. Unlike Kabul, Mazar-i-Sharif was a complex mix of ethnic and religious groups, living intermingled with each other. It was a city that had not been touched by the eighteen years of war, and had remained the most open and liberal in the country. I couldn't help but wonder how the populace of this ethnic maze would react to the brutal measures of the Taliban.

But I didn't have to wait for long to find out. Fighting started within two days. A group of Hazara men resisted giving up their arms and all hell broke loose. Three thousand Taliban were either killed or wounded, and another three thousand were taken prisoner by the end of the conflict. According to the International Committee of the Red Cross, more than seven thousand fighters and civilians were wounded on both sides.

Subsequent UN investigations revealed that the prisoners had been tortured and starved to death.

"Prisoners were taken from detention, told they were going to be exchanged, and then taken to wells. They were thrown into the wells either alive or if they resisted shot first and then tossed in.

Shots were fired and hand grenades were exploded into the well before the top was bulldozed over," said UN Special Rapporteur Pak Chong-Hyun, who inspected the graves.

The UN also reported that starved prisoners were herded into shipping containers where they died due to lack of oxygen, the bodies burned black from the heat.

The extreme forms of Pashtun chauvinism, which was ultimately accentuated by the Taliban, left a bitter taste in the mouths of many non-Pashtuns. The massacre we witnessed was a reaction to the suffocation of many years of Pashtun rule in Kabul.

Despite the aversion I had for the repression the Taliban represented, my heart melted for the boys I had met in Kabul. I couldn't even imagine them being killed in such horrendous ways. Those boys, brainwashed as they were, seemed like trained animals, viciously exploited by madmen using religion as a weapon to control Afghanistan. I needed a break from that country. I called my paper and arranged to go back to the US for six months.

Instead of going back to Kabul, I flew through Balkh Airlines to Dubai to get my flight to D.C. Dostum had put Balkh Airlines in operation with the help of the Russians, and through it he maintained a massive flow of smuggled of goods from Dubai and collected a handsome tariff.

I stayed in Dubai for two days just to shop. I couldn't go home empty handed, and that just gave my mother-in-law another few days to keep working at turning Arun against me.

Although they had settled in America when Arun was ten years old, his whole family approached me as if I were an alien from another planet. His mother didn't speak English, but his sisters were deliberately withholding, and after a few attempts to talk to them, I decided to keep my distance.

A couple days after that first visit, one of Arun's sisters called me and said she wanted to meet and talk to me, so I gave her my home address. She was the eldest of the three. Looking at a photograph of Peter on the mantel, next to photographs of my parents, she asked, "Is this your brother?"

"No, he's my ex-boyfriend."

She began sulking and after a little tense small talk just came right out and said, "You should back out from this relationship." My eyes went wide in shock, but she pressed the issue. "Arun is our only brother, and the only son of the family. It is important that he should marry an Indian girl."

I didn't know what to say—or, at least, what to say that wouldn't make things worse. But she stood there silently, waiting for some response.

"Well," I said finally, "maybe you should tell your brother to break up with me. I can't help you."

She left almost immediately after that, and to my great unease, seemed to be thinking about how she might accomplish that.

Despite the open resistance of his family we got married a few months later. I still can't understand how they managed to throw a five-day wedding for a bride they hated—or, at least, disapproved of.

After the wedding they kept their distance from me, and I never attempted to bridge that distance myself. But there were certain obligations that came with the package, which included showing up for birthdays, weddings, showers, and so on. I fulfilled my family duties with all the enthusiasm I could muster despite the boredom and isolation I suffered in the company of his people.

I tried to remind myself that this family was part of him, and I never wanted to be the cause of any schism in his life. If they didn't like me, I figured that was my problem. And as the months went on, I realized just how insurmountable a problem it was.

And that friction only increased when, after three years of marriage, there was still no sign of a baby in the future.

We tried a number of doctors and fertility clinics, but I flatly refused to use the folk remedies his family tried to force on us, everything from Ayurvedic and homeopathic medicine to specific prayers. Though Arun never said anything, I was sure that behind my back they insisted I was sabotaging the chance of our getting pregnant, lying to him while sacrificing his children at the expense of my career.

And then when a job came up for me I convinced him to move from New York to Washington, D.C. He easily managed to get a transfer to a branch of his bank in D.C., but his family made it out to be some kind of kidnapping. His sister even came to visit me again, but this time I made it clear to her that I would not listen to her complaints at all.

"Whatever decisions Arun and I make as a family are ours," I told her, managing to keep from yelling. "I don't need to explain anything to you."

That was pretty much the last tattered remnant of my relationship with his family.

And then the ultimate betrayal. I left for Afghanistan.

I have to admit that even when I was planning the trip, I was afraid it would cause further friction to a relationship that was continuously eroding. Arun tried his best to stop me, and I tried my best to convince him of how huge an opportunity this would be for me. But this time we just couldn't find a middle ground. At first his anger toward me was all on the surface—on his face and in his body language—but then it sank in and I felt a grudge hovering in the air like a Japanese ghost whenever we were together. We went through the motions of our daily routine and even made love, but there was a strange rustiness in his interactions with me.

Throughout my stay in Afghanistan he never called me, and when I called him he remained distant. Now that I was going back I didn't know if I would find a home or a house, if a husband would be waiting for me or just a disappointed stranger.

The thirty-hour flight added physical exhaustion to emotional confusion, and when I staggered out of the terminal, Arun responded with what I can only describe as mild enthusiasm to my embrace. He had always been reluctant to express affection in public so I tried not to read too much into it. He picked up my bag, and we walked slowly to short-term parking.

He asked me questions about my stay in Afghanistan, but they were all questions anyone would ask. There was no touch of love in them.

Walking next to him I noticed for the first time in a very long time that he was two or three inches shorter than me. There is something in the psyche of men that wants to have the upper hand over women, even their wives. Maybe just a tiny bit, maybe at least just in the physical sense. Then I thought that maybe if Arun were a couple inches taller, we wouldn't be having all these problems. Ridiculous.

"You're smiling," he said while opening the trunk of the car. "What's going on in that head?"

"Nothing . . . something absurd that someone had said."

Tall or short, I still loved those big brown eyes, high nose, and black hair falling on the forehead of a slim, tan body.

"Happy to be back?"

"Love to be back," I muttered an exhausted reply.

He opened his door and unlocked the passenger side for me.

* * *

Home was still home, opened like the arms of a mother, with the soothing smells that could lull me to sleep in a second—but of course not that night.

That night I rested my body next to my husband and he made love to me. In his arms after so many months I felt no expectations for a child, no mandatory exchanges or coercive maneuvers. There was only pure love, expressed by the proximities of bodies.

He kissed me on the forehead and soon he was asleep while I hovered in some kind of hypnotic super-jetlag state. Looking up at the ceiling I watched the shadow of the next-door neighbor's car pull into their garage. The woman said something in her husky voice then laughed. She was drunk and she'd brought another man home with her, apparently still celebrating the divorce she'd settled six months back. I realized that maybe I was being cruel—at least judgmental. Maybe a continuous string of anonymous booty calls was her means of coping, a way to overcome the sadness in her heart.

Arun turned in the bed and I saw his face, calm like a child. Why did our relationship seem so fragile despite being so strong in that moment? I guess sex wasn't the answer to every problem in a marriage.

Anyway, when I have insomnia I prefer to work instead of floating from one thought to another, so I got out of bed and went down the hallway to the study to write.

* * *

A few days later, I watched from the window in the study as an Indian woman parked an old Volkswagen across the street. When she crossed the street, I realized she was coming to our house. I came down the stairs into the living room, but before I reached the door, I heard a key turning in the lock and then the handle moving. I froze in the middle of the living room. A moment later she was in my house, standing in front of me.

"Oh! I'm sorry, I didn't know you were back," she said.

She was about Arun's height, with a dark complexion, wearing a long shirt and loose trousers. Her long black hair fell over her shoulders.

"How did you get a key to my house?" I asked.

"Arun gave it to me." She had a nasal voice. "His mother was worried about him and wanted me to look after things while you were away."

"Last time I checked," I said, letting all the resentment that started brewing in me to come across in my tone, "there was an adult in the house who could take care of himself."

"I didn't mean to pry in your life . . . my mother is a good friend of his mother and I was doing a favor for them . . . I guess I don't need this key anymore." She placed the key on the table next to the brown sofa and turned around to leave.

A desire to stop her, to apologize, appeared in my mind, but something in my heart protested, refusing to give any hint of approval to her surprise visit.

That evening, when Arun came home, before I could even say anything he said, "You didn't have to be so rude to Kamala . . . she was just trying to help."

"So the news got to you before I could," I replied, standing in our front hallway with my hands on my hips.

"This is not the way to behave to my people," he said, his eyebrows knitted tightly together.

He went into the living room and I followed him. "'My people' . . . since when did that woman became 'your people'?"

"You know very well what I mean."

"No I don't," I said, though I guess I did—I just didn't want to. "You shouldn't have given her a key to my house."

"'My house'?" he said, taking the same sarcastic tone I'd thrown at him. "No, no, *our* house."

"Whatever!" was all I could think to say, and my cheeks flushed hot the second it passed my lips.

To his credit, he didn't laugh at me. Instead, he said, "I just wanted to make my mother happy. It just gave her some satisfaction that I wasn't alone."

I put my hand on my head, looked at the sofa and thought about sitting, but didn't. "She calls you day and night anyway, she doesn't need to send a spy."

He took a short step toward me and pointed at my chest but didn't touch me. "You are crossing the line. I am not going to tolerate insults to my mother."

I looked at his finger and fantasized about biting it off. He must have seen the look on my face and crossed his arms over his chest.

"Yes, I know," I said, "you only tolerate insults to me."

"How is Kamala coming to our house an insult to you?"

I had to laugh in his face. "Are you really that naïve? Your mother has sent her to replace me."

"Replace you? You have a weird imagination." He took his keys out of his pocket and said, "I'm going to Salim's." Salim was one of his friends, part of the Indian community he'd made ties with after moving to D.C.

* * *

That day we fought over Kamala was the point our marriage really started falling apart. It was the day we started fighting with each other even in our silences. We had bridged the differences in our cultures, grew accustomed to the absence of a child, and weathered the separation of a few thousand miles, but the maternal scorn directed at me was finally defeating us. Kamala, who I had appropriated as a prop on the stage of our married life became a star of it, despite the fact that neither of us mentioned her again after that one fight.

We slowly slipped away from each other.

By June, my editor wanted me to tell him explicitly if I planned to go back. By that time I had come to the conclusion that another separation would be the last straw. But what we had at that moment, a marriage of cold grimaces and grunted responses, was worse than being apart.

Over dinner I decided to go with the last straw.

"If you leave again then we are done," he said calmly, putting a layer of sauce on his ravioli.

"We are already."

He put down the bowl of sauce and looked me in the eye. "I tried my best."

"I know . . ." I said with a sigh. "And I know that you blame me for this, but—"

"No, I don't," he said quickly, waving a hand at me dismissively and looking down at the table. "Our blood follows its own lead. There's little we can do about it. I thought I could bridge the gulf, but it's . . ."

"Tiring," I said for him.

A sad smile crossed his lips and he nodded. "It's a constant uphill battle . . ." Then his voice changed, got a little harder, when he said, "We need to move on. It's for the best." He stood up.

"You were just waiting for me to take the blame," I said, forming the thought even as the words passed my lips. I didn't want to accuse him of anything, but I did anyway.

He took his keys but before he could turn away, I said, "I'm leaving this Friday. Can we get this done before I go?"

He sighed and said, "I'll ask my lawyer to prepare the papers. All we have in terms of a financial settlement is this house. We can sit down with lawyers when you get back and finalize it."

"Let me know when," I said. I took a sip of wine and was surprised that my hand wasn't shaking. "The sooner the better."

XIX

The Riddle

I flew back to Mazar-i-Sharif the same way I'd left it— via Dubai. Up in the air for hour after hour, I was surprised by the relief I felt at the end of my marriage. I guess I wanted it to be over for a long time, I just didn't have the courage to end it myself. The differences that attracted us later betrayed us.

Peter had called me before I left and I expected him to meet me at the airport in Mazar-i-Sharif. But instead I found Nehal there, waving at me.

"How are you?"

"I'm good . . . Nehal, you didn't have to come to the airport, I could have caught a cab."

"Cab?"

"Taxi."

"It's fine, miss," he said with an amiable smile. "I want wife and children go round."

His awkward English gave me a smile, which I pulled back quickly.

"I hope you not mind with you in car," he said, showing no sign he noticed my reaction.

"Oh, no," I relied. "It will be good to meet them again."

He picked up my big bag, I kept the smaller one, and we walked to the parking lot where we found Laila and the two children standing near the car.

Laila called, "Hello!"

"Hi, how are you, Laila?"

"I'm fine."

I bent down, shook hands with the kids, and patted their cheeks. Shy Jamila retreated between her mother's feet.

Nehal put my bags in the trunk, and we got into the car. I sat in the back with the children.

"You have grown up a lot in a few months," I said to their son Tahir.

He smiled back at me, not understanding a word. When his mother translated for me he shyly rubbed his eyes and looked at me. Then his mother said something to him that included a thank you.

"Tank *yuu*," he said, nodding and smiling.

Jamila, who was wearing a colorful flower-patterned frock, watched the streets passing outside the window.

When we reached the house, Laila and her children went into their home and Nehal brought my bag upstairs into the guesthouse.

"Mr. Peter come too?" Nehal asked.

"Yes, I talked to him," I said. "In fact, I thought he'd meet me at the airport. Anyway, he should be here this evening."

"You need something?"

"No, I'm fine, Nehal, thank you."

When he left I took a shower. Just as I was coming out, I heard a knock at the door. I put on my robe and saw Laila through the slot of the door, carrying a tray.

"You didn't have to do that, Laila," I said, letting her in. "I'm not hungry anyway."

She put the tray on the dining table in the living room.

"You can use it later," she said with a shrug. "You will get hungry in evening. What would you like to have in breakfast tomorrow?"

"Anything . . . but no *parathas*, I prefer slices."

"Okay."

"How was the city in my absence?" I asked as Laila busied herself in the kitchen.

"Peaceful . . . just some disputes here and there . . . but we are very worried."

"Why?"

"The things they did to the Taliban . . . horrible, horrible . . . don't know what would they do if they ever take over Mazar-i-Sharif. . . . You are here for news. Do you think they will come back?"

"I think they'll do their best to get a hold on the north," I said, knowing that wouldn't make her feel any better. But if I were in her position, I would want to know the truth. "They expect another clash in the spring."

"Spring is not far . . . Allah is merciful whatever he brings on us."

I remained silent. Their tendency to bear the man-made calamities of life in the name of God was tiresome.

* * *

Peter arrived from Kabul with Edward later that evening. I was anxious for any news from the south.

"From everything I've seen and heard," Peter told me after he'd finally settled back into the apartment, "the Taliban are planning an assault on the north. After losing so many of their fighters last year, they've started a comprehensive campaign to recruit new men. The *madrassahs* in the Afghan refugee camps, and in some areas of Pakistan, have been closed so they could send their remaining *talibs* to Afghanistan."

I sighed and thought, but didn't say, *That probably means the Taliban fighters are getting even younger than they are now.*

"They're also coercing Pashtun families all over the south to send their sons," Peter went on, "and in some cases all but at the point of a gun. They closed all the roads to the north, too. We had to fly from Kabul to Dubai and then back up to Mazar-i-Sharif by Balkh Airlines."

"But if they've closed the roads . . ." I started, then looked over at the tray Laila had left on the kitchen counter.

"There will be food shortages here, if there aren't already," Peter confirmed.

We sat in silence for a moment, and it seemed Edward had drifted off to sleep sitting up on the sofa.

"Please tell me Delhi Durbar is still open," Peter said finally. He had discovered the Indian restaurant, during his last stay in Mazar-i-Sharif. "I want to go there . . . now."

"Ugh," Edward scoffed, his eyes still closed, "I hate Indian food."

"Then you aren't invited," Peter said with a false frown.

"Goody," Edward said as he hauled himself up from the sofa. "I'm going to bed."

"There's food in the kitchen," I told him before he could go. "Laila brought it this morning."

"Thanks," Edward said and staggered tiredly to the kitchen.

"Shall we?" Peter said, standing and holding out his hand to help me up.

We got into the car Peter had left in the care of Nehal, and he drove us through a city bustling despite the sense of impending doom that hovered over it.

Christmas tree lights ran around the name of the restaurant, one color chasing the other to be chased by another.

The only waiter, in a white uniform, asked us if we'd like to sit in the garden at the back or inside. We chose the latter and he led us to a table far back, close to the kitchen, in the large room. The restaurant was empty.

The waiter brought us menus, filled our water glasses, and left. A few pieces of white paper were pasted, one over the other, on the printed prices of the menu. As food prices rose, a new piece had been added until they grew into thick bundles. The new prices were probably four to five times higher, but even then they were half the price of a cheap dinner in the US. Peter recommended chicken vandaloo that was served with rice and a *nan* along with a *somosa*.

"So, how was your break from beautiful Afghanistan?" Peter asked with a smile.

"Good enough."

His smile faltered. "You don't sound very enthusiastic."

"No . . ." I sighed. "It was all right."

"How's Arun?"

"He's fine, I guess . . ." Then I realized I had to elaborate, and that eventually I would have to start saying this out loud to people. "We aren't . . . together anymore."

He looked at me carefully, but seemed confused when he started to ask, "You . . . are good with this, or. . . ?"

"It wasn't working," I answered, though it wasn't much of one.

He nodded and gave me a world-weary little smile. "Sorry to hear that."

We chatted about different things over the dinner—the state of war, politics back home in the States, some gossip about mutual friends and rival reporters. He told me Arshad, whom he'd met in Kabul, had asked about me. The food was good, and in the end it was just nice to be somewhere with someone. I hadn't realized how lonely I'd been.

On our way back he stopped to buy some cigarettes at a *paan* shop. *Paan* was primarily an Indian pastime, but some Afghanis were fond of it too. Small pieces of areca nut, aniseed, and colorful sweetened coconut wrapped in a betel leaf were eaten after meals. I never had the courage to try it.

On the stairs he said to me, "Won't you be lonely tonight?"

A naughty smile crossed his thin lips.

I remained silent, but secretly wanted to laugh.

When we went into the house, I went to my room and closed the door.

He came into the room and closed the door behind him. Darkness cloaked us both.

"I want you," he said in a husky whisper. "I've always wanted you."

I remained silent. I smiled and sighed at that cheesy line. No one had ever said that to me. I felt like the heroine of a Hollywood romantic comedy, which I realized was a welcome change from feeling like a victim in a Hollywood thriller.

He stepped to the bed and sat down. I could see only the silhouette of his body.

"Do you want me to go?" he asked.

He waited a few seconds for my answer then stood.

"No," I said.

* * *

In the middle of July, I realized I'd skipped a period. Besides the break in the cycle there was a sense in me that something was out of the ordinary.

One day I went downstairs and knocked at Laila's door. Jamila opened it and then ran inside, giggling. A minute later Laila appeared.

"Please, come in," she said, clearly surprised to see me there.

A narrow hallway led to a living room on the left side and the kitchen door opened to the right. After the living room, there was another small hallway with doors to two other rooms.

In the living room she motioned to a big sofa with orange and blue flower patterns on a white background. "Would you like to have tea . . . or something cold?"

"No . . . no, Laila. I just need to talk to you."

She sat, attentive, overly formal. I felt my upper lip twitch, then she tipped her head to one side and her face softened. I caught a sob in my throat and said in as calm and even a voice as I could, but too fast, "I need to see a gynecologist. Do you know any good ones in the city?"

"Are you pregnant?" she asked, her eyes wide—with surprise but no judgment.

I remained silent.

"I will go to my lady doctor tomorrow, she is good. Why don't you come with me?"

I cleared my throat and asked, "Don't we need an appointment?"

"No . . . you will just have to pick up a number and wait."

"Okay," I said with a shaky smile, "it's settled then."

* * *

The next day Nehal dropped us at a clinic on his way to work, where my suspicions were confirmed within an hour after our visit to the clinic.

One question incessantly rang in my mind: Whose child was it?

The number of weeks the doctor told me I was pregnant provided no clarity. Twentieth century technology made it possible for me to share beds with two different men in the same week who were thousands of miles apart from each other.

It can't be Arun's.

We hadn't gotten pregnant in seven years, I doubt we could get pregnant at the very moment of our separation.

But that first night I'd spent with Peter, we had had no protection.

I expected Laila to ask a series of obvious questions, too, when I came out of the doctor's office, but she remained silent.

Once we were settled in a rickshaw, I told her the news and asked her not to say anything to Nehal. I didn't want him to mention anything to Peter—or anybody else for that matter.

I wasn't ready to tell Peter yet.

I wasn't ready to establish a permanent connection with him.

I decided right then in that rickshaw that I would leave Afghanistan before I started to show. Despite the fact that the scale was tipping toward Peter I wanted to be sure about the identity of the father before I said anything to either of them.

Till then, the child was mine alone, and a secret I shared only with Laila.

XX

The Empathetic Man

I was running along a street that had butchers' shops on both sides. The bodies and heads of cattle and poultry hung on iron hooks, blood dripping from them. Men stood behind the carcasses, laughing. I turned and saw a ball of fire coming from the sky right at me. I ran into an alley to get away from it but when I got to the other street, I found it waiting for me.

I woke up just as it hit me, my body shaking.

My clothes were sticky with sweat. I sat up in bed. The chirping of birds on the pomegranate tree fueled my pounding headache.

Peter wasn't next to me—then I heard him whistling in the bathroom. I put on my robe and opened the door to get a cup of coffee. I offered thanks to God when I saw the coffee pot, almost full, in the kitchen. It was rare that Peter was out of bed earlier than me, which made it rare that he made coffee in the morning.

He sat at the dining table.

"Good morning," I said.

"Good morning." Seeing me in my robe, he asked, "Staying in today?"

"I have a headache . . . I may leave a bit late."

I poured myself a cup of coffee, vaguely aware that I wasn't supposed to be drinking anything with caffeine anymore. One cup won't hurt, I told myself.

"I thought I better let you sleep a little bit more," he said, flipping through pages in one of his notebooks.

I remained silent.

"What's wrong?" Peter looked at me as though he sensed something was wrong.

"Just a headache," I said. "I didn't have any big plans today anyway."

I took my coffee into the bathroom and took two Ibuprofen tablets then went back to the bedroom. A knock on the front door—time for Nehal Khan or Laila to bring breakfast. I heard Nehal talking to Peter.

"You're worrying too much, Nehal," Peter said, his voice much louder than our host's. "They only go after people who openly resist them."

"They are bad people, they go after who they want . . . do you know when they come?" Nehal asked.

Over the rattle of the plates, Peter said, "Nobody knows what they're up to this time."

Footsteps passed my door, heading for the kitchen, then I heard Edward say, "Your wife is a superb cook."

"Thank you."

Peter came into the bedroom after a few minutes. Finding me back in bed he asked, "Is it getting worse?"

"No, I'll be fine in an hour or so."

"Do you want some breakfast?"

"No, not now."

He took his bag from the corner, put the notebook he'd been flipping through into it, and zipped it closed before slinging it over his shoulder.

"Okay, bye," he said, looking at me sideways, obviously expecting me to say something else.

"Bye," was all I said. But I did manage a smile.

He left the room and in the hall said to Edward, "I'll meet you downstairs. Bring your stuff."

I listened to them leave then dozed off again.

* * *

I woke up with a shudder in my heart. A loud knock came from somewhere. I struggled to differentiate between reality and dream.

"Please, please, open door . . . I know you are there."

It was Laila—banging on the door as if she meant to bash it open.

I dragged myself out of bed, came out of the bedroom, crossed the living room, and opened the door. She rushed in.

"They are in the city! They are killing everyone . . . a neighbor tell me they are killing everyone in the government!"

"They can't just kill everybody," I said, shaking my head, rapidly coming out of my sleepy stupor. "They only attack people who openly resist them." Peter had said that—though I wasn't sure I believed him when he'd said it, and I could tell Laila didn't believe me now.

"They are! They are killing *everybody*. I called husband again and again but no answer. My neighbor has told me that the main bazaar is full of dead bodies." She started sobbing.

"Don't worry," I said lamely. "I, uh . . . I'm going out. I'll stop at Nehal's work and tell him to call you."

"Thank you . . . thank you very much." She didn't seem at all relieved.

"Can you do me a favor and make some coffee?" I asked, just to keep her busy. Her hands were shaking and she wasn't breathing but panting. I was worried she would actually go into shock.

"Yes . . . yes."

I went to the bathroom, took a quick shower, and started getting ready.

Laila knocked at the bedroom door while I was dressing.

I opened the door, said, "Come in, Laila," and she stepped in, holding a tray.

"Coffee is ready and I made your breakfast hot too."

"Thank you," I said, doing everything I could think of to appear calm. "I'm not hungry, though. I'll just have some coffee. Thanks."

She handed me the coffee cup and I took a sip before tying my sneakers. I found them more practical on the rocky roads and dirt patches of Mazar-i-Sharif.

I finished my coffee and put my camera in my bag. Laila stood watching me the whole time, her arms wrapped around herself, her lips quivering.

She walked out of the apartment with me, begging me again to make her husband call her.

I locked the door and promised her that I would.

Leaving her to stare after me I took my old Fiat, an Indian model, and turned right toward the market. I intended to go downtown to see what was happening in the city but thought of stopping at the neighborhood bazaar to pick up a few things I needed before the fighting closed the whole city down.

All the shops in the bazaar were already closed. There weren't even any stalls along the road in front of the shops, or the otherwise ever-present cart vendors. The street lined with cheap restaurants and *chaiwallas* had never seemed to sleep before, just dozed for a while before dawn. Now it seemed like a ghost town. The shutters were closed, almost all with locks on them.

Cries and curses drifted in the air and a few seconds later a few men ran toward me. I stopped the car and locked the doors, but they all passed me by. Another few seconds later, another group of men, these wearing black turbans, ran toward me with weapons on their shoulders. One of them howled, and all of them stopped. They encircled my car and waved at me to come out of the car.

I felt my jaw quivering and I started sweating even though the morning air was still cool.

With a shaking hand I pointed out the word "journalist" written in Pashto and English across the windshield. One of them came forward and knocked at my side window then beckoned me to open the door.

Peter's words echoed in my head: *They only attack people who openly resist them.*

I opened the door.

The man in the black turban beckoned again, a command that I step out of the car.

I wrapped the small *chadur* I was wearing around my head and shoulders and stepped out of the car. I took my passport and press credentials out of my bag and waved them in a slow circle so all the men in front of me could see it.

A man with a huge scar on his left cheek seemed to be leading them. He called somebody else from the circle and another man standing behind me came to the front. Their eyes were cold and their stern expressions made their cheeks seem sunken, their faces skull-like. Their loose shirts and trousers, mostly browns and blacks, hung on emaciated bodies.

"Who are you?" the short man asked in English.

"I am a journalist," I said, surprised I could speak through a throat tight with fear.

"I know you are a journalist. What is your name and nationality?"

"Rachael," I said slowly. Then I swallowed and added, "I am an American."

The leader said something to the man who was questioning me, which he promptly interpreted for me. "Where are you going?"

"Downtown."

The leader said something else to him, but his cold green eyes stared deep into mine. I wanted to run, but knew I couldn't, shouldn't . . . wouldn't.

"You will cover yourself properly," the man said, and he looked me up and down as though just then seeing me, and finding me some kind of dirty, unwholesome thing. "The Taliban will not tolerate obscenity."

Another string of words from the leader, then the translation with a thin, cruel smile: "Go back home. Nobody here can guarantee your life until the betrayers of Islam are tamed according to the rules of *Shariah*."

I nodded, though I had no idea what part of my dress was offensive to them. I was wearing a long skirt with a long Afghani embroidered shirt and a small *chadur* to cover my shoulders and head, only my face and hands could be seen. Did they expect me to wear a *burqa*?

"I am a journalist," I said, surprised at my own courage, "and according to international law I have a right to cover the news."

The leader reacted even before it was translated for him. He moved a step toward me, took his rifle from his shoulder, and hit the side mirror of my car with its butt. I covered my face and sat down on the seat of the car, afraid I would be the next thing he would hit.

He yelled like a lunatic, spittle flying and spraying on my face. The man close to the front passenger seat shook the locked door.

"Open the door," the interpreter said to me.

I bent down the other side and pulled up the lock.

The man opened the door and unzipped my bag. He took out my cameras and held them above the roof of the car to show his leader, who waved him over. The man took the bag and the cameras to the leader, who threw everything on the street and started trampling them with his heavy boots.

"Please don't do that," I said, my voice weaker now. A tear was forming in the corner of my right eye. "You can't do that."

I bent to pick up my things, but then he turned the barrel of his rifle toward me, which made me freeze.

The translator looked at me then him, and said, "You must go . . ." Then, I thought—maybe imagined, his voice softened just a little and he added, "Don't argue."

I pulled my feet into the car, closed the door, and started the engine. The armed men started walking in the direction I came from. Leaving my broken cameras behind, I started driving downtown.

At one corner a group of men and women appeared so suddenly in front of me I had to swerve to avoid them. But in these narrow, labyrinthine streets, I ended up scraping along the wall of a house. Something hit the roof of my car—I wasn't sure what it was, maybe something falling from the house I'd sideswiped—pinging on the metal.

The crowd of people started running. A woman screamed—a thin, exhausted wail. A man fell bleeding to the street and rolled, then a woman tripped over him and there was blood on her *chadur*.

Someone was shooting at them.

Then the ping-ping-ping sound on the roof of my car again.

Someone was shooting at us.

I laid down as low as I could on the floor of the car and wrapped my arms around my head. I wasn't sure I was breathing. There were more screams, the hard crack of gunshots, then a silence that was somehow even worse.

I stayed with my head down until my leg started to cramp. I sat up slowly, ready to throw myself back down on a moment's notice. A few men with black turbans burst through a door across the street, then I heard shots coming from the house.

My car's engine was still running. Five people lay motionless on the street, but in that moment there were no armed men, so I reversed the car and sped away.

At the end of the street I saw an old man sitting near the dead body of his young son, crying and mumbling.

When I hit the main road there were more bodies of men, women, children, and even dogs and donkeys lying on the sidewalks and sometimes in the middle of the street. Blood collected in small pools. Across the street, fire moved fast from one house to the next, engulfing each one. A woman ran along the sidewalk, the wrist of her daughter, maybe eight or ten years old, in one hand and a sack in the other.

I decided to go back home, but was afraid the car would attract too much attention—any attention was too much. So I stopped at the side of the road, got out, and like the woman dragging her crying daughter, ran as fast as I could.

I hadn't gotten as far as a block when shots rang over my head. I thought I was using every ounce of adrenaline, but somehow managed to run even faster—just a few feet before a strong hand grabbed my hair and pulled me into a narrow flight of stairs. A whimpering cry came out of my mouth and I fell down, my cheeks flushing hot.

"You are safe." An old man with heavy moustache bent down and shushed me.

I was out of breath. I tried but couldn't say anything. A stocky woman stood outside the door of an apartment at the top of the stairs.

"Come up, it's not safe here," the man said in excellent English.

I touched my forehead. I was bleeding. I stood up, trying to catch my breath.

"Come upstairs," he said again.

I didn't move.

"You can trust us, it's not safe here."

I followed him.

The woman closed the door behind us.

"My name is Muqadar, this is my wife, Harriett."

"You shouldn't be out there, they are behaving like wolves," Harriett said while handing me a glass of water.

I drank silently.

"Come with me. I'll clean your wound," she said.

"It's okay, it's just a cut."

"Why don't you freshen up and clean it yourself, bathroom is right there." She pointed at the door down the hall.

"Thank you."

I went to the bathroom, which was next to a tastefully furnished bedroom. I could see a part of the room—a dresser with beautiful woodwork and a bed with a brown bedspread that had a large pink flower in the middle.

I struggled with the handle to the bathroom door then stopped, took a deep if shuddering breath, then turned it and walked in.

I took a few minutes in the bathroom just to breathe, then washed my face and tidied my hair and clothes. When I came back to the living room, I settled down on the brown sofa.

"I saw you running on the sidewalk and I knew you would be

in trouble. They have lodged a pickup right across the road, they are there since the invasion," Mr. Muqadar said.

"I need to get back home," I told him.

"Not now, if you love your life," Harriett said, while putting a tray of snacks and tea on the coffee table in front of me.

"Can I use your phone?" I sat forward fast, only just then thinking to call Laila.

"It's not working since the last few days," Harriett said with a defeated shrug.

"Where do you have to go?" Muqadar asked.

"Just behind Chowk-e-Shadian."

"Stay here, wait for the evening," he said. "Once it will be dark, I'll tell you a short cut. Most of it goes through a building of one kind or the other. You will have better chances to get to your place safe."

"But you are welcome to stay here as long as you want to," Harriett said, then she exchanged glances with her husband as though she felt he was rushing me out of there.

I did start to calm down, even in this strange, dimly lit apartment with these two strangers. We talked while Mr. Muqadar drew a map to get me home, all three of us content to take our minds off what was happening outside. Mr. Muqadar, a native of Mazar-i-Sharif, had spent most of his life in Germany, where he married Harriett. Their children were scattered all over the world and the couple was now regretting their decision to spend their senior years in Mazar-i-Sharif.

As the sun went down, dark clouds rolled in and with them rain and thunder.

"I have to go," I said finally and Mr. Muqadar nodded. His wife looked down at the floor, frowning.

I took the map from Mr. Muqadar and said, "Thank you." I looked at Harriett and said, "Thank you both."

They forced uneven smiles onto their faces and gave me their blessing as I slipped out their door and into the darkness.

Mr. Muqadar was right. Most of my way went through the passages through apartment buildings, opening into alleys. The deep darkness the rain had given to the night was helping me not be seen, but I was also afraid it might make me stray from the path, and reading the map was usually impossible. I made my way mostly from my memory of it.

At one point I was sure I'd lost my way, but on the very next turn I was in front of the house.

I moved fast through the gate and knocked on the first floor. Laila opened it without delay, as if she was standing by the door, looking out to see her husband—or anyone coming up the stairs.

Before the door closed behind me, she was talking in bursts between panting breaths. "Did you see him? Is he all right? Is he coming home?"

I put my hands on her shoulders, ignoring the rain dripping from my drenched clothes. "I couldn't go very far," I huffed, still out of breath but struggling to appear calm. "Conditions on the streets are . . . not good . . ." I knew how stupid that sounded. Why was I trying to be so distant—so much like a reporter? "He might have stayed in his office . . ." I said. "He might have stayed in his office building."

"What's happening outside?"

I didn't know what to say that wouldn't terrify her.

"Tell me, please." She was crying.

I took a deep breath and told myself that if I were in her position I would demand to know the truth, to know *everything*. "They are killing everything that moves on the street. I spent the whole day in a strange couple's house."

Laila staggered back. Still holding her by the shoulders I eased her into the living room and down onto a chair. She wept.

Her children came out of one of the rooms at the end of the hallway. Jamila hugged her mother's knees and little Tahir stood close, surprised, not understanding what was going on.

The door opened and Nehal rushed into the hallway, breathing heavily, bleeding from his shoulder. He fell down, pointing at the door, saying something to Laila.

Laila moved forward fast, took Nehal's keys, which were still in the lock, and closed the door.

"They are after him," she said to me.

Both children were crying now.

Gunshots came from somewhere out on the street. I had already seen them follow men into their houses—I knew what was coming.

"Tell the children to go hide somewhere . . . maybe in the basement," I said to Laila.

Laila followed my advice, but Jamila kept moving her head sideways. *"Haramzadgi,"* Laila yelled at the girl, which turned her crying into uncontrollable sobs.

"Go with them, I'll help Nehal," I told Laila.

But before she could move, Nehal said something to Jamila, he seemed to be whispering in his fragile state. Jamila took her brother's hand and went into the room they'd come out of.

Shots again—definitely outside the house now.

Laila and I took Nehal to the other bedroom as fast as we could.

Someone was pounding on the door.

We laid him in the closet. Laila took off some of her clothes from the hangers and threw them over him to make him at least a little less obvious. He was unconscious now, he had apparently lost a lot of blood.

We closed the closet door and went back into the living room. They were still pounding on the door—over and over and over again.

I went to the door, and Laila tried to stop me.

"It's no use," I said. "It's better to open the door."

I turned the two locks, and the pounding stopped.

Three men rushed in, shouting at the same time. Rainwater poured off them. One of them was a pudgy man with white whiskers and some years behind him, but the other two were young, in their mid- or late twenties. The taller of the two young men stepped to Laila and put his rifle over her shoulder and the older one pointed his at me.

"There are no men in the house," I kept repeating slowly, and as calmly as I could, in case any of them knew English.

Laila, two feet away from me, was probably saying the same thing to them.

I hoped she was.

The young man standing a little behind the two bullies pointing rifles at us seemed familiar to me. His large eyes seemed sad. He used his sleeves to brush water from his hair. The other two wore turbans.

The older man pushed Laila with the barrel of his rifle and repeated his question, which had to be about the man of the house.

An image came to me unbidden: the stadium . . .

And then I realized I'd met that young man in Kabul during my interview with the Taliban troops. He had come from Pakistan and seemed one of the least enthusiastic about the war.

I turned to him, my hands still up, and said, "I met you in Kabul . . . I interviewed you . . . with Mr. Arshad." Hoping he would recognize the name, I repeated it, then repeated it again.

It was less than a second but I saw in his eyes that he remembered me.

The other man shouted his question at Laila again, his voice getting increasingly shrill.

I stepped back, very slowly, and pointed at Laila. I took off the *chadur* Laila was using to cover herself and pointed to her belly to try to convince them she was pregnant. I had no idea if this appeal would work. They were shooting everything that moved on the street. I wasn't expecting much sympathy from them, even for a pregnant woman, but I had nothing to lose.

The young man I met in Kabul said something to Laila's accuser, and there was a heated exchange between them.

The man from Kabul stepped forward, aimed his rifle at the other man then turned his head and looked straight at the man who was pointing rifle at me.

The man pointing his gun at Laila's said something in a very agitated tone.

A shot made us all jump. I sucked in a breath and held it—he'd shot Laila.

But instead of Laila, the man who'd been shouting at her fell to the floor in a heap and the next moment the man from Kabul turned around and shot his other comrade in arms.

I took one step closer to the screaming Laila and the older man pulled the trigger as he fell—the bullet buried itself in the ceiling. Laila's knees buckled and I grabbed her and together we sank to the floor, not sure what had happened just a heartbeat ago.

The man from Kabul looked at us for a few seconds, then he took the rifles from the fallen men and emptied their shells into a satchel that hung from his shoulder. He took other things from his dead comrades' bags, but I couldn't see. Tears blurred my vision, and Laila's sobs filled my ears.

He went to the door then stopped and looked at the pool of blood there. He turned and saw the trail of blood in the hallway, leading to one of the bedrooms.

He followed it fast, his AK-47 up in front of him, to the bedroom. Laila rushed after him, grabbing at his legs and saying, "Nah . . . nah . . ."

He dragged her along with him a few steps but then broke away from her.

Laila beat the floor with her hands, repeating, "Nah . . . nah . . . nah . . ."

She started hitting herself in the head. I grabbed her hands, helped her to sit, and wrapped my arms around her. Two gunshots rang out and Laila screamed so loud my eardrums rattled. She shuddered in my arms and slipped back to the floor.

The man from Kabul came out of the bedroom with the sheet from her bed. He closed the eyelids of the man that had threatened Laila then covered his body with the sheet. He didn't even look at the other man's body, which lay with his legs folded inward and limbs hanging awkwardly at his sides.

He turned to us and said, *"Hits kas."*

No man.

He left, and closed the door behind him.

I rushed to the bedroom to check on Nehal. He'd been shot in the head and chest, but something told me he'd died before the men ever burst in, from loss of blood.

We found Laila's children under Jamila's bed. Jamila still held her brother's hand tightly, whispering for him to be quiet, then we took the stairs at the back of the kitchen that led to the upstairs apartment. We took every care not to let the children see their father in that condition, but we were unable to shield them from the bodies of the two in front of the door.

Gunshots rippled through the air, punctuated by the thud of mortar shells or other munitions, but nobody came near the house.

"Maybe we should try to go to my brother's house?" Laila said.

I shook my head and told her, "It's not safe on the streets. And besides, they may have the same problem we have here. No one and no place is perfectly safe today."

Laila shook her head, but said, "You are right."

An hour later Laila seemed to have regained her courage. She went down and called her brother's house, but nobody answered.

In these moments of relative peace I started to worry about Peter and Edward, who were still out there somewhere. It wasn't until evening that we heard the phone on the first floor ringing. Laila ran for the stairs, but I stopped her, pulling her back into the bedroom I shared with Peter.

"Stay with your children," I said, touching the side of her face then glancing over at Jamila and Tahir, who slept fitfully on the bed.

I didn't wait for her to answer, just ran for the door, down the straits, then into the apartment thinking I'd either go slow and maybe miss whoever it was or go fast and run into another AK-47.

I did the wrong thing.

I answered the phone.

"It's Edward," the voice on the other end of the line said, "Laila?"

"It's me," I said through a huge breath I didn't know I was holding.

"Rachael," he said, and he sounded both relieved and frightened.

"Where are you? I asked, sure the two of them were still together.

"Hiding," he said and the absence of the word "we're" in front of that made me clench my teeth. "In a hotel," he added, then there was silence.

"Edward?" I said, my eyes starting to burn. "Are you there?"

"I'm here."

Not "We're here."

I couldn't say his name, couldn't ask . . .

"They shot him," Edward said. He sounded tired. Broken, somehow. Tears poured out of me and I went to my knees, the cord from the phone stretching up over me to move my hair off my forehead. "He was trying to talk to the Iranians who'd been forced to move out of the consulate building. And they shot him. They shot them all."

XXI

Another Massacre

Sometime in the fall of 1998, we were ordered to attack Mazar-i-Sharif again. This time around we had several Pashtun guides who had lived in the city and knew it well. There was no chance of our troops getting lost in the numerous dead ends of the city.

These guides also knew which parts of the city were most heavily populated by the Hazara community, which was the main target of our attack. Our leaders said they wanted to send a message to the Hazara population that the lax ways of the past would not be tolerated in the future, and to cement that it was necessary to take a hard hand. We were also instructed to be particularly vigilant in hunting the supporters and employees of the Dostum government.

I knew that was all a facade. Their real intention was to take revenge for the previous year's losses. And I couldn't blame them. I lost Ahmed, Rehman lost his friends, we lost everyone we knew from the *madrassah*. . . . We didn't know many people outside the Taliban anymore, so those fallen brothers were the only victims that mattered in all this. It seemed as if our tiny little world was blasted in one go and turned into ashes. It was not only their deaths that had made an impression on our minds, but also what they had gone through before they were put to death. They had been starved and then thrown in wells and tankers to rot. In fact, Ahmed was lucky, he had left early and with honor, in the face of a hail of bullets. He had made his mark, but the rest of the *talibs* from our *madrassah* had no mark and no grave, their bones were entangled with each other somewhere deep in the dirt of Mazar-i-Sharif.

We reached the outskirts of the city in the early morning. We came across a few hundred troops that were neither prepared for nor even expected us. They were cut down like a fresh crop of wheat, fast, with one sweeping blow.

Just after this onslaught of ours we were ordered to move through the city as fast as we could and bring down as many Hazara men as bullets would allow. We were told not to worry about Uzbeks as long as they didn't get in our way.

It was around ten in the morning when we entered the city. The people were unaware of our arrival, and were occupied by their day-to-day business. This invasion was very different from our entry into Kabul, where the local population had already locked themselves inside their houses.

We opened fire and the natives started falling down. At this juncture it was difficult to differentiate between men and women, let alone Hazara and Uzbek. Each and every breathing being on the street was under a shower of our bullets, and every house and shop had the marks of our atrocities on its walls.

Our pickup, with eight men, stopped in front of a government office. On our way in we shot three men who were in the front room. These targets stopped seeming like people. I couldn't think of them as men with families, children. They were obstacles in our way, and for me, in the way of this all finally being over. We moved into the hallway and started checking offices on both sides.

A door opened at the end of the hallway and three men made a run for it. Before we opened fire they turned right into another hallway. Suhrab Khan beckoned Rehman and I to come with him and we moved fast into the hallway. The rest of the men stayed to keep the hunt in the building moving forward. When we turned right we saw a door leading out of the building. When we came out we saw the men getting into a black car, which soon moved for the gate of the building. We fired at the car but all our shells hit the roof of it or entered the wall behind.

We ran to our pickup and jumped in. Suhrab Khan drove us away to follow the car. The car turned right into the very first street, they knew that they were safer on the side streets. We kept following them and shot the car twice.

The sun was setting and it seemed darker than usual. I looked up at the sky. Clouds were gathering, surely bringing rain.

The pickup stopped with a screech and we fell all over each other in the bed. The black car we were following stood sideways, blocking our way. When we jumped down from the pickup we saw the three men running into the street behind the car. Rehman and I jumped onto the trunk of the car and opened fire. All of them fell down.

Thunder rumbled and rain started pouring down.

We jumped back onto the street and hopped into the pickup. Suhrab Khan started the truck but it didn't move. I heard "Haramzadag!" from the driver's seat.

I stood up to look into the street. One of the men was running away, and before we opened fire again he turned right onto another side street.

Suhrab Khan reversed the pickup, sped it up, and turned onto the first street that took us in the direction the man had escaped. The wipers of the pickup made rhythmic creaks when they came to the extremities of the windshield, and the drops on its small roof played *tabla* with an even speed.

He couldn't run faster than our pickup, and if we ended up on the right street we would find him.

Drenched and tired, we stopped at a crossroads where four streets met, looking around in the darkness, futilely trying to find the man.

"There are many more men on the streets to kill," I said, "we should go back to the main street."

"He works in a city office, we are not letting him go," Suhrab Khan barked from the driver's seat. He didn't care, he was safe from the rain.

Rehman fired a few shots, startling me, then he shouted, "There! There he is . . . he went into that house!" Rehman pointed to a two-story building at the end of one of the streets.

"How can you see anything in this darkness?" I asked.

"I saw him! I saw him!" he insisted like a child.

When we reached the house we found no easy way in. Suhrab Khan and Rehman started kicking the door. After a few blows we heard the locks inside the house moving away from their sockets. A tall woman opened the door. We rushed in. Another woman, covered in a *chadur*, stood a few feet away. I could sense her fear.

The woman who had opened the door wore a long shirt with mirror-work and a black skirt. She covered her head and shoulders with a silk *duppatta*. Suhrab Khan pointed his rifle at her, while Rehman, standing next to Suhrab Khan, held his rifle on the other woman.

"Where is that man?" Suhrab Khan asked the woman who opened the door.

She replied in English.

"Where is he?" Rehman asked while pressing his rifle to the shoulder of the woman in the *chadur*.

"No man is here," she replied in Dari.

"Don't lie to me!" Rehman said.

The foreigner kept repeating the same phrase in her language—I realized then how surprised I was to find a foreign woman in Mazar-i-Sharif.

"They are lying," Suhrab Khan said, and placed the barrel of his rifle directly on the foreign woman's head.

The woman nodded and said something to me. I didn't understand any of it but thought I heard the name Arshad.

She repeated the name three times.

I blinked, the memory coming to me as if thrown at my forehead from the woman herself. It was the American woman who talked to us in Kabul, asking all sorts of questions. Arshad was the Afghani journalist who was interpreting for her. I didn't want to let myself feel sorry for her, some busybody reporter from a world away, who seemed to think reminding me of our meeting would save her life. She didn't seem to realize that their only chance of survival depended on her producing a man—any man—that we could kill instead. She stepped back a little and pulled the *chadur* from the other woman's waist.

She kept saying something, pointing at the pregnant belly of the other woman as if we were blind and didn't know the woman was pregnant. Did she actually believe that shaming us in this way would do any good for either of them?

"I don't care!" Rehman shouted at the woman like a lunatic. "I'll kill all Hazara women to kill the seeds of all Hazara men! They killed all my people . . . tell me: *Where is the man?*" He pushed her down to the floor with the barrel of his rifle.

A voice inside me began to speak. I had sowed a crop of doom for a woman I recognized, who had been polite to me, and another whose fate brushed with mine through some accident of history. Maybe I had already killed the father of her unborn child. The death of this woman right here would add to the burden my soul had been carrying for so long. A man lost here and a man lost there was the way of the war, but she didn't have to lose her life—and definitely not her innocent baby's life. And to what end?

I pointed my rifle at Rehman and asked him to let her go.

"What are you doing?" Suhrab Khan demanded.

"There is no use killing a pregnant woman . . . we can search the house to find the man."

"You are not the one who gives orders here," Rehman growled.

"I'm not giving an order, I'm making a request. But I will kill you if she falls."

"There is no way I'm letting her go . . . she needs to—"

His eyes seemed to bulge from their sockets and his forehead was full of folds.

"Rehman, don't," I said.

"Tell me where—"

I shot him. Then I turned and shot Suhrab Khan. He had had no time to comprehend what was happening, the bullet went right through his left temple. Blood sprayed everywhere.

A sort of peace came over me, but only for the space of a

heartbeat. I had just killed myself, I thought, as surely as I'd killed Rehman and Suhrab Khan. In that moment I realized then that they may very well have been the last two men on Earth I actually knew.

I looked at the women, squatting on the floor, covering their ears with their hands.

I turned around and went for the door. Why did I look down? There was a puddle of blood a couple feet from the door, mixing with the rainwater that poured off our clothes. I hadn't noticed it before. I was sure it didn't belong to either Rehman or Suhrab Khan, their bodies were too far from it. I looked down the hallway. A trail of blood led to one of the rooms at the end.

I followed it. The Hazara woman grabbed my legs. I dragged her with me for a while but soon shook her off me.

I went into the room and looked around—there was no place to hide except the closet. I opened it. A lot of woman's clothes were on the floor, all wet with blood. The face of an unconscious man peered out from one end of the pile of clothes. I shot him twice then went back into the front room.

"No man," I said, and came out of the house. The Hazara woman started beating her head like a lunatic.

I never learned how to drive so I had to walk back on foot. I shot the tires of the pickup so no one else could drive it. I went in the direction we had come from to get to the main street and hopefully find the surviving men of my terrible clan.

XXII

The Drug Dealer

A week after I'd given a suspicious Rustam Khan a fictitious account of the deaths of Suhrab Khan and Rehman, he called me in and introduced me to a tall man with a long beard as black as night. "This is Ibrahim. From now on you will work with him. He will let you know what you are supposed to do."

"Get your things," Ibrahim said without a word of greeting. "We leave for Herat immediately."

A few minutes later, we were in his pickup.

We reached Herat in the early afternoon. Two men sitting on a *charpie* under the trees outside a big house stood up to receive his orders. He greeted them and told them to get us some food.

He took me to a room that was full of cardboard boxes, big and small. He opened one and took out a paper bag and showed it to me.

"Do you know what this is?" he asked.

"No."

"White gold."

"Gold?"

"Yes . . ." he replied, his expression flat, emotionless, "this is heroin."

I shook my head and couldn't help but say, "What are you doing with heroin? We are against drugs . . . we burned so many poppy f—"

"That was past," he interrupted. "Now that the whole of Afghanistan is in our hands we need money, and this is the best thing to sell."

I shook my head again and asked, "What do you want from me?"

"You will go with me across the border to Pakistan . . . I need

235

somebody who speaks Urdu well to help me to market this."

"They are hunting for me in Pakistan," I said, relieved at finding a way out of this. "I can't go back."

"Who is hunting?"

Then I realized I may have made a mistake telling him I was a fugitive, but it was too late.

"Who is hunting for you?" he asked again.

"Police."

"Why?"

"I ran away from the *madrassah* once."

"Don't lie to me! Police do not look for people who run away from a *madrassah*."

"I ran away with a girl."

He stopped to think about this, then sighed and asked, "When did you come to Afghanistan?"

"Four years back."

"The police are not so efficient there," he said with a shrug. "They don't look for people for so long."

And with that, I was a drug trafficker.

* * *

Two days later we travelled through the passages in the mountains, and on the cheap crowded passenger vans to get to Peshawar. We took the train to Lahore from Peshawar Cantt.

In Lahore, we went to the mausoleum of Data Ganj Bakhsh, a Sufi saint, and under the beat of *qawali*—songs in his praise—we traded our "gold" with a man who appeared to be a beggar sitting outside the mausoleum with a dirty metal pot in front of him.

From Lahore, we took another train the whole night to Karachi. On the beach, near a posh neighborhood, another exchange took place. A man who took tourists on camel rides took out a bundle of 500 rupee bills that were tucked under the seat fastened over the hump of the camel, and handed it over to Ibrahim.

After this exchange I asked him to let me go and see Museabate. The slum was not far from that posh neighborhood.

"But you better get back before evening," he said, that same stern, emotionless look still on his face. "You can't slip away. I have many eyes in this country."

"I know," I said, even though I thought there was at least an even chance he was lying. After all, if he had all these "eyes" in Karachi, why had he brought me in the first place?

When I reached Rehmatea's hovel, I knocked on the wooden panel.

"Who is it?" Her harsh tone was as alive as before.

"It's me . . . Raza."

She pulled the sackcloth aside to look at me, and blinking said, "Raza . . . come in."

She embraced me and then brushed her fingers along the scar of my forehead.

"How are you?" I asked.

"I am all right."

"How is the child? How is Perveen?"

Massi Museabate frowned and looked me up and down then seemed to very carefully choose her words. "Your son's name is Faiz . . . he is in the *madrassah*. Perveen is all right . . . I went to see her last month."

All of a sudden I felt exhausted. I sat down on the *charpie*.

"Couldn't you do anything to stop that vulture getting hold of my son?" I asked, not looking up at her.

"I tried," she said, and I heard the defensiveness in her voice. "I went to the orphanage, but they were not ready to let me have him. They said I was not a kin and I couldn't feed him. They said that I would turn him into a beggar."

I barely heard her. I said, "I want to see him, will he let me see my son?"

"No . . . if he finds out that you are here, he may . . ."

I waited for her to complete the sentence but she didn't.

"What would he do?"

"He may send a message to Shahbaz Khan, and collect that price on your head."

Seeing my agony, she patted my shoulder and said, "That *madrassah* is the only place for the child. They won't let me raise him, and you certainly can't take care of him."

She was right—at least about the second part. How could I bring Faiz with me back into the grip of the Taliban, and nothing but war? Still, just the thought of Bayfazal touching that innocent child . . . *my* child . . .

"I will kill that man . . . I have killed many, I will kill him too."

"And what good it will do?" Rehmatea asked. "All those children he feeds and teaches will be on the streets to beg, or the orphanage will take them and this time who knows where Faiz will end up."

Tears rolled from my eyes. "I want to see Perveen."

"It's better you don't," she said, and again, she was probably right. "If they identify you, you will be in a terrible mess."

"Then why am I here?" I asked, not expecting an answer.

"You have visited me," Rehmatea said, an unfamiliar smile on her face. "You have come to know you have a son, and that Perveen is all right. That can be reason enough." After a pause she added, "I'll tell her you came."

I shook my head then stood. "I should go," I said, but before I went out I remembered that fatal diary, the diary I had burned in the camp fire. "Where did my m—where did Tara go? Why did she leave me behind?"

That little smile was gone from Rehmatea's face then, replaced by a frown. "Her condition was very bad, so I asked an NGO to look for her parents. They somehow found them."

"And she left me behind?"

"She had no choice, your grandfather was not ready to accept you."

"Don't call him my grandfather . . . and don't call her my

mother," I said, without the strength to make it a demand. "She was a selfish woman."

"No, she wasn't. She was on her deathbed, she had no choice."

"Did she ever come to see me?"

"Your grandmother came often, and sometimes when your mother felt better, she came, too. But after two years, all the money—and the visits—suddenly stopped."

"Money?"

"Your grandmother sent me some money every month."

"And you accepted it?"

Rehmatea shrugged. "I am a poor woman, remember. I didn't have enough money to feed myself let alone take care of a child."

"So you gave me away when the money stopped coming."

This was met with a deeper frown, and I saw anger coming into her face so she looked more familiar. "I gave you away a long time after the money stopped coming. I did my best. Stop trying to find somebody to blame." Another pause, then she waved her hand in front of her and added, "At least, stop blaming me."

I took a deep breath, my eyes closed.

She was right.

"Do they still live in the same place?" I asked.

"I don't know. So many years have passed . . . they might have moved away. What would be the use of going there? Your mother is not there anymore, she is not in this world anymore."

"There is nothing to lose, either . . . *Allah Hafiz*."

She grabbed my arm, her hand weak and sweaty. "Why don't you stay. Let me make some tea for you."

I shook my head. "I have to close the chapter you have opened by giving me that diary."

Still holding my arm she said, "I tried my best to save you from the truth, but you insisted on knowing. . . . Many times I thought of destroying it, but I never could."

"Well," I said, "I have done your job."

She let go of my arm. "Be safe," she said as I was going out.

* * *

Long lines of cars were parked on both sides of the streets in the posh neighborhood of Defence. I turned onto the street written on one of the envelopes my mother had sent to Rehmatea and started looking for the house number. Very few of the houses actually had numbers, but almost all of them bore the names of their residents. I did not see the name Farooq on any of the plates. When I reached the end of the street, I turned around, carefully looking both ways again.

A woman got into a car. A man whose rusty clothes showed his status as a worker bee opened the gate for her. I stopped in front of the house.

"What do you want?" the man asked me in a harsh tone. The combination of a turban, the scarf on my shoulder, and a long beard probably made him think I was there to ask for money for some mosque or *madrassah*.

I did not respond. I took the photograph from my pocket and looked at it carefully.

The woman reversed the car and came out of the porch. When she straightened the car I moved toward her.

She turned her head to me with a question on her face. Her hair was tied loosely in a loop behind her head. I kept looking at her face. I didn't know what to say.

"Sorry, *Maulana*," she said, "I just have this at the moment." She took out a five rupee bill, and reached out of the car window to give it to me.

"No, *Khatoon*," I said, as politely as I knew how. "I am not here for money."

"What then?" She was already getting impatient.

"Are you Tara?"

"Tara?" She went pale. "Who are you?"

"My name is Raza."

Her carefully trimmed eyebrows made a full curve, emphasizing her astonishment at hearing my name. "Raza? How do you know Tara?"

I didn't know what to say.

"Who are you?" she repeated.

I took out the photograph and pointed to the girl sitting on the floor on the right of the elderly couple. "Is this you?"

"Yes," she said, squinting at the photograph. "How did you get this? Who are you?"

"Are you Tara's sister?"

"Who are you?" she asked, her tone accusatory. I heard fear in it.

"Tara was my mother."

Her mouth and eyes went wide open. She looked at me from head to toe and then beckoned me to stay there. She parked the car on the side of the street, got out, and motioned for me to follow her. We went into the house and stopped in front of a door on the side of the main door.

"Wait here, please," she said and entered into the house from the other door. A couple minutes later the door in front of me opened and she invited me in. The large room had a three-seat sofa and a few chairs scattered on the other side of it. A rolled carpet lay along the wall and two paintings leaned against the wall over it. I sat at the corner of the three-seat sofa. She sat opposite me on a chair.

We remained silent for a while, then she asked, "How have you come to know about this house?"

"The woman who raised me gave me a few letters of . . . of my mother's that have the return address."

"And how did you get this photograph?"

"It was in the diary my mother had left behind."

The man, whom I had seen at the gate, brought a tray with some snacks and tea. He looked at me with suspicion, as though I were a stray dog as likely to bite her as lick her hand.

"I live in America," she said while pouring a cup of tea for me.

"I am here to sell this house and wind up everything."

I wasn't sure why she was telling me that.

"Is there anything I can do for you?" she said while handing me the cup.

"I don't expect anything," I said. I wasn't really sure how to answer her. I didn't really know what I wanted. I didn't expect my mother to be alive, or to somehow be welcomed into this family that long ago abandoned and forgot me. I ended up just sitting there.

"I wish I could do something for you . . . I can give you some money."

I didn't want her to think I had come there for money. "Can you tell me about my mother?"

The woman shrugged and said with a faint smile, "She was my elder sister . . ." She seemed to be struggling to find the right words. "She died a year after my mother brought her home."

"Did she ever talk about me?"

That brought a sad smile to her face. "That whole year she *only* talked about you, but my father never allowed her to bring you home . . ." She sighed and the smile went away with a shake of her head. "We are not bad people, but—"

"Don't worry, I am not here to blame anybody. And . . . and your mother, can I meet her?"

"She passed away a couple of years after Tara's death."

And with that I knew the reason Massi Rehmatea stopped getting money.

A man's voice came from inside the house: "Mama . . . Mama?" A young man entered and froze in place, not expecting to see me there.

"What is it, Haseeb?"

"Can I take the car?" he asked, still looking at me.

"I need to go for shopping, *beta* . . . I'll drop you wherever you want to go."

"All right," the young man replied, then with one more

suspicious look my way, he left.

The sister of my mother did not introduce her son to me. In different circumstances he would call me his cousin.

"Thanks for talking to me," I said as I stood up.

"Hold on." She went out and came back with a pen and paper. She wrote something on it and held it out for me. "My address in America. Phone and email is there, too. . . . If you ever want to talk, feel free to write or call me."

I took the paper, smiled, and nodded, then left the room. She followed me to the gate. *"Khudha Hafiz,"* she said when we reached the gate.

"Khuda Hafiz," I replied, and left the house in which my mother had spent the last year of her life.

XXIII

The Addict

We took the train to Lahore. It was the same train on which I'd left Karachi with Perveen. The tea cabin was busy but the stall that sold food a few feet away was the busiest on the platform.

I could have gotten up and run back into the city I'd grown up in, where Perveen and my son lived, but I remained there on the bench next to Ibrahim, inactive, impotent.

It was the same bench, too, on which I'd sat with Perveen as we dreamed of a life of possibilities away from the *madrassah*, away from her brothers, and away from her husband-to-be. The life we'd found after our elopement was without the people we ran away from, but it was still far from what we'd dreamt it to be. It was barely less a nightmare for both of us.

I looked up. A shadow flew away in the sky, probably a bird who had lost her way, searching for a refuge in which to spend the night.

I wondered why I didn't just let the war have me. Ahmed threw himself into the path of bullets to be done with it, why didn't I? Ahmed didn't have anything to live for, did I?

Within a single breath I knew the desire to see Perveen and our child kept me alive.

But no matter how much I wanted to be with them, I couldn't do anything for them. All they would see was the ugly face I had acquired in this war, the same face that went all over the world as the face of the Taliban, the face of a murderer who took lives not only in the war but also in the peace, the face of a fugitive who felt safer in the arena of a foreign war than on the streets of his own country.

"You want tea?" Ibrahim pushed me out of my reverie.

I nodded and he made a *V* sign with his fingers to the man

behind the tea cabin.

A couple minutes later a boy about nine years old brought two small glasses of tea in a carrier made of wire. He handed one to me.

This boy was probably luckier than my son. He at least breathed outside the walls of a *madrassah*.

The train arrived and people started to board. Ibrahim handed the cups back to our little waiter, paid him for the tea, and took the bag he'd been keeping between his feet.

I took up my satchel and followed him.

All throughout the night I stared through the window at the dark night outside. The slums along the track seemed endless and the flickering lights of the hovels fought unsuccessfully against the endless blackness. And then there were fields that demanded tremendous sacrifice from farmers who were still unsuccessful in feeding the downtrodden denizens of the city.

We stayed in Lahore for a day and then left for Peshawar. When we arrived in Peshawar, Ibrahim rented a room in a cheap hotel near the station. He slept throughout the day and I tried to as well, but sleep remained aloof. My mind was buzzing with thoughts that refused to go away.

When he finally woke in the evening, Ibrahim said, "I have to go and meet a friend who lives here . . . I want you to stay in the room. Do not let my bag out of your sight, and do not leave the room under any condition."

I nodded.

I started pacing back and forth across the room. I wished I had holes in my head through which I could dispel all these thoughts. I would tell them to leave this house and take away the past and present that reside in it, which were stuck in there and imposed their judgment day and night, behaved as if they were separate entities and could stand alone without me.

I tripped on Ibrahim's bag. I picked it up and put it on his bed. I walked away from it but when I'd paced to the far wall, my eyes fell on it. It was half open, and its rusty zipper whispered of the precious contents inside it, offering me a refuge from my own mind for a few hours.

I threw it on the floor and pushed it under the bed.

* * *

I didn't know why I was so cold and wet. I struggled to open my eyes but my eyelids contracted under the attack of some brilliant light. And then I felt as if somebody had thrown me in a stream of water. I heard a voice coming from a far place, scolding me.

"You idiot, if you wanna die, use your gun, not my stuff!"

And then another wave of the stream pulled me out of my stupor.

I was sitting in the bathroom in a puddle of water.

He threw another bucket of water on me and then slapped me.

"Moron, why didn't you just tell me, I would gladly send you across this world, why waste my gold."

I threw up all day.

In the evening he took the bag to go out to ply his trade.

"You have wasted a lot of money on the very first trip . . . I don't want to drag you with me for the exchange, but don't do anything stupid while I am away."

The next day we left Peshawar and four days later we were back in Herat.

* * *

The world I was in, different from the world I actually lived in, was a refuge. Or maybe this world was real and the other one was just a nightmare. I was at peace here, anyway, mindless, on a playful journey full of rhythmic and adventurous happenings. The place where thoughts had no judgment, not even a stable perspective, where there was no effort and pressure, and where even the weight of the body containing the tormenting soul seemed to be absent.

When I came out of the journey the stolen drugs from Ibrahim's room had taken me, I found myself behind bars with ten addicts just like me. We were starved and ignored the whole day. In the late afternoon a man came and called over one of the addicts. An hour later he called another one. At night they gave us some food but offered us no answers in response to our questions about the absent inmates.

The next day, one by one, all of them disappeared. I was left alone to pace the cell.

In the late afternoon the man came for me. He took me to a room and pushed me in. Three men were waiting for me. There was a bathtub full of water in the middle of the room, a large bucket of ice lying near it.

I was told to take off my clothes. Their eyes surveyed me from top to bottom and then before I could move or speak one of them hit me with his fist, and then the other one. They spared my bones but punctured my flesh and turned it into a field of red, painful stains. Their dark hearts and primitive minds had no mercy.

Once they were satisfied with the effect the punches and slaps were creating on my body, they threw me in the water and poured the ice over me. The cold water started to coagulate the blood, and turned them into pink sores. My body was as torn as my heart, covered with cruel cuts and unforgiving bruises.

A few days later, when the sores on my body had turned into scars, I left for another trip with Ibrahim.

XXIV

Boston

I stayed with a friend in Washington, D.C. I was just there to resign from the paper and take care of a few last brushstrokes of my life in the capital before moving to Boston with my mother. I wanted some time away from war, politics, and journalism. I wanted to have my baby, and plan for the future away from all that.

My mother was seventy years old and still active. She hated the idea of living in a retirement home. Moving in together was a welcome change for both of us.

When my son was born I named him Sebastian. His dark skin and curly hair told me as surely as any DNA test who his father was. Crying in my arms, I felt as if he was taunting me, telling me how quickly and thoroughly he could throw me out of my comfort zone and force me to revisit a path I wanted to erase from my life.

Despite knowing that half of his perfect, beautiful little being came from Arun, I put Peter's name as his father on the birth certificate.

"This isn't right . . ." my mother said just about every day. "You need to tell Arun."

And with those passing days I grew more and more irritated.

"This is not for you, or for him. This is for Sebastian," she said one day.

"I thought you hated Arun," I shot back.

"I never said that." She sat down on my father's recliner to rest her knees.

"There were plenty of times when you made that abundantly clear without saying it."

My mother sighed and said, "It doesn't make any difference now whether I liked him or not . . . he is the father. He deserves to know, and Sebastian needs to know who his father is, sooner or later."

"As if this is the first single-parent home in America," I grumbled. I kneeled on the floor and folded the clean laundry while Sebastian dozed in his little bouncy seat. Despite the harsh tone of our words, the fact that we were "yelling" at each other so quietly made me smile.

"Don't behave like a child," my mother said. "If you want me to shut up I will, but you know better."

She never mentioned Arun again after that half-whispered confrontation, but her silence only kept the argument alive inside me, however preoccupied I was with Sebastian.

I knew I didn't want to establish any new connection with Arun. Sharing a child would tie us together forever, creating complexities in my life for which I just wasn't ready.

One night I had the same dream I'd had in Kabul. A child, divided in two parts from the middle of the forehead to the feet, like a cardboard cut-out, standing between Arun and I. The baby seemed confused. A part of him ran for me, and the other to Arun. The part that reached me turned into a whole boy, but the two halves had different features.

This time the child asked me, "Am I Sebastian?"

I came awake with a gasp, asking myself, *Why did I name him Sebastian?*

I realized only then that Sebastian was a name that could be both Western and Indian. Did I subconsciously choose the name for that obscure reason? It seemed farfetched, but I was unable to drive the thought from my mind.

A few days later, I called Arun.

I found him in a good mood. "Hey! You're in D.C."

"No," I said, "Boston."

"Good timing. This is my last day here."

There was a silence I wasn't sure how to fill, a sudden awkwardness.

"I'm moving to New York," he said, then, "after the wedding."

"Wedding?" I said, just to make sure I'd heard him right. I didn't know in that moment if I found that to be good news or bad news. I filled the next uncomfortable pause. "Congrats. When's the big day?"

I cringed, feeling way too casual, but he seemed to take it in stride and said, "Today."

"To—" I started.

"This evening, yeah," he said and I could sense that he sensed how weird this was for me, or maybe it was just weird for him, too. "It's just a small . . . thing . . ."

"Well, best wishes from me," I said, cringing again at how canned that came out. Before I could think better of it I asked, "Is the bride Kamala?"

"Yes."

A desire to hurt him came to me fully formed in that instant. "Well, I just called to tell you that I gave birth to your child six months ago."

"What?"

"I found out I was pregnant when I got to Afghanistan that last time." I didn't pause, just bulled right through so he couldn't respond. "I didn't call you because I didn't want you to worry about me, being pregnant in a war zone and everything."

Then there was a long silence.

"Arun? Are you there?"

He hung up on me.

I was ashamed of what I'd done.

* * *

The phone rang while I was putting Sebastian to bed. I heard my mother exchanging social graces and I figured it was one of her old lady friends. A minute later she came into the nursery and took Sebastian from me.

"It's Arun."

Sebastian rubbed his eyes and protested the exchange, but my mother waived me out of the room.

I picked up the phone and tried to sound as neutral as possible with one word: "Hello."

"Why would you do this to me?" Arun started right up. "Was living with me so bad that you would have this kind of animosity toward me?"

"I'm not sure what you're complaining about," I cut in, feeling a bit taken aback.

He took a deep breath, then said, "Couldn't you tell me you were pregnant?"

I needed to think of something that would stop him in his tracks, and I tried, "I wasn't sure whose . . ." But I couldn't say it. I heard him take a breath in to speak, so I jumped back in with, "This isn't the time to talk about this. Once you settle in in New York, after the wedding, we'll talk."

"I cancelled the wedding," he said as if it were the most obvious thing in the world.

Blinking and shaking my head I said, "No, no, no . . . please do *not* do that. If you think we can get back together because of Sebastian, you're just . . ." I wanted to say "nuts," but went with, "wrong."

"His name is Sibtain?"

"Sebastian."

"I know, but we pronounce it *Sibtain.*"

"Arun," I said, "go get married . . . we'll talk later."

"No, it's too late anyway. Her people already know about my decision. When can I see him?"

I shook my head, knowing he couldn't see me, and told him, "It's up to you. I'm not working for now, and my mother is always here."

Without pause he said, "I'll be there tomorrow, sometime in the afternoon."

"Okay," I said, still shaking my head.

He said, "See you," and hung up.

Into the empty line I said, "I shouldn't have told you about Sebastian on your wedding day."

* * *

Sebastian was asleep next to me while I read on the living room couch when the doorbell rang. My mother went to answer it, but I stopped her with a hand on her wrist. I put down my book and found Arun standing outside with a small bag on his shoulders and a plastic bag in his hand. I opened the door for him.

We exchanged short hellos and I led him to the living room. He exchanged graces with my mother next then sat down next to the baby. He picked Sebastian up and touched his cheeks with the tips of his fingers then kissed him on the forehead. Sebastian moaned for a moment but fell right back to asleep.

I wasn't actually breathing at that moment, I think.

"Would you like some tea or coffee," my mother asked in her hushed whisper.

"Tea, please," he whispered back.

I sat down on the chair across from him and took a deep breath. My hands were shaking.

"I didn't understand," he said. "What were you not sure about?"

I hung my head and sighed. "I lived with Peter White . . . you remember Peter White from . . ." He nodded, his attention still on Sebastian. ". . . in Afghanistan . . . in Mazar-i-Sharif. I wasn't sure whose baby it was until he was. . . . We had tried so many times and I didn't expect it to be yours."

"Until he came out half-Indian," Arun said. There didn't seem to be any animosity in his voice, but that wasn't quite true when he continued, "You slept with him before our divorce?"

"Don't be ridiculous."

"What makes you sure now?"

"Do you think I'd call you if I wasn't be sure?"

"Let me have the custody," he said, and the words thumped into me. "You're too busy to take care of him."

A part of me wanted to pummel him to death with my bare hands, but instead I sat there and, I think, calmly told him, "I stopped working before he was even born. I have nothing in my life but Sebastian. You don't have to worry about him, or me."

"But I still would like to have custody."

"That's not going to happen," I said instead of murdering him on the spot.

"How do you expect me to establish a relationship with my child when you're in Boston and I'm in New York."

"It's *our* child, not yours," I said, as if explaining the situation to Sebastian, not his father. "Look, I don't want to keep him away from you. I wouldn't have called you if that were the case. You can visit whenever you want. Maybe, some time, y'know, way in the future, you can maybe take him with you for part of the holidays or something." That felt wishy-washy, but this didn't: "I'll have primary custody."

"Sooner or later, you will have to go back to work," he said, taking his turn at being condescending. I guess I owed him that much. "You know that and I know that. Sibtain will be better off with me. I have a whole family to take care of him."

"You mean your mother and your sisters?" I said, and it came out like a felony accusation.

"Yes," he said with a shrug.

I remained silent.

"What's wrong with them?" he asked.

"Sorry, Arun, I won't give him up." Did he really not get that?

"Nobody is asking you to give him up," he said. "I'm just asking you to let him live with me, and you can be the one to visit whenever you want to and maybe take him for maybe some of the parts of the holidays."

"No," I said, then had to add, "and I just love it when you make fun of me."

His face changed, darkened. "I don't want to go to court, but I will if I have to."

"Well," I said, standing up from the chair and reaching for my baby, "then I guess we'll leave it up to the lawyers, then."

He kissed Sebastian and carefully put him back on the sofa. He stood up, still carrying his bag.

"Here are some things for him," he said, holding the bag out for me.

I remained silent, arms crossed in front of me, and kept my eyes on him, ignoring the bag.

He showed himself out.

XXV

Caves

Something happened in America.

Everyone was talking about it, but no one seemed to know anything. I ignored all the chatter at first—America was a million miles away. To me, it may as well have been another planet. For me, then, all there was to existence was the war and orders and moving from place to place in pickup trucks, and sometimes being shot at and sometimes shooting at people—or even shooting at nothing: buildings, clumps of trees, the sides of mountains . . . just to shoot.

A boy younger than I was when I was first brought to Afghanistan said that he had just come from Kabul and had seen it on TV there: building with smoke pouring out of them, and martyrs in planes destroying entire cities. Then an older man said it was just one building, and someone else said it was three buildings, and another said it was four. But the implication was the same—we had brought the war to America. I just wasn't quite sure which "we" had actually done it.

Or why.

Every day after that, for day after miserable day, we heard about the threats of reprisals from the American president until everyone expected the onslaught of A-bombs every time a plane flew overhead. Then I heard that the Americans only wanted some Saudi man, whose name I had heard a few times during the war between the south and the north. If they could have him, they would leave us alone.

That didn't seem possible to me, but what did I know of what America wanted? And even then, many of my brothers seemed all too happy for the Americans to attack, eager to prove themselves against "a real enemy." Just a teaspoonful more madness in a country that had long since gone well and thoroughly mad.

As time passed, the boys who had come from across the border from the *madrassahs* and who were now men with hearts without empathy and brains full of images of war, started going back home.

I was the only one left alive from *Roshni Kay Minar*. Fifteen died in the war and one I killed with my own hands.

Even if I decided to go back, where would I go? I couldn't even show my face anywhere near Perveen. And Faiz? Even if I was able to take him away from that horrible man, what would I tell him about myself?

Soon, foreign jets filled the sky of Afghanistan, and bombs rolled down, one after another after another. No corner of any city and no space of any wilderness was safe. They turned the turmoil we had created into havoc.

When American soldiers started driving tanks across the land my leaders had killed thousands to possess, my Brotherhood started leaving their strongholds in groups to take refuge in caves in the mountains. I left with Ibrahim and about a dozen others.

And I was a caveman now. We all were, vicious in killing our own kind.

Every few days, a few of us went out to get our ration of food from the ragged network that tried to support us, and on the way down and back up, we never missed an opportunity to loot the people on the roads at gunpoint, as rare a sight as they were. And every now and then, some of us would go down to plant landmines on the side of the road in expectation of a military caravan moving from one part of the country to the other.

Once I was told to go with a group that was planning to raid a nearby village to get supplies. On our way down the mountain I sat down on a rock to rest. Something inside me was telling me to sit there and let the rest of them keep walking.

A large bird turned circles in the blue sky right over my head. It was probably a hawk, looking for prey. I watched him for quite a while but it didn't go away, just kept flying in circle after circle over my head.

I stood up and looked around, searching all around me in the barren, rocky land. Not a soul to see. I looked up again to find the hawk, but it was gone.

A power greater than me was whispering in my heart to let the fear go and allow the change to happen, to take me away from that place.

I started going down the mountain. At the root of the hill I found a path leading to the main road. Once I reached the road, I looked both ways, but there was nothing to see. I turned in the direction of Kabul and started walking. Some time later—I don't know how long—two American tanks rumbled toward me.

I kept walking.

* * *

I turned off the recorder.

Telling his story made him relive overwhelming emotions. I could see that it had exhausted his already torn heart, tortured body, and tired mind. Did he regret his agreement with me? Did he hate me for convincing him to go through that ordeal?

But when everything was said, and every bit of his secret was captured on tape, he just looked at me.

I responded to his eyes. "I'm a woman of my word. I'll do my best to get your son out of there."

Epilogue

Faiz

I flew to Islamabad and met Arshad. We had already exchanged a few emails, and I had provided him with the information Raza had given me about the *madrassah*.

The flight to Islamabad from Boston via New York was late, and I found Arshad waiting for me in the lobby when I reached the hotel after spending more than twenty-four hours in the air.

"Do you want to rest a couple of days before we fly to Karachi?" he said after the usual greetings.

"No, we should leave tomorrow."

"Okay, I'll see that you are checked in . . . have some rest."

We arrived in Karachi late the next afternoon. I wanted to visit the *madrassah* right away but Arshad insisted that nothing could be done at that hour of the evening.

We rented a car from the airport and settled down in the Marriot Hotel, located next to the US consulate. I don't think I slept a wink that night.

The *madrassah* that had loomed so large in Raza's life was only a few miles south of the hotel.

When Arshad pressed the bell, a boy of about fourteen appeared in the window of the gate. Arshad asked for Fazal and the boy disappeared.

A couple minutes later the window opened once more. The same boy wanted more details from Arshad, then he went away again.

We waited another few minutes and then were invited in.

Beyond the gate sat a two-story building with a large yard, half of which was covered with prayer rugs stacked four feet in height, running from one wall to the other. Behind the *madrassah* rose the minarets of a mosque.

We were led to a room with some cane chairs and a wooden bench. The walls were painted a shiny green color from the floor to the height of an average man. The rest, including the ceiling, was a muted yellow. A fan was running at its highest possible speed. Despite the obnoxious rattling noise it made, it was a pleasant relief from the scorching summer heat.

We stood there in the middle of the room, waiting for Fazal, the man Raza called Bayfazal.

A man with a long beard and shaved head appeared.

"As-salāmu 'alaykum," he said to Arshad.

"Wa-'alaykum-us-salām," Arshad replied.

He beckoned us to sit down.

After a few polite words, a heated exchange started between the two men.

Arshad turned to me and said, "It's done. We need to give him ten thousand rupees . . . around two hundred dollars."

"I expected him to demand more," I whispered, not sure if this Bayfazal could understand English. "What did you say to him?"

"He demanded a lot . . . but I threatened him that I will send every possible institution of the government to investigate the *madrassah*, and find the deeds behind this camouflage."

"You should do it anyway," I said with a wry smile.

Arshad did not reply.

That horrible man insisted on getting the money in dollars. I didn't have enough with me so we went out to a nearby bank. On our way Arshad said, "All *madrassahs* are not like this one."

"But this one is . . ." I searched for the word but could only think of ". . . notorious. You need to do something for the sake of those children."

"Poverty is the real culprit," he said, shaking his head. "It drives people to these institutions . . . you may be very familiar with the gang activities, here in this new phenomenon these children end up in *madrassahs* instead of going onto the streets and joining gangs."

"I don't know where you're going with this," I said, touching his arm so we could pause in the street. "Are you justifying—?"

"I am just saying," he interrupted. "These *madrassahs* provide a lot that society in general cannot . . . or *does* not."

We started walking again and I asked, "And that gives them the right to exploit these children and send them off to war at the age of, what? Thirteen? Fourteen? Twelve? Younger?"

"No, it does not. But you must know if one *madrassah* is closed, how many children will be on the street, children that have nowhere to go?"

"So we should let the *madrassahs* do whatever they want," I said, shaking my head, at the same time knowing I wasn't being completely fair to Arshad.

"I am not justifying anything," he said. "I am trying to confront the reality on the ground."

I remained silent. We were about to enter the bank.

When we got back to the *madrassah*, Fazal counted the money very carefully. Twice. Then he called somebody in and a man with a dyed moustache and beard came in. I wondered if this was the man Raza called "the Executioner." He went out again after listening to the orders of his master, and brought back with him an eight-year-old boy.

It had to be Faiz, but in that moment I realized I had no way of knowing for sure.

He wore a dirty navy blue long shirt and loose trousers.

Jallad pushed the child slowly toward me.

I felt anger bloating inside me. I could have slapped the two men, but instead I held the hand of the child and touched his dirty cheek.

Arshad said something to the child and he replied in a tiny, timed voice, "Faiz." He kept looking at Arshad and I, trying to grasp the reason for our presence and his summons to that room. It was then that I started to see Raza's features in that little face.

"Do you have some clean clothes for him?" I asked Bayfazal.

He moved his head from side to side, smirking.

I took off Faiz's shirt, and dropped it on the floor.

"We need to go," I said to Arshad. I didn't want to stay in that deplorable place one more minute, and I didn't want Faiz to be there one more second.

We went to a mall not far from the *madrassah* in an upscale neighborhood on the coast of the Arabian Sea. The soothing sound of waves reached to the street where we parked the car.

I bought clothes for Faiz and we went to one of the restaurants on the second floor of the mall for lunch. While we were waiting for our food I tried to change Faiz's clothes but he kept slipping away from me, refusing to get undressed. Arshad picked him up and took him to the restroom. A few minutes later, Faiz appeared in black shorts and a red and blue shirt, with a clean face and hands.

"Can you find a family that can provide a stable environment for him?" I asked Arshad as the boy happily ate his lunch. He looked at some of the food as though he'd never seen it before.

"I can try," Arshad replied, "but it will take time."

"Would it be a good idea to take him with me?" I had been thinking of almost nothing but what I should do once I found little Faiz. All I knew was he couldn't stay in that horrible *madrassah*, and he certainly couldn't join his father in a military prison. His mother surely would have kept him if she could.

This was a boy without a family, with no place in the world to go.

"I don't know . . ." Arshad said. "If you take him with you, then he is yours for life. It will be very harmful for him if you change your mind later, and he will end up here again, no matter in a house or a *madrassah* . . . I advise you to give it a serious thought."

I watched children playing on the beach, running away from the waves, shouting and laughing at each other. Faiz, sitting close to the large window of the restaurant, looked at them with envy.

"Do you want to go there?" I asked him, pointing to him, then to the beach.

I think he got the gist of what I said, but he just looked at Arshad. When Arshad conveyed the message in Urdu, he nodded. If I brought him back with me, he wouldn't even know the language. It would be like being transported to an alien planet, or being yanked a hundred years forward in time.

We finished our lunch and went across the street to the beach. Within minutes he started to come out of his shell a little and started running round the beach in front of us. His exchanges with Arshad became longer, and he seemed to be more at ease.

When we went back to the hotel, Arshad took Faiz to his room, and I went to mine. I couldn't call my mother. It would be the middle of the night in Boston.

* * *

In the evening I heard a knock on my door.

"Come in, it's open."

Arshad came in with Faiz and said, "I have to visit my niece— she lives here. Would you be all right with Faiz for the evening?"

"Yes, I'll be fine."

I took out a drawing pad and crayons I'd bought in the airport on my way to Pakistan and placed them in front of Faiz. Once he was busy coloring, Arshad sneaked out and I called Boston.

"Mother, how are you?"

"I'm good."

"Is Sebastian all right?" I heard tittering from the other side— Sebastian quicker responding than my mother.

"He's just fine. When are you coming back?"

"I don't know yet, but I'll be back as soon as I can," I said. I paused for a breath then said, "Mother, I need to tell you something."

After another short pause, she said, "Honey? Are you all right?"

"I'm adopting the child."

I looked at Faiz, engrossed by rubbing blue crayon on yellow, excited by the change in color to green.

There was a silence on the other side. "Mother? Mother, are you there?"

"Yes, I'm here. Please don't do this."

I couldn't help but smile at that. What else should she say? "I've thought about it very carefully . . . I can afford another child."

"I *implore* you not to do this. A foreign baby?"

Still smiling, I said, "This isn't the first time somebody has adopted a child from another country."

"I know that . . . but you have Sebastian, remember? Why would you want to take responsibility for another child?"

"I don't know . . ." I said. "Somehow I feel responsible."

My mother sighed and so did I. Then there was just the hiss of the intercontinental phone line.

"Look," she said finally, "I know that man saved your life, and you had to fulfill some promise to him, but you can make arrangements there—a boarding school or an orphanage, or . . . some . . . family."

"I know, but I've decided. If it bothers you, I'll move to an apartment, but I'm bringing him with me."

Exasperated, she said, "We have a big house, and you don't need to move. But have you thought about how this is going to play out in the custody case? Arun's lawyers have already made some very convincing arguments about your absence from his life, before the divorce, and the possibility that you'll do the same to Sebastian."

"That's just stupid," I spat into the phone. I looked down and Faiz was looking up at me, his big eyes wide. I smiled at him and he went back to coloring. Then I continued in a calmer voice, "Our life before the divorce has nothing to do with our life after the divorce, and the court knows I resigned long before Sebastian came into this world and have not worked a day since then."

"She said, on a phone call from Pakistan," my mother said, and I cringed a little.

Then Sebastian started crying in the background.

"I need to feed him," my mother said.

"Okay. I'll call you tomorrow."

"Give it another thought, okay?" my mother said. "Bye-bye."

My mother had a real talent for creating doubt in my mind.

* * *

Faiz was asleep on my bed when Arshad came back.

"Do you want me to take him to my room?"

"No . . . no, I have decided to take him with me. Can you tell him what's going to happen?"

"Sure . . . feel free to call me or knock at my door during the night in case he wakes up and you need me."

"No, I won't," I said, committing myself. "We need to start dealing with each other despite the language barrier."

* * *

The next morning at breakfast, Arshad chatted with Faiz for quite some time. During this exchange Faiz kept turning his head to look at me.

"I think he understands more than we think," Arshad said. "He is very afraid of going back to the *madrassah* and this will help him to accept any new stable environment . . . it may take time but he will be fine with you."

* * *

A big rusty gate led to an open space with two huge papal trees. The jail itself was covered in peeling yellow paint. Arshad talked to the guards standing outside the gate. One of them opened the door inset in the gate and led us through a corridor lined with the doors of prison offices. We met a man in a suit in the office at the end of the hall. Arshad knew him, and he was expecting us.

This man led us to another open space. On the other side there were bars, covered on both sides with chain-link mesh. A couple dozen women sat on the floor behind the bars. Some of the women were covering their heads, others neither cared how they appeared nor had any concern about the privacy of their inmates, speaking loudly to their visitors. Many had infants with them.

The officer took us to a woman who was sitting close to the wall in the corner. Her head was covered with a *duppatta*. There were circles around her large eyes.

She looked at Faiz, and said something to him. Her eyes were moist and it was obvious that she was struggling with her emotions.

"Rachael Brown," Arshad said, "this is Perveen."

The girl smiled at me and I had to wipe a tear from my eye.

"She wants to know why are you doing this?" Arshad said.

I looked at Perveen, not Arshad, when I said, "Raza helped me and I made a deal with him that I would help his child."

After listening carefully to Arshad's translation, she started talking to Faiz again, but he just said a couple words back. He seemed reluctant to show any affection for her.

Then Perveen looked at me and nodded.

"Tell her that I will remain in touch with her, and let her know about Faiz from time to time," I said to Arshad. I took out my business card and started to hand it to Perveen, but Arshad gently pushed my hand away from the bars.

"No . . . no, don't give her anything," he said, nodding to a guard whose bulging stomach was pushing his pants down. "I will send it to her through my friend along with my contact information," he assured me.

Perveen walked away crying and so did I. Faiz looked up at me, but not at his mother, with concern. I squeezed his hand and smiled, and he smiled back.

Roundfire

FICTION

Put simply, we publish great stories. Whether it's literary or popular, a gentle tale or a pulsating thriller, the connecting theme in all Roundfire fiction titles is that once you pick them up you won't want to put them down.
If you have enjoyed this book, why not tell other readers by posting a review on your preferred book site. Recent bestsellers from Roundfire are:

The Bookseller's Sonnets
Andi Rosenthal
The Bookseller's Sonnets intertwines three love stories with a tale of religious identity and mystery spanning five hundred years and three countries.
Paperback: 978-1-84694-342-3 ebook: 978-184694-626-4

Birds of the Nile
An Egyptian Adventure
N.E. David
Ex-diplomat Michael Blake wanted a quiet birding trip up the Nile – he wasn't expecting a revolution.
Paperback: 978-1-78279-158-4 ebook: 978-1-78279-157-7

Blood Profit$
The Lithium Conspiracy
J. Victor Tomaszek, James N. Patrick, Sr.
The blood of the many for the profits of the few... *Blood Profit$*
will take you into the cigar-smoke-filled room where American
policy and laws are really made.

Paperback: 978-1-78279-483-7 ebook: 978-1-78279-277-2

The Burden
A Family Saga
N.E. David
Frank will do anything to keep his mother and father apart. But
he's carrying baggage – and it might just weigh him down ...

Paperback: 978-1-78279-936-8 ebook: 978-1-78279-937-5

The Cause
Roderick Vincent
The second American Revolution will be a fire lit from an internal
spark.

Paperback: 978-1-78279-763-0 ebook: 978-1-78279-762-3

Don't Drink and Fly
The Story of Bernice O'Hanlon: Part One
Cathie Devitt
Bernice is a witch living in Glasgow. She loses her way in her
life and wanders off the beaten track looking for the garden of
enlightenment.

Paperback: 978-1-78279-016-7 ebook: 978-1-78279-015-0

Gag
Melissa Unger
One rainy afternoon in a Brooklyn diner, Peter Howland
punctures an egg with his fork. Repulsed, Peter pushes the plate
away and never eats again.
Paperback: 978-1-78279-564-3 ebook: 978-1-78279-563-6

The Master Yeshua
The Undiscovered Gospel of Joseph
Joyce Luck
Jesus is not who you think he is. The year is 75 CE. Joseph ben
Jude is frail and ailing, but he has a prophecy to fulfil ...
Paperback: 978-1-78279-974-0 ebook: 978-1-78279-975-7

On the Far Side, There's a Boy
Paula Coston
Martine Haslett, a thirty-something 1980s woman, plays hard on
the fringes of the London drag club scene until one night which
prompts her to sign up to a charity. She writes to a young Sri
Lankan boy, with consequences far and long.
Paperback: 978-1-78279-574-2 ebook: 978-1-78279-573-5

Tuareg
Alberto Vazquez-Figueroa
With over 5 million copies sold worldwide, *Tuareg* is a classic
adventure story from best-selling author Alberto Vazquez-
Figueroa, about honour, revenge and a clash of cultures.
Paperback: 978-1-84694-192-4

Readers of ebooks can buy or view any of these bestsellers by clicking on the live link in the title. Most titles are published in paperback and as an ebook. Paperbacks are available in traditional bookshops. Both print and ebook formats are available online.

Find more titles and sign up to our readers' newsletter at http://www.johnhuntpublishing.com/fiction

Follow us on Facebook at https://www.facebook.com/JHPfiction and Twitter at https://twitter.com/JHPFiction